Book News

Sign up for exclusive updates and offers at
news.jljarvis.com

Get the Audiobook

The Enemy

The Enemy

Highland Soldiers 1

J.L. Jarvis

THE ENEMY
Highland Soldiers 1

ISBN (ebook) 978-0-9858554-0-6
ISBN (paperback) 978-0-9858554-2-0
ISBN (audiobook) 978-1-942767-28-2

Published by BookbinderPress.com

Chapter 1

A Walk Down the Aisle

Dunross, Scotland, June 15, 1679

Mari wore only her shift and bare feet. They had taken the rest. With nothing to confine them, her dark chestnut waves tumbled over her shoulders. The beadle sent her on her way with a prod of his beefy fingers. She fixed her eyes forward and walked down the makeshift aisle in the barn that served as kirk for today's secret meeting. Whispers wafted in waves as she passed by each row of parishioners and pressed toward her goal. On she proceeded past a grim gauntlet of narrow-eyed elders to arrive at the stool of repentance. It was oaken and plain, with a hole in the middle. A commode: meant to inflict shame. She sat on it and folded her trembling hands on her lap. Her bare feet were flat on the ground, and she pressed her knees close together. Her moss green eyes drifted over the congregation. Skin like cream and full lips of a muted rose hue softened the dread from her features to her detriment. She appeared almost untroubled, which would only inflame the kirk elders as they meted out accusations and determined her punishment.

Steps away stood the minister, a lanky man with keen eyes that could shrivel a soul. His stentorian scolding rang out through the barn, where a few dozen people sat on folding stools watching.

"Marion McEwan, you are charged with engaging in the sinful act of fornication. Confess and repent of your wickedness before this assembly now. Name your partner in sin so he might likewise be brought to justice."

Her gaze drifted toward him, but lips never parted to break the long silence.

"Speak or suffer the wages of sin. It is your choice. No one else can save you," he said, with an edge that grated through his tone.

When no answer came forth, his wrath simmered. "Marion McEwan, hear me now. Confess your sin! Repent before God against whom you have transgressed or be cast out from this congregation!"

The minister's indignation rang into the heavy oak rafters. "Fall down before God. Show your tears of remorse! Name your partner in sin that he might share your utter disgrace and plead for deliverance from the fires of hell!"

Still she offered no words of repentance, nor a name of the father. A gust from the moor blew out the candle she held in her hand.

Suddenly quiet and measured, the minister's voice intoned his contempt, rising and falling with well-practiced effect. "Are you so shameless and prideful to think you can raise this wee one with no father and no kirk? Will you wallow in your blasphemous ways rather than swallow your pride? We can have you imprisoned, and when you are released, you will be an outcast! Do you hear me? Cast out from your kirk and your kinsmen! Your only hope is confession. Repent now and be delivered from—"

The minister stopped mid-rebuke as a shadow eclipsed the main source of light coming in through the doorway. Before muskets could be raised, a fierce Highland dragoon strode in. Hair, dark and wild as his mood, was lashed back, but the wind caught loose waves. A daunting form, he was draped in plaid colors of earth, dried bracken, and heather. Powerful legs took him in a few strides to the minister, who found his chin caught in the crook of the Highlander's elbow as if in a vise. Fear-numbed faces looked on. A handful of parishioners by the back wall lifted their muskets, but lowered them as three more kilted men appeared in the doorway with doglock pistols aimed at them. The Highlander whirled about and took stock. Satisfied that his men had matters under control, he pressed a pistol to the minister's temple. One man rose from behind and lunged at the Highlander. He was dispatched with a sharp backward jab of his elbow.

"Blinking *eejit*! Are there any more fools here?" The Highlander brandished his pistol. "Look outside. Do you see the rest of my men at the top of that brae?"

Heads turned toward the doorway. The setting sun blazed from over the brae. "If these lads and I dinnae join them soon, they will thunder down here and strike down all who dare hinder us." Confident he had secured their attention, he went on with chilling calm. "Let us leave, and I will neither kill nor report you for this illegal meeting today. But stand in my way, and the whole High-

land Host will descend and hunt down every man Jack of
you."

His eyes met those of the minister's son, and he
allowed himself a brief moment to burn his scorn into the
man's onyx eyes. He was tempted to pummel the
scoundrel, but not today. He would leave this one to the
vengeance of God; or better yet, to the sorry lout's wife.

Sweat beaded the minister's forehead as the Highlander shoved him toward the stool of repentance. Mari
watched, her face now drained of color.

"Kneel," he ordered the minister. As he did, the Highlander kicked his feet out from beneath him, making him
fall face first into a pasty of cow dung and hay. A noise
from the back caught the Highlander's attention. With a
sudden pivot, a flash from a musket caught his eye just as
one of his men returned fire with his pistol. The musket
shooter clutched at his grazed arm and watched his blood
darken his sleeve as he slid his back down the wall in a
faint.

As the Highlander wielded his pistol to keep other
foolishly brave souls at bay, he cast a quick glance at Mari
McEwan and his deep brown eyes softened. "Come, lass."
He held out a strong hand and she took it. While rising,
she faltered. With a sure grip, he steadied and guided her
up to his side while he took in her unsteady state.

Without warning, the Highlander stomped his heel
on the minister's hand, which had inched its way down to
his belt and grasped a knife hilt. The Highlander relieved
the reverend of his knife and, with an easy yank, pulled
the offending hand onto the stool. With a shuddering
stab, he pinned the minister's sleeve to the seat of the stool
of repentance.

Mari's eyes drifted half closed as she swayed. The Highlander circled her waist with his arm as the burnt-out candlestick fell from her limp hand. "Steady, lass," he said as he tightened his grip.

With a weak glance up to him, she whispered, "I'm fair done."

Shoving his pistol into his belt, he scooped her up into his brawny arms. Warmth softened his eyes as he looked at her, even as his jaw tightened. Now livid, he strode toward the door with a few well-placed dark glares that forbade any to stop him. "Shoot me and you'll shoot her as well," he said, casting the words over his shoulder with conviction and measured haste. Once outside, he hoisted her onto his large gray drum horse, and then mounted behind her. His men backed away, pistols pointed, then mounted their horses in a run as they all galloped off toward the brae. Soon they were but silhouettes against the last remnants of the day's sun.

THE MINISTER FINISHED WIPING the dung from his face and returned the handkerchief to its owner.

"Someone do something!" said a man who showed no signs of moving himself.

"Dinnae be daft," said the reverend with biting impatience.

"We should follow!" said another.

"And do what-complain to the authorities that our illegal worship meeting was interrupted by the king's royal dragoons? He has the law on his side. And as long as we meet against the law like this-outside of the kirks that were taken from us-we can do nothing!"

Thomas settled his shaken new bride in a stool, and then turned his attention to the men's discussion. "We were fortunate, aye? They could have killed every one of us on the spot and been thanked by the crown for their service." His words were met with spontaneous nods of agreement, for while he was an accomplished student of St. Andrews University and therefore deemed worth their attention, he was also the minister's son.

"Right you are, Thomas," said the Reverend Blackwell.

"We shouldnae act in haste," his son added.

"Thomas is right," said an Elder. "'Sufficient unto today is the evil thereof.' Better we rally and fight for freedom another day!"

"And what if it were your daughter spirited away? Would you just let her go?" said Margaret McEwan, the young woman's mother.

"*Whisht*, Margaret," said her husband, Archie, in a low voice. Discreetly, he gripped her arm.

Thomas said, "She brought it upon herself-and on us."

"How so?" asked her father as he leapt to his feet. Now it was Margaret who clutched Archie's arm to restrain him.

The minister said, "One has to wonder why the whole Highland Host has descended upon us for one girl."

"The whole Highland Host?" said her mother. Mouth agape, Margaret looked first to him, then her husband.

The reverend ignored her interruption and continued,

"Highland barbarians came seeking your daughter. What has she done to draw such interest, I wonder?" He gave her a knowing look.

"*Och*!" Margaret fumed and opened her mouth to protest, but Archie tightened his grip on his wife's arm. She closed her mouth and looked down to the ground to conceal her anger.

Reverend Blackwell studied her with sharp eyes. "It's clear now where your daughter gets her rebellious spirit. Hold your tongue, Mistress McEwan, or you will find yourself taking your daughter's place on the stool of repentance."

Margaret took in a sharp breath to reply, but Archie's quiet, throaty grunt cautioned her to hold back her rage.

Having dispatched his authority, Reverend Blackwell continued, "Thomas is right. Marion brought this upon herself by consorting with those savage Highlanders. Ah well, we ken who the father is now, do we nae? My only surprise is that he came to claim the wee bastard and its mother."

Several of the men nodded.

Archie quietly asked, "Can we nae send a party to search for my daughter?"

The reverend shook his head. "The wages of sin have been paid on this day. I'll nae stand in the way of God's judgment."

With a sideways glance toward her husband, Margaret whispered through tight lips, "Archie, you'd best take me home before I say what I'm thinking."

As they rode from the kirk, Mari turned and looked over the Highlander's shoulder to see whether anyone followed.

He said, "Dinnae look back, lass. 'Tis bad luck."

"Aye? Well my luck couldnae get any worse." Had she been stronger, she might have laughed, but instead she leaned wearily back against the Highlander's solid chest, secure in the strong arms that held her.

He glanced down with a soft smile. "Have I not changed your luck a wee bit?"

"Aye, so you have." She let her eyes close and she rested against him, this Highlander, royalist, and papist from whom she drew strength and support. He had done more for her than her own people this day, and the truth of that ached.

Beneath the waving grasses, the uneven moorland made for a rough ride. Unaware she was doing so, she clutched his arm tighter as each wave of pain struck. Despite effort to conceal it, a small moan of pain escaped.

He leaned his cheek against her hair, his voice quiet and low. "We'll slow down as soon as it's safe. Then we'll find a place for you to rest."

"Ensign?" she said faintly.

"Aye?"

"I cannae see the rest of your men on the brae."

"No? *Och* well, the sunset's too bright. You wouldnae see them." His mouth twitched up at the corner. "Even if they were there."

Chapter 2

The Highland Dragoons

Two Months Earlier

Mari McEwan crossed the moors with her brother, Jamie, and his sweetheart, Ellen. They were on their way to an illegal outdoor church meeting, which the Covenanters called a conventicle. She walked ahead, while Jamie and Ellen lagged behind, stealing fond looks.

"How much farther have we to walk?" Mari turned back and caught Jamie planting a kiss. Mari cleared her throat loudly, causing Ellen to flinch.

With a grin, Mari raised her eyebrow and said, "'Tis a good thing we're going to worship."

Ellen rushed over to Mari as they continued on their way. "Marion! You willnae tell anybody?

Working to keep a straight face, Mari said. "Tell what? That you've succumbed to the sins of the flesh, and you lust for my brother?"

Clapping her palm to her mouth, Ellen gasped and said, "Marion!"

Jamie put a light hand to Ellen's waist to guide her over so he could walk between them. To Ellen, he said, "Dinnae mind what my vexatious sister says." His eyes lingered fondly before he turned to give Mari a withering look.

Unfazed, Mari hooked her arm into her brother's. "I ken that you love her. 'Twas only jest, Jamie."

His expression hardened. "'Tis nae right to jest about sin. And you know how I love Ellen. I'd marry her today if I could, but we'll wait till we've had a proper courtship. You'd do well to consider the same." His jaw clenched as he looked straight ahead and walked on.

He had seen her a few days before with Thomas, the minister's son. They'd been talking, nothing more. He and Thomas were friends, so she saw little reason for Jamie to disapprove. But he did, and he would not discuss it. Ellen leaned back so Jamie would not see her catch Mari's eye and give her head a slight shake to dismiss Jamie's harshness.

Mari smiled back, and then turned to face forward before Jamie could see their exchange. Ellen was good for Jamie. She hoped that Ellen's gentle nature would soften Jamie's austere temperament. The two were a good match, as any who knew them agreed. More important than that, they were deeply in love. Mari envied their confidence in it. Never once did they doubt that their feelings were real and would last forever.

Mari's affections, in contrast, were unsure and secret except to her young man. It was how he insisted it be. He would never have brought her to worship like this. They hid how they felt from the kirk—perhaps for good reason, but it made her feel wicked. The kirk elders were stern and unyielding, and her life surrounding the kirk was an uncomfortable fit. She only came to these open-air meetings for Jamie, to serve as a chaperone. Otherwise, he could never have brought Ellen. He paid well for the favor in farm chores. In truth, although she would never admit it to Jamie, she would have done this for either of them. She loved Jamie, although, as his sister, she felt it her duty to take every opportunity to point out that Ellen was far too lovely and good for the likes of him.

Jamie clutched Mari's wrist. "Jamie," she protested, as she tried to twist her arm free. But she followed his eyes to the distance, and fixed her eyes on it. With increasing apprehension she watched. Kilted horsemen bore down upon them.

"Accursed Highland dragoons!" Jamie spat the words out.

There were no trees to conceal them on this part of the moor. If they tried to run, they would only look more guilty. Either way, the horsemen would catch them. Their only chance was to face them and hope they could talk their way out of suspicion.

Without taking his eyes from the approaching horsemen, Jamie said, "Ellen, give me your Bible."

"Jamie, no." She clutched his hand. They both knew that the mere possession of a Bible would put them in danger. They could be called upon to swear an oath renouncing everything they believed in—everything they had sworn before God to uphold. If they did not swear it, soldiers had the legal authority to kill them on the spot.

ELLEN WAS CARRYING the only bible among them. Mari had accidentally left hers at home. She and Jamie had bickered about it after leaving. When she realized she'd forgotten her Bible, Mari had taunted him with wide eyes. "I'll just share with you, Jamie." She'd grinned at his glare, knowing that sharing a Bible afforded her brother the chance to touch Ellen's hand, which was as much intimacy as could be had in a kirk service—even if that kirk service was held in a field.

Mari continued to torment him. "Of course, I'll need to sit in the middle to be able to see it. My eyes are so weary from sewing." She put her hand to her brow with a pitiful sigh.

"*Och!* Brilliant! You'd have me court Ellen with you in the middle!"

With feigned sweetness, Mari said, "But Jamie, are you not there for the worship?"

"Aye, to worship my Ellen 'neath the braw moon and stars." He glared at her sideways. "With my daft wee sister between us!"

Mari had grinned broadly, thoroughly satisfied to have irked her brother.

BUT NOW, as three Highland dragoons approached, there was only one Bible that concerned him.

"Ellen, give it to me," Jamie told her with quiet urgency.

"I cannae, Jamie. I've already hidden it."

Knowing full well what she was risking, she met his

eyes and showed him the depth of her love in a look. His expression pled for what could not be, for the dragoons were upon them. It was too late for the Bible to change hands. Jamie gripped Ellen's hand and pulled her beside him as the dragoons came to a stop.

"Good evening," said Jamie, with dark caution in his eyes.

Two of the soldiers dismounted, while one remained on his horse. The three men were a fearful lot, with skin mottled and leathered by their austere existence, but it was their leader who made Mari shudder. He had the features of someone who might have been handsome in his youth. But his nature had etched brutal lines in his features, from which two eyes reflected a cavernous soul. To Jamie he said, "It's a bit late to be out for a walk."

"It isnae too late for us."

The dragoon's tone sharpened. "Where are you going this evening?"

"Home."

"Where is that?" asked the second. He had the look of a man who had fought hard battles and survived with even harder emotions.

"Dunross," said Jamie as he eyed the Highlander.

"Dunross?" asked the leader, dismounting.

Jamie nodded warily.

"Search them," he ordered his men as his eyes went from Ellen to Mari.

One soldier wrenched Ellen from Jamie's grasp, while another circled and grabbed hold of Jamie from behind. Mari lurched toward them.

"Stay back!" commanded the one on the horse. With

his pistol aimed at Ellen, he said, "I'll shoot them both." Mari warily did as directed.

In the struggle, Ellen's Bible dislodged from beneath her jacket and fell to the ground.

"What's this?" asked Ellen's captor with a smirk.

Jamie lunged toward him, but the heftier dragoon had his arms hooked about Jamie's from behind. Jamie struggled in vain.

The one on the horse aimed his pistol at Ellen.

Helpless, Jamie clenched his teeth in terror for Ellen.

"Will you swear allegiance to the king and acknowledge him as head of the church?"

Ellen steeled herself with steadfast grace and was silent.

"Say it, Ellen," said Jamie in a low voice. "They're only words."

Tears shone in her eyes as she looked at him. "Jamie, I cannae."

The dragoon twisted her arms further back with his iron grip, and spoke in her ear. "Swear allegiance."

The leader studied her for a moment and then said, "Never mind. She can swear by her actions." He dismounted and pulled out his flint and steel. "There's a chill in the air. Start a fire for us, lassie."

He thrust the flint and steel at her. Reflexively, she took them with trembling hands. He gestured toward the Bible, which lay on the ground, the wind whipping its pages. Her captor released her with a shove to the ground. "Light it."

Ellen's back stiffened.

The leader echoed the command. "Light a fire for us, lassie."

When Ellen did not respond, the leader grabbed her chin in his rough hands and pulled her up to face him.

"No," Ellen whispered.

Jamie watched with horror.

Mari saw her chance. All were focused on Ellen. Mari bent over and lifted a large rock with both hands. She was close enough to strike the man holding Ellen.

"Set it down." The leader clamped his arm about Mari's waist. She let the rock drop on his foot. He cried out a curse. She pounded her fist back to his groin and took off in a run. In a few strides, he caught up and lunged for her, knocking her down to the ground. She tried to scramble away, but he climbed over her and took hold of her hair. She reached behind her neck and grasped his wrist. She tried to roll over. She fought with her nails and teeth to be free, but he pinned her face down to the ground with his body.

Mari lay beneath him, unable to see. Ellen screamed, and Jamie let out a deep wail. "Do what you will to me, but leave her alone," pleaded Mari.

He replied with a backhanded slap that struck her ear with a painful ringing. She lay still, trying to work through her pain to think what to do next. A rough hand took hold of the folds of her skirts and pulled up. Jamie called out Ellen's name. A shot sounded.

The man on top of Mari shifted his position as he lifted his head to see where the shot came from. Sounds of a struggle subsided, followed by rhythmic grunting that made Mari's stomach convulse. A single sob came from Ellen, and then another shot fired.

"Your turn, minx," said the dragoon as he flipped her onto her back like a rag doll in his brutish hands. As he did so, Mari felt the hard shape of his dirk. As she put her arms about him, she slid his dirk from his belt and completed the embrace with the dirk in her hand. He moaned with pleasure and reached up with one hand to paw at her breast while his hand clutched its way up her thigh. Bile heaved to her throat.

Feeling her spasm, he said, "You like that, do ye?"

He let out a grunt as she thrust the dirk into his back. When he cursed, she pulled at it to strike him again, but it stuck. He reached back for her hand as she freed the dirk. With a thrust, she sank it into his side. He wrapped his hands around her neck. As he tightened his grip, she gasped and choked. His mouth opened. Sounds came from his throat, the beginnings of words never finished. His grip loosened and he fell upon her, limp and uncon-scious. She pried his hands from her neck, panting for air.

Hearing his grunts through the darkness, one of the others laughed. "Kilgour, need some help over there?"

Mari pushed and squirmed until she was free, then she slipped silently out of earshot and ran into the night.

Moments later, she heard hoof beats behind her. She rolled down a peat hill. There was a cave not far away. Behind, a voice cursed the soft peat that was slowing the horses. At the foot of a brae was a burn. Once there, she would know her way. She and Jamie had played here as children. As soon as she heard the water trip over the rocks, she knew she did not have far to go. Following the sound to the water's edge, she soon gained an advantage by being on foot. She deftly maneuvered along the bank, over boulders and around gnarled trees. Not far ahead was a small cave. Just as the horsemen were nearly upon her, Mari slipped inside its moss-covered entrance, edging her way to the back of the cave. Cowering against the cave's wall, she forced herself to take slow, quiet breaths as she listened to the men, now on foot, leading their horses outside the cave.

JUST AFTER DAWN, Mari stepped inside the farmhouse. Margaret rushed to her. "Marion! Where is Jamie?"

"Mum." She had been strong through the night, but no more. With the helpless face of a child, she said, "Jamie's dead."

When the story was told, her mother sat in her rocker and stared at the fire, while tears pooled in her father's eyes as he sat at the table and stared at his hands. It was a good while that passed before anyone spoke of what had to be done.

"I must tell Ellen's family," she said.

"Aye. Bring her father and some men to help bring the twa souls home to be buried."

"Father, you ken we cannae. The English Royalists willnae let Covenanters bury their dead."

A deep sob came from Margaret as she wept her first tears.

Archie said, "*Och!* I willnae leave a child of mine on the moors for the crows." He stopped, unable to compose himself.

"No, Father." She rushed to take hold of his hands to console him. "We must wait for the gloaming. Then we'll go find him. 'Tis no but a few miles from here." Her eyes teared.

"We used to play hide and seek there. *Och*, how we'd

go crawling and climbing. I hid last night in a wee cave Jamie found years ago. It saved my life."

A long silenced passed.

Archie tamped down his emotions. "Tonight, then."

Chapter 3

The Minister's Son

Thomas Blackwell arrived with his mother. He carried a basket of oatcakes, chicken pie, jelly and tea, which he handed to the maid as they all took seats in the sitting room.

"You're very kind, Mistress Blackwell. Thank you," said Mari's mother.

"Not at all, Mistress Thomas." She laid her hand on Rowena's for a moment in silent sympathy. As she withdrew it, she said softly, "Reverend Blackwell is gathering men to go out after dark and bring Ellen and Jamie back home where they belong. They will wait until dark, to avoid suspicion. The Highland Host are all about us. No one is safe." With a sharp intake of breath, she stopped, her eyes darting about before settling on her clasped hands in her lap.

Rowena nodded. "Aye, 'tis a truth we ken well."

Mistress Blackwell said, "Your Jamie was a brave martyr."

"I'd rather he were alive."

The maid arrived with tea. While Rowena started to pour, Thomas spied Mari through the window and excused himself.

Once outside, he approached her, taking care to arrive at a suitable distance from her so as not to prompt tongues to wag. "May I walk with you, Marion?"

When his eyes met hers, his thirsty gaze lingered too long to mistake what lay behind them. "Where are you going?"

"I thought if I walked I might keep my mind off of it."

His lips parted, but the question that burned from his eyes was not forthcoming. "May I walk with you?"

Mari hesitated. To go walking together would draw notice, which they had both worked to avoid.

"I cannae let you go walking alone after—they're all around us, Marion. It's not safe, and well you know it."

With a nod, Mari went on her way walking with Thomas beside her. In silence, they followed a path that led over a hill and past a small copse of trees. When they were well out of sight of the farm, Thomas took Mari's wrist and led her into the trees, out of sight. Pulling her into his arms, he cradled her head in his hand and planted kisses on her forehead. "My dear Marion. I'm sorry." A long while passed as Thomas stroked Mari's hair back from her brow. He touched her hairpin and her hair tumbled free.

Mari looked up in sudden shock, as she reached up to put her hair back in order.

His hands grasped her wrists. "Don't." Burning eyes bore through hers. "Let me touch but your hair as it falls in long strands over your breasts."

"Thomas! You musn't speak like that!"

Thomas slowly coaxed her hands to rest on his shoulders, and her reached round her neck and combed his fingers up her scalp, through her hair to the ends, guiding the strands to the front as his fingers released the ends gently to land on her breasts. "*Och*, Marion, you're a beauty." He breathed in as he leaned close and whispered in her ear. "You're mine. You know that you are."

She lifted her chin as his breath warmed her ear. A tear slipped down her cheek. "My brother and Ellen have died. Thomas, how can I think of anything else?" She took a step back on weak knees and found her back against a tree.

"Let me comfort you, Marion." Thomas pressed the full length of his body against hers. "'Tis right that you should come to me. For you're mine, and you know it." And he combed his fingers once more into her hair and he pulled her to him. "You belong to me. Say it." His body insisted before his voice did, and he put his mouth on hers and his tongue in her mouth.

Against thought or will, her lips parted to his as a thrill shot through her. His hands were on her, drawing her closer as he kissed her until her head swam. Her heart ached as an image of Jamie's dead body flashed through her mind. Mari gasped at the thought. Thomas stiffened against her. "Marion, you've been mine since that day you gave yourself to me. Let me have you again." He fumbled with the cloth that covered her corset, slipping his fingers inside, but not reaching the tips that he sought. His voice edged with frustration, he said, "Take it off. Let me touch you."

His insistence made her uneasy. She tried to move away, but was pinned against the tree. "Thomas, no." Pressing her palms to his chest, she tried to wriggle free, but he had her securely pinned with her arms in his grip and his body against hers.

"But you liked it before," he whispered, as he kissed her neck. Pressing his groin against her, he slid his hands down to her skirts, clutching and pulling the fabric to get underneath.

"We should never have done it. If the church elders knew-"

"But they don't. And they're not here now, are they?"

"But it's wrong. What you want is for husbands and wives, which we're not." She looked boldly at him.

He would not meet her eyes. "Do you think I would marry a woman who thinks she can lead me around like a bridled horse? Well, I'll marry when I'm ready. Don't force your will, Marion. I'll marry when I'm sure that you love me enough." He took a step back.

Mari put her clothing and hair back in order as he talked.

"The Bible speaks of a virtuous woman. You'd do well to read it and study it well, for you're lacking some traits that a future minister's wife needs to have."

Her last vision of Ellen haunted her mind, and the thought of being touched now sickened her stomach. She had loved Jamie and Ellen, and now they were gone. What right did she have to give in to pleasures of the flesh? How many times had she heard Thomas's father preaching about the wages of sin? How could Thomas continue to ask this of her when he knew it was wrong? She said, "Perhaps I am not the virtuous woman you would wish me to be, but to ask it of me now isnae virtuous, either."

Thomas scoffed. "I've been patient with you, but you vex me sometimes."

As he said it, his face took on the look of his father while preaching.

Mari could not absorb what she was hearing. "I vex you?"

"Aye, woman, you do." He looked stern and unyielding.

In that moment, Mari saw her future with him, being told of her failings by a man who would never see his. It took her breath. When she could speak, she said, "Jamie and Ellen are dead. You found me in a moment of weakness. I'm sorry for that. Please show some respect for the dead, if you won't for my wishes. Jamie wouldae approve. I willnae do what you wish on his grave."

Her words silenced him, and his eyes grew cold and dark. Turning, he offered his arm. Mari shook her head. "We shouldnae be seen touching." She lowered her eyes for a moment, and then turned toward her house and walked back alone.

Chapter 4

Crying the Banns

May 4, 1679

Two weeks after Jamie and Ellen were buried, five Highland dragoons in gray waistcoats and plaids rode southwest from Glasgow atop pale gray horses. The officer in charge sat tall with broad shoulders and a comfortable confidence. From his blue bonnet, dark hair was pulled into a tie at the nape of his neck. Looking straight ahead, he spoke to his men, who flanked him two on each side. Keeping pace with the ensign's brisk canter, they rode with abandon, invigorated by the bracing wind that swept over the moorland. Rounding the top of a gently sloped hill, they came upon the ashen remains of a Beltane fire from a few days before. Charlie flashed a broad smile. It was, by far, his most dangerous weapon. He cocked his sand colored head as though deep in thought, but a mischievous grin lurked just beneath the surface. "Alex?"

"No," Alex summarily answered, for he knew what was coming. Alex was older by a year, with the mighty build and bearing of a formidable warrior, which made him an unlikely subject to tease. But everyone has a moment of weakness at some point in his life. For Alex, there had been only one—one which Charlie remembered in brilliant detail.

"Hughie, you remember, do you not?"

"No, I saw nothing," said Hughie, holding up a flexed palm to distance himself.

"*Och*, aye, now I recall, Alex." Charlie took his time, grinning broadly. "Remember, Alex, when you drew the oatcake marked with coal?"

Even Duncan, the quietest of the group, had to suppress a snicker.

Charlie went on. "Three times. You only had to jump over the flames three times. But you just about did a damned sword dance over the flames." He smiled with unbridled pleasure. "'Twas a braw dance, that was, laddie."

Alex lunged forward to urge his horse over toward Charlie, but Duncan grabbed the bridle of Alex's horse and stopped him.

"Aye, it was," Charlie said, relishing the moment. "And when your plaid caught fire, it burned brighter than the bonfire. Or maybe it was just the reflection from your bare arse when you pulled the burning plaid off!" By this time, not one of them could keep from laughing.

Alex said dryly, "Aye, laugh all you want, Charlie. But if you had some bollocks of your own, you'd do the same to protect them."

Unscathed, Charlie grinned.

They rode along quietly for a moment or two, until Callum, their leader, said, "Do you not want to ken where we're going?"

Duncan said, "South."

Callum glanced at him sideways and proceeded as though the answer were yes. "Archbishop Sharp was murdered yesterday on his way to St. Andrews. He was in a carriage with his eldest daughter when a band of Covenanters shot him, then dragged from his carriage and —in front of his daughter—stabbed him sixteen times until he was dead."

Hughie said, "In front of his daughter?"

"And they call Highlanders barbaric," said Duncan.

Charlie cocked an eyebrow. "Daughter? What does she look like?"

Alex pulled off his bonnet and swatted Charlie with it.

"They were led by Hackston of Rathillet and Balfour of Kinloch. The others were poor men—probably weavers. At least one of them is from Ayrshire, so we've been sent here to find him and anyone with him."

"He's in Ireland by now, I'll wager," said Duncan.

"Aye, I'll wager you're right," Callum said.

"But Callum—I mean, Ensign MacDonell—" said Duncan, with a hint of sarcasm.

Callum cast a wry look sideways. They'd all been boyhood friends, but he outranked them now. While his friends did not mind, it made Callum a bit uncomfortable. Knowing this, they took turns raising the point now and then for their own entertainment.

Hughie grinned as he watched Duncan, whose only sign of amusement was a slight curve at the corner of his mouth. A gentle breeze brushed blond strands back from Hughie's brow, exposing the fresh face and bright eyes of one who still found excitement in battles. At seventeen,

Hughie was sure he had lingered too long at home, and was excited to be on this adventure. "Callum, what are we to do here if the weavers we seek are in Ireland?"

"Our orders are to quash any Covenanter activity that we find."

"And I'm sure there's a brilliant plan to accomplish that," Duncan said dryly. He was a practical man, which some mistook for pessimism. But in matters of battle he was most often right.

"Aye." Alex laughed as he brandished his sword. It caught the light as he sliced the air deftly toward imagined Covenanters. "We'll accomplish the task with the well-applied tip of my sword here, here, and... here—Sorry, ma'am. I was aiming for your daughter. You, uh, might want to tuck those back into place."

When the snickering subsided, Callum explained, "The curates have a list of everyone in the parish. We're to investigate those who fail to attend Sunday services."

Duncan lifted dark, knowing eyes to meet Callum's. "Investigate. In English, does that mean to beat or hang them?" he said dryly.

"We willnae harm anyone without good reason. We're not like that, and you ken it," said Callum sternly.

"We may not have a choice," Duncan said.

With a spark in his eye, Charlie said, "Aye, we do. We'll just ask them politely to trot their wee arses into the English kirk. I'm sure that will work nicely."

"I say we use the same manners they used on our parents when they were wee children. Thousands marched into our homes with their civilized manners and burned our chapels and families. But we are the barbarians," said Duncan.

Hughie said, "Now we're marching onto their land and forcing them to go to a different church. How is our cause any better?"

"You ask too many questions," said Charlie.

"No," said Callum. "It's a fair question. The difference between the Presbyterians and us is that we fight for our clan. If our clan takes on the king's cause, then that cause is ours. We honor our clan, for without our clan and our honor, we are nothing. It's simple and true."

"We can keep our minds simple enough—some of us more easily than others," Alex said with a sideways glance toward Charlie, "but dinnae expect welcoming hugs when we get there."

With a sharp look, Callum said, "That's why we willnae let down our guard, ken?"

The men all gave a nod.

Callum went on. "I ken you've all heard of what goes on—robbing, reiving, and the like. That willnae happen with us, or you'll answer to me. And that goes for the women. Treat them like our own."

"That's been my plan all along, to treat them like me ain!" said Charlie.

"Like our mothers and sisters," added Callum, reprovingly.

Charlie held his arms up in defense toward Callum. "I was joking!"

Shaking his head, Callum smirked. "You're a sorry swine."

THEY MADE camp on a hill overlooking the farms of Dunross. While they worked, Callum said, "We'll bide here for a while."

"And do what?" Alex asked.

"Watch and wait."

Alex, looking unusually serious, said, "Can you not tell us more about the man we are looking for—perhaps what he looks like?"

"Aye." Callum looked at him frankly. "We got a detailed description from the Archbishop's daughter and servants: average height, average build—wearing bonnets or hats." Callum rolled his eyes.

"Well that narrows it down to half the stinkin' men in Scotland," said Charlie.

"Aye, but I do have a name," Callum added.

"A name? Well, you might have mentioned that sooner," said Alex.

"James McEwan," Callum said with a sly glint in his eye.

"See that farm down there? That's where he lives, and that's where we will quarter ourselves when the time's right."

ARCHIE FERGUSON WAS A TACKSMAN, with one of the larger farms in the area. Because of this, his farm was often used to host Covenanter meetings. But today it was quiet, except for the usual workings of the farm. People were once again going about their everyday work, but now Jamie and Ellen were gone. Two weeks had passed, and the weeping was over—except for occasional moments when, in an instant, tears would well up unexpectedly. But the grief was still fresh.

Janet Ferguson greeted Mari and her mother and accepted the basket of shortbread Margaret offered. They sat outside weaving straw baskets and talking, sometimes as though nothing had happened. It bothered Mari to feel this way, but it was the way to go on, she supposed, else her grieving mind would unravel. And there was something comforting about hearing the two older women talking about other things—normal things—that concerned other people in the kirk.

"They'll be crying the banns for Thomas Blackwell and Agnes Bell."

"No! Agnes?"

"Aye."

"With Thomas—the minister's son?"

"Well! I didnae ken they were even courting."

The two women were so engrossed in the news that they barely noticed Mari get up and leave. She made it past the corner before she vomited. Wiping her mouth, she leaned her head back against the wall and closed her eyes, catching her breath, her palm on her abdomen. As she salvaged her composure, she sensed something and glanced up to discover the dairymaid, healer and midwife, Grizzal MacRorie, standing not far away, staring at her.

Since childhood, Grizzal had frightened Mari, with her brusque and often hurtful ways. "Some people just dinnae like children," her mother had told her. But Mari thought this woman simply did not like people, for as Mari grew up, Grizzal continued to express her annoyance whenever it suited her and regardless of its effect. But today it was Mari who had little patience. She met

Grizzal's eyes squarely and said, "Have you no work to do?"

The woman stared straight back at her and, with a knowing look, said, "Aye." But she made no move to leave.

"Then why didnae you go do it?"

"*Och*, I was just thinkin' o' sumpin' me mither used to say."

Not wishing to seem rude, but in no mood to hear more, Mari gave a polite nod and walked back toward the house.

Behind her, still within earshot, she heard Grizzal say, "What's done in the corner will come to the hearth."

Mari needed no help feeling queasy, but she willed herself to get past the door, around the corner, and far enough past the buildings and workers to somewhere private where she would not be further observed. Her head spun for a moment. She clung to a tree. *No, I willnae boak here.*

She walked past the byre through the field densely dotted with yellow buttercups in bloom at her feet. She came to an oak, where she leaned on the far side of it, wiping her tears. Then on she walked into the shade of the woods, where no one would hear her weep. Tears freely flowed as she found herself by the cool water. She pulled the fillet from her hair and dipped it into the water, then pressed it to her red eyelids and cheeks as she continued along the worn path. The path was well traveled, but not at this time of the day, when the farmhands were working. No one would trouble her now. She followed the path to a high cliff from which water poured as if from a spout between two steep walls of rock. Mari stopped to be sick again, then finished her climb to the top of the falls, where she stood and watched water pound the rocks far below.

She leaned against a large tree and cried out, knowing that the roar of the waterfall would drown out the sound. No, it could not be, and yet she had wondered, but tamped down the thought and the fear that now roiled inside her. It could not be true, but when Grizzal as much as said it, she knew that it must be. She was with child—an unmarried sinner. Before long, it would show and bring shame on her parents, who had endured so much heartache already. The kirk folk would judge her, and her parents as well. She wept until she could cry no more. She gazed at the water approaching the falls, and a strange calm came over her. The water was smooth, almost as if it were still, and it soothed her. She stepped closer to watch it. The power of it mesmerized her. Closer yet she stepped, wondering at the way the clear water seemed to slow just before it sprayed over the ledge in a seemingly solid white mass. Her handkerchief slipped loose from her hand. Caught by the breeze, it billowed and seemed for an instant suspended in air before resting on the surface until the water swallowed it.

She had not planned or imagined this, yet she was here. It made sense to accept the immediate pain in exchange for the rest, which would last beyond her life and cling to the wee one. The wee bastard. When would that label lose its grip on her child? She could not bear to imagine their two lives, the unending judgment and pain —and the loneliness. Who would have her now? Worse yet, anyone who would have her would do so without love. Someone would have need of a wife to do farm chores, and her parents would marry her off. She had ached from loneliness before, but there had always been hope of it ending. Now there would be no end. She would live life alone, never having known love.

She peered down at the rocks below. In mere moments she could join Jamie and Ellen. She reached out her hand and let the mist from the waterfall settle on her smooth skin and calm her. She seemed apart from herself. The cool moisture dulled her pain. She stood there for a very long while. Her toes crept closer. One step, then another. Now was the best time to do it. No one would ever know why. They would think it was an accident. Her parents would not be shamed. If she waited, her family would suffer more, and that kind of suffering would be worse to bear. This would spare them. Yes, she was a coward, for she would also be spared. The torment of keeping the secret until the inevitable public disgrace was too much to fathom. She leaned forward and took one last step.

Chapter 5

Rock of the Raven

An arm clamped about her waist and pulled her back from the cliff to a patch of ground under an oak, the branches of which stretched to the ground forming a canopy over them. Callum held her there, with his arms wrapped around her waist from behind, solid arms and soft words.

She screamed and struggled against him, legs flailing, heels kicking his shins.

"Easy, lass. Shh. I'll not harm you, but I'll not let you harm yourself, either." He held her and said soothing words in his deep voice until she stopped struggling.

"There now," he spoke calmly. "We're going to step away from the cliff, ken?" He cautiously loosened his hold, but she pulled away toward the cliff.

"No." He spoke firmly, but quietly. "Sorry, lass, but you're not going that way." He heaved her up into his arms and carried her safely away, and then set her down. Her cheeks were flushed, and her nostrils flared. She made a few attempts to get free, but soon gave up and sat still where he had placed her. He took a seat between her and the waterfall, gripping her wrist, just in case.

With a steady gaze, he looked into her frantic eyes. "Now, let's just sit down and rest for a bit."

Contempt mixed with panic as she looked at his hand on her wrist. "I'll have naught to do with you, soldier."

"I'm not asking you to."

As moments passed, she no longer struggled, but instead settled into a despondent slump. "Why will you not leave me alone?"

"I was not in the mood to watch you die."

"You didnae have to watch. You could have just gone away."

He gave her a rueful half grin. "No, I could not do that either."

"Why not?" She glanced at his uniform coat and plaid of a Highland dragoon with mixed fear and contempt. "You kill people all the time. Why do you care?"

"Because—you were not meant to die like that. Your life is worth more."

Her eyes darkened. "Do you think me a fool? I ken what you're after." She scrambled backward and turned, trying to get up and run.

"No, lass." He clamped a firm hand on her ankle, which may as well have been a leg iron for all she could move.

Given no choice, she turned toward him and sat, but her eyes flashed like a threatened creature facing its hunter. Her pulse throbbed in her neck as she took in gasps of air.

Taking no small offense, his tone bit through the words. "Listen, lassie. When I take a woman, it isnae by force." His eyes narrowed as he continued. "I just saved your life, you ungrateful beastie. I dinnae need a grand thank-you, but I could do with a wee bit less kicking and clawing."

To his astonishment she seemed almost to smile, assuaged by his words.

He returned his own perplexed smile. At this point, he became acutely aware of his hand on her ankle. Slowly, he lifted his hand, but flexed in readiness should she run. With an admonishing look from beneath his dark lashes, he said, "No more jumping off cliffs, now?"

While she shook her head, large tears filled and then dropped from her eyes. He withdrew his hand at once.

"I ken you meant well over there," she said in a quiet voice. Her eyes settled upon the waterfall, and a tear slipped from her lashes. She turned away as tears fell faster than she could wipe them away. "I'll be fine now. Please leave me alone."

"No."

Guileless green eyes met his for a moment and pierced him with their sorrow. Doing her best to discreetly wipe her nose on her sleeve, she said, "Well then, prepare to watch me die, although now in less haste and with far more pain."

His mouth twitched, suppressing a grin. "You are not going die."

"What makes you so sure?"

"Because it isnae your time yet."

"But it's your time to blether," she said, frowning.

He grinned. She was no longer weeping, and he seemed to have gained a small measure of trust. "If it were truly your time, you wouldnae have to work so hard at it, would you?" He leaned closer and looked in her eyes.

Her expression softened, but her sadness stayed close to the surface. A breeze tugged at some strands of silk tresses. Callum was troubled by a sudden impulse to gather the thickness of hair in his fist and inhale.

She said, "You can leave. I willnae jump."

He looked away and thought through the more sensible actions of standing and leaving, but he was reluctant to do so.

He said, "When you first saw me, you were frightened."

"Aye, and why would I not be?"

"I had just saved your life, for one thing."

"And for what? I ken all about you Highlanders."

"Oh. And you ken about me, do you?"

"I have no cause to believe that you're different from the others."

"Which others, lass?"

"The other Highlanders. They're all about us, and you ken that already."

He did. He was one of eight thousand who had descended upon the inhabitants of this part of the country to quell Covenanter activity on behalf of the Crown.

He said, "We all come from different clans. We're not all the same, ken?"

She scrutinized him with suspicion, but something in his gentle gaze drew the words from her. "I'm sorry."

"There's no need to apologize—except for the kicking and clawing." He touched his forearm as though examining a fresh wound. As she caught sight of his grin, she smiled back, her first real smile, and it pleased him. He wondered what she might have been like had he met her in happier times.

She looked offended. "You find me amusing?"

"Aye." He smiled genuinely. "It's not a bad thing."

She met his eyes with a less guarded look. "Stop, please." She looked away toward the water pounding over the edge of the falls.

He said, "I was looking at you—"

"I ken that. It's called staring, and I dinnae like it," she snapped.

He grinned to himself and continued. "And I thought, as you stood on that rock with your raven black hair, that you looked—"

"It isnae raven black. It's plain dark brown."

"There is nothing plain about you, lass." From the sharp look he received, he returned to his story in haste. "Seeing you there on that rock made me think of a raven."

"So now I'm a crow?"

"No, lass." He shook his head, smiling, and started to say that she was too lovely for that, but stopped short. Flattery neither impressed nor pleased her. "Our clan motto is Rock of the Raven. I was reminded of home. I felt as though I had been drawn to that rock—to the raven on that rock—for a purpose. You see, where I come from in the Highlands, 'tis said that the cry of the raven can foretell things."

"Soothsaying is wicked."

Callum winced. She did not make conversation easy. In fact, he was beginning to wonder whether conversation was worth all this effort.

"What sorts of things can it foretell?"

She'd surprised him with that. "Ah, well, it could mean the coming of an important guest or good fortune. It can also foretell of a battle, a loss, or a death."

"The raven isnae very specific then, is it?" said Mari, beginning to smile.

"Ah, but look at us now. You're not... flying off that cliff over there, and I'm—" He paused to rephrase what would have sounded like more idle flattery. He would not tell her that he was sitting beside a young woman whose beauty was different from any he'd seen. Nor would he marvel at how she intrigued him. "And I'm glad that you're not... there—but here." He inwardly groaned at how poorly that came out. He was not used to feeling awkward.

She said nothing, but her frown made it clear. He was overstepping his bounds, but he could not shy away. "Tell me, lass, what's so bad as all this?"

"I cannae speak of it."

"Whatever is troubling you, it's not worth doing that."

She shook her head gently, but said nothing.

He tried to accept her silence, but only managed to make it look so. It should be enough, Callum thought, to have helped her. It was not. He wanted to know her, and to see her untroubled by whatever had brought her to this desperate moment. "You couldnae shock me."

"Nor will I."

With a sudden lurch, she rose to her feet. Callum leapt up after her, fearing she had changed her mind about hurting herself. But instead of running toward the cliff, she ran in the other direction. Callum caught her by the waist, as she bent over and vomited. Once more, he was reduced to awkwardness. He should withdraw, he decided. But she put her arms over his for support. Callum circled her waist with one arm and pulled her hair back with the other. By the time she was done, she was weeping and he was behind her, soothing her with deep, quiet words in her ear.

She wiped her mouth with her hands and said, "May I please go to the water—just to wash?"

Her pitiable plea struck his heart. He cast his eyes doubtfully at her. "Only if I hold onto you." He trusted her, but with a fair measure of caution. He took hold of her wrist and led her a safe ways upstream from the falls, where he allowed her to kneel by the water. Having planted himself between her and the cliff, he released her to splash water on her face and sip gingerly from cupped hands. When she was finished, Callum offered a bit of his plaid, and she dried her face and hands with it. Her eyes softened to his as he offered a hand to help her up, and then led her away.

Once seated beside her under a tree, he studied her and considered his next words with care. "It's not an illness that sickens you, is it?" he said, knowing the answer.

Once more, silent tears dropped from her soft moss green eyes as she shook her head.

"Does the father ken?"

When she did not answer, he imagined the father abandoning her and his rage erupted. "Will the cursed scoundrel not claim the wee thing as his own?"

"He doesnae ken, nor will he. Ever."

Her bitterness brought him to a hush. "*Och*, lass. Did he force you?"

Callum fought the impulse to reach for her hand and to pull her to him. He wanted to comfort her, to take on her burden—if only for a moment.

She averted her eyes and softly said, "No."

Abruptly she rose to her feet. Callum followed, unsure of where she might go next. He would not let her return to the cliff. At the same time, his mind raced as he tried to absorb what she had told him.

"It isnae right to talk like this with a strange man." She stood poised to leave, yet hesitant.

She was right, of course. She was vulnerable, and that made him want to help and protect her. That, and her large eyes and raven silk hair drew him to her. He had shown honor and no small restraint in his actions toward her. He had saved her life and stayed with her to help her calm down. He had done the right thing. Now, before he did the wrong thing, he needed to step away.

She would need to be escorted home. There could be other Highlanders about. What gentleman would not do as much? It would be wrong to leave a lady out here in the woods unprotected, so Callum decided to see her home. And then, while she was turned away from him, he leaned down and brushed his lips on her silken hair and inhaled.

She turned her head and, finding his face so close to hers, took a step back, but not before her gaze drifted down to his mouth. Her lips parted. "I must go."

He forced himself slowly to take a step back. This put her a bit more at ease, but she looked about as though lost. Whether unsure or unwilling, neither of them left. With each moment that passed, the thought of taking her into his arms grew more tangible. His thoughts turned to yearning. His instincts were not serving him well, and good judgment was waning. The fact that she lingered was not helping him live up to his former claims about duty and honor.

At last, with her eyes cast to the ground, she said softly, "I dinnae ken where to go."

He sighed. It was no more than sympathy that he was feeling, he told himself. But he was, in truth, relieved that she was not leaving him yet. "Have you no home?"

"Aye, but if I go there, I will have to behave as though nothing were wrong. I'm not ready to do that quite yet."

"You could stay here with me for a while. We could sit here—or go for a walk."

He could see in her eyes that she doubted his motives. And why would she trust him? She had told him that she had been with a man, by choice, and conceived a bairn, but would not tell the father. A man might draw conclusions about her, and yet he did not. Her pain and her spirit moved him. The fact that she kept her distance from him and her wits about her proved she had not given up. If she chose not to tell the father, she no doubt had good reason. He suspected a broken, but proud, heart, for which he admired her. She had faced the path on which this decision would send her, even if she had faltered today. Callum hoped she would find her way down that rough road. More than that, he wanted to help her. No, that would be madness, he corrected himself. That was not why he had been sent here.

She said, "I'd like to go away from this place."

Callum nodded and got up and offered his arm, and they walked through the tall grasses.

"If Jamie saw me out walking with a Highlander— and a royalist soldier, to boot—*och*! He'd save me the trouble and throw me over a cliff himself!" She nearly laughed, but soon sobered. She reminded herself that he was gone.

"Jamie? Is he the wee one's father?"

"*Och*, no! He's... he was my brother!"

Callum nodded, trying not to reveal his relief—until he reminded himself that her Jamie was the same James McEwan suspected of murdering Archbishop Sharp, and whom he had been sent to find.

Mari's expression clouded. "He was killed by a Highland dragoon." The way she said Highland left no doubt of the common contempt with which they were held in these parts. Her eyes swept from his plaid to his royalist uniform jacket and up to his eyes.

He felt as though he had been punched in the gut. He may not have been there, but in her eyes it could have been he. Already stories spread of the Highland Host who now quartered themselves in the area, seeking to quell Covenanters. There were many clans in the Highlands, and as many standards of behavior. But in her eyes, he was no different from any of them.

"I'm... sorry."

"They shot Jamie. They—had their way with Ellen, and then they shot her. She was a good friend to me. She was Jamie's true love."

He reached out his hand, barely brushing the tips of his fingers to hers.

She slipped her hand away. "The next day we went to bury them, but they were gone. We found Ellen's body outside of the kirkyard, where the heathen are buried. Then the men sent me home. Women cannae go to a funeral. So I went home without even saying goodbye." Her breathing grew heavy as her eyes filled with tears.

"We never found Jamie. They do terrible things, you ken." Her eyes darted toward him. "Of course you do."

He did. Although he had not been party to such deeds, it was not unusual to behead and dismember the bodies and send them to their hometowns for display as a warning. She had every reason to despise Highlanders. If she found out he had followed her here, she would spurn him as well. In these days of illegal meetings outside on the moors and in the hills, wandering off was suspicious. He had been sent here to put an end to Covenanter meetings and their illegal activities. He had not found her by chance by the cliff. He had been spying on her. When she had wandered off, he had followed her. He was doing his duty. He would not be sorry for that.

She stopped walking. "By being here, talking with you, I betray Jamie and Ellen. It's like turning my back on their memory." Bitter tears led to gut-wrenching sobs that shook her lithe body until he could stand it no more.

He put his hand lightly on her shoulder. When she did not flinch or scoff—either of which he expected—he gently enfolded her in his arms. It was for comfort, as one would comfort a sister. He told himself so, and he nearly believed it. But she clung to him as a drowning person would cling even to an enemy. She clutched folds of his sleeves in her fists, and he held her clinging form against his, not as one would comfort a sister. Good sense flickered and faded. He touched her chin with his thumb and forefinger and it tilted up. Her eyes opened to his, and with that, he was lost. He lowered his lips to hers, soft, barely touching. And he was undone.

She placed her palms on his chest and pressed him away.

He pulled away with a guttural whisper. "*Och*, lass." Slowly, he shook his head and smoothed a stray hair from her cheek.

She looked down as she mumbled a breathless good-bye, and then she was gone.

Callum kept his eyes fixed on her until she had gone out of sight, then he leaned his head back against the tree with a heavy sigh. "Bloody hell, MacDonell. You've made a pish of it now."

Chapter 6

A Dangerous Path

Mari ran until she was sure she was out of sight and had not been followed. Then, slowing her pace, she tried to sort through what had happened. "When will you learn?" she scolded herself. She had always been prone to dreaming. She had been told often enough to resist such sinful imaginings, but she had persisted. Love was one such dream for which she would pay dearly. She had longed for what Jamie and Ellen had shared. Thinking she had found it, she had been fooled into a love that was false. It taught her that love could not be trusted. Men could not be trusted. She had too easily given her heart. That was a mistake she could not make again. If she ever gave her heart to another, it would take a long time before he earned her trust. And yet, before she gave her heart and body to the bairn's father, she had known him her whole life. Even that had not been long enough.

And this man—this Highlander—was a stranger, a royalist enemy. He had happened upon her at a vulnerable moment. He could have taken advantage of her, but he had not. Savage Highlander or not, she would have gone over the edge of the falls to her death had it not been for him.

How could she even have thought to do that? Yes, she wanted the pain to be over, but now she could see that she did not want to die. She wanted, more than ever, to live. He had given that to her. If a stranger could care that she lived, perhaps someone might one day care for her, too. Where, minutes before, she had felt only despair, she now felt a small bit of hope.

She drew in a quick breath as she touched her lips. She could still feel it—his kiss. The kirk folk would say she was wanton. But the kirk folk would say it with or without this particular kiss. Still, this was not at all like her. A stranger! What had possessed her—his fine face and braw body? No, although he did possess both. He was kind when he need not have been, and that won her trust. When he touched her, a thrill went through her; and that won her heart. She had not meant to give it, but with him she had forgotten to guard it. That frightened her most.

He would never kiss her again because she would not see him. He was gone, but she would not forget him. She would always remember his kiss, and that he was her enemy.

CALLUM MACDONELL STORMED into camp with a scowl that not only caught his men's notice, but further reduced them to silence.

"We break camp in the morning," he told them as he stormed about, packing and moving things.

"What happened to 'bide here for a while—watch and wait?'" Charlie asked.

"No need now," Callum summarily said. No one hastened to ask for the reason, but they all exchanged quizzical looks. They had never seen him like this, so they tried to stay out of his way. No one wished to be first to step into the path of his fury.

It was Duncan who, late in the evening, found Callum sitting alone on a rock looking into the night stars. He sat down beside him. The nearly full moon cast shadows of trees on the ground.

Lifting rueful eyes, Callum said, "He has a sister."

With a blank look, Duncan said, "Who?"

"Jamie. That's what they call him."

It took Duncan a moment before he gave a nod of understanding. "James McEwan?"

"Aye."

"They call him that, do they? And how do you ken?"

"She told me herself."

"The sister?"

"Aye!" Callum barked.

Duncan turned to face Callum directly, but said nothing. There was no need, and Duncan was not one to waste words. Nor was he one to waste emotion, or at least the expression of it. He knew that any chiding due Callum would be self-inflicted. What Duncan did best was to listen.

Callum said, "So you see, there's no need to camp here when at least one of them kens that we're out here."

"Aye, that makes sense."

"I had no choice but to speak with her," Callum said defensively.

"I dinnae doubt it," said Duncan in his calm way.

"It couldnae be helped. More than that I cannae explain without betraying a trust."

"But that's not what troubles you." Duncan studied Callum.

"No." Callum stared into the night. "I did the right thing, to begin with."

The last part caught Duncan's notice. "Beautiful lass, is she?"

Callum looked up at the stars, and then down at the shadowy ground. "Aye, she is."

Duncan studied his friend. What a pitiful creature he appeared to be now. They had grown up together. If anyone knew Callum, it was Duncan. But never had he seen his friend in such a state.

"Callum, there's no one I would rather have beside me in battle. But women can cloud our good senses."

"*Och!* A dark thundering cloud."

Duncan let out a rare laugh. "Aye."

Callum stared out over the moors at the farm. "I followed her from one of the farms. I thought she might have been taking a message or supplies to her brother."

"But she was not."

Callum shook his head. "We're to quarter ourselves on her damned farm tomorrow."

Duncan considered their plight for a few moments. "Now that you ken her, could you not use that to get information about her brother's whereabouts?"

"She thinks he's dead."

"If she's telling the truth."

"She is."

"How can you be sure? You're a royalist. Why would she trust you?"

Callum leveled a dark glare at Duncan. "Trust me. She was telling the truth."

"He's bound to contact someone at home sooner or later."

"Aye." Callum nodded gravely. "And when he does, I will betray her, and then I will lose her."

"You just met her. Would the loss be so great?"

Callum turned to his friend with a look of misery that more than answered his question.

Duncan winced. "Just look out for the lads. You've embarked on a dangerous path. They'll follow you no matter where you take them. So be mindful of where that might be."

FOR THE REST of that day and the morning that followed, Mari's traitorous heart would not rest. She begged silent forgiveness from Jamie and Ellen each time her thoughts strayed to the stranger. She stayed busy, hoping to distract herself. When that did not work, she found solace in knowing that she would not see him again. Once she accepted that fact, she let herself think of the Highland soldier. He would never be near enough to trouble her again, so her heart would be safe.

Except when she dreamed. In the night she awoke, reaching out for him. And in the dark hours when dreams hung in the air like a fresh mist, her heart and her longing were for him.

The next morning she went walking across the land she and Jamie had explored as children. Such grand adventures they had had on the wild Scottish moors! She went now as a penance to remind her what was proper. For once in her life she would do the wise thing and not love. Love was not like it sounded in stories and ballads. Love was a hollow ember that burned trust and hope, leaving only a fool with an empty heart and full belly. And a hungry one. Mari set out for home with a full bowl of porridge on her mind.

She arrived there to find soldiers in plaids—Highland dragoons roaming the grounds as if it were their right. Other royalist Highlanders had descended upon nearby farms and estates, but her family's farm had escaped notice. But that was before Jamie and Ellen were killed. Now both their families were suspect. Five men were to be quartered here, and her family would have to house and feed every one of them.

Mari rounded a corner of the byre and bumped into a Highlander. Others were standing nearby, looking as though they'd had a few drams. Even though they were not the dragoons from the moor, they were royalists just the same. The sight of them brought a flush of panic to her face as the feelings returned of her last evening with Jamie and Ellen. Her heart pounded. Had they been sent to finish the job they had started? She told herself it could not be. They would have been waiting for her, not standing about drinking whisky and laughing. But she could not gain control of her fear.

"Easy, dearie." Alex steadied her by taking hold of her

shoulders. She had bumped into him, and seemed about to stumble. She pulled free and continued on her way.

She was soon flanked by a soldier on either side, arms hooked in hers. On her left, Charlie said, "Dinnae mind my friend there. Alex has spent so much time reiving cattle, he dinnae ken how to woo a real woman." He laughed and dodged a smack on the back of his head from Alex.

She glanced nervously from one to the other.

"Charlie, dinnae frighten the lass," Duncan said gruffly.

"Dinnae be daft!" Charlie grinned and began to sing. Alex joined in. Hughie picked up his fiddle and played. Charlie took hold of her waist and whirled her about in a dance. She grew dizzy and gripped his arms just to stay balanced.

It's of a shepherd's daughter,
Kept sheep on yonders hill.
A squier's son came riding by,
And he fain would have his will.

You and I, you and I,
He fain would have his will.

"He took me by the hand,
And by the silken sleeve,
And gently laid me on the ground
Before I gave him leave."

You and I, you and I,
Before she gave him leave.

"Since you have had your will of me,
Pray tell to me your name,
That when my baby it is born
I can call it by the same."

You and I, you and I,
Can call it by the same.

"Sometimes they call me Jack," said he,
"Sometimes they call me John,
But when I'm in the fair king's court
My name is Sweet Will-yum."

You and I, you and I,
Can call it Sweet Will-yum.

THE MEN WERE STOMPING and singing and passing her, spinning, from one to the next as they danced. She tried to pull away, but could not get free. This was what the minister called promiscuous dancing. She had been cautioned against it since she was a child. If anyone saw her, she would surely be called before the kirk to answer for this sinful display. The savage Highlanders laughed as the bodhrun beat quickened. A tear slipped down her cheek.

Abruptly a pair of strong hands gripped her dance partner's shoulders and pushed him aside. Alex whirled about and pulled back his arm for a punch, but a fist caught his jaw unawares and he staggered back a step, and then lost his balance and fell to the ground.

Callum took her hand firmly and guided her protectively behind him. She followed his lead, at the same time relieved yet unsettled by his sudden presence as she steadied her breathing. She did not want her heart to leap just because he was near. Women were not supposed to feel such desire! But the strong shoulders in front of her fell at eye level, and made her want to lean closer and breathe in his scent, touch the leine that hung over his back, and feel the skin underneath it.

"This lady isnae for the likes o' you lot, ken?"

"Aye," came their submissive replies as they exchanged glances. When those looks hinted at grins, Callum quelled them with a glare.

Still sternly eyeing his men, he said, "They'll not bother you again, lass." Barely glancing at her, he looked back at the men to deliver one more look of warning.

He offered his arm. Mari hesitated, but seeing his men looking on, she took it, both for protection and so she would not humiliate him in front of the men he had just rebuked for her sake. But his touch made her nervous. She rested her hand on an arm that was hard with muscles. And it was warm. Callum guided her around the corner of the byre and stopped, turning to her.

"Lass." The deep voice he had used with his men was now gentle. His eyes softened, but maintained a cautious reserve. "Dinnae judge them too harshly. The lads were only having some fun. They didnae mean to upset you."

"Aye, well—" She stopped herself before saying that they had indeed upset her. Instead, she forced a nod of

acceptance as she took a step backward. "Good evening."
She set off in brisk strides toward her house.

"Lass!" he called after her. He lowered his voice and
said to himself, "You need not run from me. I'll not harm
you."

The heavy door closed.

Chapter 7

Not Forgotten

"Is that you, Marion?" asked her mother.

"Aye." Having escaped to the safety of her home, Mari feared, from the tone of her mother's voice, a request would soon follow.

"Sally is ill. Would you please do the milking?"

Mari inwardly groaned, but said in a pleasant tone, "Aye, Mum."

"But mind you, stay clear of those Highlanders."

"Aye."

She stood at the door for a moment, heaved a sigh, and set out for the field, where she gathered the cows and led them back to the shed. Before long, Callum was there, too conveniently timed for mere chance. He grabbed a spare milking stool and sat beside her. Mari cast a deliberately indifferent glance, and began milking the poor cow with marked vigor and flushed cheeks, yielding little milk but increasing frustration.

"Easy, lass."

Gently, he put his hands on her wrists, which she

slipped away quickly. His amusement showed only in his eyes, which settled on her for a moment, unseen. He took over the milking and yielded much better results.

Now fully vexed, she said, "I've been milking cows since I was a wee child. I think I must ken how to do it by now." She refused to look at him except for his hands, upon which her eyes rested.

"Aye, but you looked about to pull the teats right off of her."

Her head snapped toward him. Now flustered, she glanced away just as quickly. She could not let him see how he affected her.

"You've got to help her relax so the milk will come down."

A blush tinted her cheeks. "Do you think I dinnae ken that?"

He cast a gentle grin toward her, but refrained from comment. The Highlander then proceeded to stroke the cow's udder with his palm. His hands were large and well formed, and his touch was gentle. Mari's mood softened, the realization of which unsettled her more. She got up and moved on to the next cow, where she fought for composure.

A long while passed before either spoke. Mari lost herself in the rhythmic spraying of milk into the pail. Callum finished the first cow and moved on to another. Mari listened, but would not watch him walk by.

The late afternoon sun was nearly gone when Callum finished. Mari was not quite done with her last cow when he sat down beside her.

"I'm sorry about the dancing. The lads meant no harm."

"Aye, so you said." She stopped milking and looked at him. She wished she had not, for his eyes held a power that disturbed her. She lowered her eyes, only to notice his lips and recall how they felt when they had kissed. Steeling herself, she said, "We dinnae indulge in singing and dancing."

"I'm sorry to hear that." He studied her in a disquieting way.

Mari returned to her milking. "Our ways are very different from yours in the Highlands." She said this as much to herself as a reminder that he and his men had invaded her home with their wild Highland ways. They were different. They could never be anything to each other—not that she had ever thought they could.

"We are nae as different as you think."

His voice resonated too close to her ear. Deep and rich, its timbre weakened her. She missed a beat in her milking. "Aye, we are, and there's no changing that."

She got up to empty her pail. He took it, and she let him carry it for her. Then she chided herself for having done so. Everything was too easy with him. Every touch, every look, and every word that he spoke won her heart before her will could prevent it.

"Lass, I'm not your enemy." But as he said it he looked away, for he knew he was wrong.

She flashed a look of triumph and said, "You are my enemy, and you ken it. You Highlanders moved into our homes as if you belonged, but you dinnae belong. We dinnae want you here, and we'll never forget what you've done!"

"I have a duty to my clan, and this is part of it. I willnae apologize for that."

"How could we lowlanders possibly matter to you or your clan way up there in the Highlands?"

Anger flared as he interrupted her. "I might ask you the same. What did we matter to you when thousands of Campbells—your fellow Covenanters—marched into our homes? And your people did not merely quarter there, as we are doing here. They killed our women and children and laid waste to our glen. And we have not forgotten. You've suffered a loss, and I'm sorry. But you are not alone in the suffering of losses."

Her eyes flashed in protest, while at the same time her feelings of guilt kept her silent.

His eyes met hers directly. "My mother watched your blessed Covenanters destroy everything our family owned. Then they murdered her mother. When her father fought back to defend her, they murdered him, too. My mother was spared because she ran into the hills and escaped them. But other bairns and their mothers were killed. And what had they done to deserve it?"

Mari said, "I dinnae ken about that. The Covenanters I know are good men who fight for our freedom to worship."

"By destroying ours? Lass, I dinnae care a whit about whether you pray to that hedgerow over there. But while your Covenanters hide behind the skirts of religion, they are plotting to bring down the monarchy, and that I cannae abide."

"I have not heard talk of that."

"Aye, well it may not have made it to your wee world here, but it's there just the same."

His arrogant tone made her bristle. "In that case, our

'wee world' can hardly be worth your trouble. So why are you here?"

"Because our chief called us to serve."

"He calls, and you fight—without question?"

"The more trust a man has, the fewer questions he need ask."

"And you trust that what you are doing is right?"

"Aye. It's a matter of duty and honor to my chief and to our king."

"Aye, well that sounds very manly, but explain to me this: Monarchs go back and forth—from Catholic to Episcopal to Presbyterian. If the king is divinely appointed by God, then why cannae God make up his mind which church he should go to?"

He took firm hold of her shoulders and looked as close to anger as she had seen him. "Say what you will to me, but dinnae let others hear you talking like that. Some might call it treason."

She quashed an unsettling fear as she lifted her chin and spoke her mind. "*Whisht!* That's a convenient answer when you've not got a real one."

His eyes hardened. "A real answer? Here's my real answer: Your Covenanters slaughtered my kinsmen and now threaten my king, and I will fight back."

"They may have been Covenanters, but they were not my people. How can you blame me for that?"

"How can you blame me for the death of your brother and friend? And yet I see it in those bonnie green eyes of yours, lass." His frank gaze bored through the fierce indignation that brightened her eyes and colored her cheeks.

Her lips parted. The sight transfixed him. "Marion," he said tenderly, lifting his eyes to meet hers.

"How did you ken my name?"

He glanced off to the side. He had been sent to find James McEwan; he knew every name in her family, as well as her neighbors, but he could not admit that to her. So he said, "I've heard them calling you that."

She studied him for a moment. "Oh."

His eyes searched hers. She was wholly uneasy. They'd met when she was at her weakest. He knew too much about her. And now, just by looking at her, she felt his gaze through to her heart. She could not let him affect her so. Chest pounding, she turned away and picked up a pail of feed for the chickens as though he were not there.

"Mari—"

She kept walking.

He called after her. "Mari will suit, I suppose, as I willnae be given time to say more."

Had she not been so distraught, she might have smiled as she went outside to feed the chickens.

Chapter 8

Traitorous Heart

When, some while later, Mari was obliged to return and complete her chores, she entered the byre and exhaled in relief to not see him.

"I would have a word with you."

Mari flinched at the sound of the quiet, firm voice from the shadows behind her. She turned around to find Callum, arms folded, leaning casually against a timber post.

She let her eyes meet his. A mistake. His gaze burned into hers. She diverted her eyes to the empty chicken feed pail in her hands. To set it down in its proper place would bring her nearer to him, so she clutched it tensely. Dusk was settling in, cloaking them both in its shadows.

"I cannae talk with you here, or anywhere for that matter." She quickly glanced at him, but the way he was staring at her made her more ill at ease. She impulsively pivoted away, but he grasped her wrist before she could escape. The pail dropped with a shallow clang. She froze, unwilling to turn toward him. Twisting her hand, she tried to free herself, but he pulled her gently yet firmly to face him. When her eyes met his, he frowned to see her expression. Silence stretched between them, broken only by the thrum of her heart in her ears. He studied her hand as he held it.

She hated the way that with only a touch he dissolved the emotions she wielded against him and drew others she could not control. She tried to slip her hand from his to escape, but he held it and stroked it with his other hand.

"Let me go, please," she said weakly. She looked about to make sure no one was watching. *He is your enemy. Your brother and dear friend are dead!* But her logic rebelled. *He did not do it, any more than I killed his kinsmen. We both share similar grief and lack similar guilt. But still, we are opposed.*

"Mari." He paused, searching for what to say next that would not set her into flight. In an effort to distract her and put her at ease, he said, "Do they call you Mari?"

"No."

"Then I will."

"Sir—or rather, Soldier... "

She was flustered, which gave him hope. He regarded her with quiet confidence. "Ensign."

"Ensign," she said, but then paused, blushing as she forgot what she had wanted to say.

"MacDonell. Although, after I've been kissed, I tend to answer to Callum." A grin tried to form on his lips, but he checked it.

"Ensign MacDonell, you asked for a word with me. Now that you've had it and more, would you please let me go?"

He stared at her hand for a moment, then looked away with a troubled expression. "I must tell you something."

"No, please do not. What happened before was a mistake. There is no more to say."

He frowned, even though he agreed. "It's not that."

He stopped himself before blurting it out: *Your brother is alive.* He had not planned it, but his good sense seemed to fail in her presence. He wanted her to know there was hope. He had the power to ease her grief. And yet, what if her brother were not still alive after all? He could be mistaken. He struggled to make his thoughts clear. Did they have solid proof? Who in St. Andrews really knew James McEwan? What if someone, under threat of torture, had offered up his name, knowing he was dead? People did desperate things to avoid torture. What better way to appear to cooperate and yet not put another at risk than to say that a dead man had done it? If he proceeded to tell Mari that her brother was alive and it turned out not to be true, he would cause her more grief. And if James were alive, why had the lad not told his own family? If he did not want his family to know, did Callum have the right to tell them otherwise? Callum could not help but question his own motives. What would he more likely ease, her suffering or his conscience? No, it was too dangerous. There were too many questions attached. To speak now, without knowing the answers, could yield unexpected and uncontrollable results. He was not ready to risk Mari's heart or the lives of his men. Suppositions were dangerous things.

Mari said, "If you have something to say, please say it now, before someone sees us."

He loosened his grip on her wrist and stroked the edge

of her sleeve with his thumb while he searched for the words. In a quiet voice, he said, "Mari," and lifted his eyes to meet hers with a smoldering look.

Unable to hold his gaze, she glanced down, now spellbound by his thumb as it stroked the folded edge of her sleeve. "You are too familiar, sir. If someone saw..."

With a reluctant nod, he withdrew his hand. "Forgive me. You've bewitched me."

She swung her arm to slap him, but he caught her wrist neatly and held it. "If I'm to be struck, I'll first ken the reason."

"You accused me of witchcraft and disguised it as flattery."

He was nonplussed. "I said what I feel."

"As though I were to blame for your lack of control." As she said it, the heat rose to her face. The mere thought of control or lack of it implied emotions she could not properly think, let alone speak: carnal emotions that scared her, most of all because she felt them, too.

He peered at her while he forced down his anger. "I assure you, as I stand here, I dinnae lack control, even though it may be put to the test at this moment." He leveled a probing look. "Lass, have I given you any cause not to trust me?"

Mari's fingertips trembled in his sure hand. "Not yet, but I've heard such words before. People behave in one way, but they change once they get what they want."

"Mari." Callum took a step toward her, but she stiffened, so he stopped. What he wanted to do was take firm hold of her shoulders. Instead he spoke with forced calm. "Look at me. Really look at me, and tell me you truly believe I would speak false words to you."

Tears welled up in her eyes. "I believe that you would. You're a man, and men lie."

He interrupted her. "Mari, I willnae lie to you. Nor will I hurt you."

"No one ever says in advance that they'll hurt you. But they do just the same." She cast her eyes to the side to avoid his.

"I am not like the bairn's father, if that's what you're thinking. Nor will I pay for his wrongs." His temper sparked, and he clenched his jaw as he tamped down his anger. Had he not pulled her from certain death? How could she not trust him, when all he wanted to do was to help her? Ah, but now he was not being truthful to himself. He wanted much more than that, he was forced to admit. *Eejit, the lass is in pain. Give her some time.* But that was one thing he could not seem to do.

Mari said, "I'm not asking you to pay for what he did. I'm just asking you to leave me alone."

"Is that truly what you want—what you feel in your heart?"

As she gazed at him, she knew that the answer was no. Lest he see it in her eyes, she looked down—anywhere but at him—but not before her eyebrows drew together. The light caught her moist lashes. "I dinnae trust feelings."

He softened his voice. "Mari. My feelings are true."

No one called her Mari, and somehow the way that he did made her heart pound. She fought it and lifted her eyes to stare boldly, but faltered and looked down again. "It's my own feelings I dinnae trust." Silent moments passed, so she looked up to see his reaction. His gentle look gripped her heart.

Callum felt a surge of relief from her confession. She

had as much as declared there was something between them.

"You're a soldier," she said.

"Aye," he replied.

She said, "In battle, if someone sank a dirk into your heart, could you choose how it would feel?"

"No, but I'd let the wound heal."

She cried, "But not all wounds heal."

"*Och*, lass." He was beginning to wish he could sink a dirk into whoever had hurt her. "This one will." He reached out to wipe a tear from her cheek, but she turned to avoid his touch.

He nearly said that people did not die from broken hearts, but then he thought of how he had met her, when she was about to do just that. He wished he could make her forget, but how could she when the memory grew in her belly? Until her heart healed, his attentions were no better than salt for her wound. *Walk away*, said a voice in his head. *Now*.

Despite that, he heard himself say, "I willnae hurt you like the bairn's father did. You must trust me, lass."

She practically scoffed, and that wounded him. "People who ask for trust seldom deserve it. Forbye, my past is no business of yours."

"It's my business if he stands between us."

Her bitter tears shimmered. "Us? There is no us. And do you truly believe that the wee one's father is all that stands between us?"

"So there is an us!" He grinned in triumph, but quickly saw she was in no mood to be grinned at.

"Mari," he said, running a thumb along her wrist as he studied it. "I've laid bare my heart." He could not quite believe it himself. He gazed at a strand of hair that lay on her brow and reached up to touch it. His hand lingered, stroking the smooth strands of hair.

"Stop that!" she snapped as she took a step backward, but her foot caught a crack in the cobblestone floor and she faltered. With firm hands, he caught her waist and steadied her. She took in a small gasp and kept her eyes focused straight ahead, at his chest. She leaned as though pulled closer to him. Correcting herself, she took a careful step backward until he released her.

When she would not meet his gaze, he studied her troubled brow, her flushed cheeks and the lips he had once tasted. Stillness hovered between them. "Mari, I dinnae want to hurt you. Believe me."

"I do." In a soft voice she added, "But you will."

Callum said nothing. No words would change her mistrust. Not today. Not for a very long time. Yet he stood there, not wanting to leave her. He would stand there until she forced him to go.

Mari's brow furrowed as she exhaled with resignation. He had already seen her at her lowest. Nothing she said now could be worse. It would be a relief to have someone to talk to. "He said he wanted to marry me."

Of course he did. Callum's eyes shut for an instant. There was really no need to hear more. But until she told him, it would loom there between them. He could not share his particular thoughts at the moment, for they were too harsh. So he held his tongue. She glanced toward him, almost as though she were rolling her eyes from self-loathing, but also checking to see if he looked poised to flee. That charmed him—that and her eyes, which were green and quite round. He had no plans to flee.

She spoke in a quiet voice, with little emotion. "He came by one day, on his way to speak with my father to ask for my hand, or so he said, and I was fool enough to believe him. There's a burn not far from here, with a thicket of trees beside it. It was a grand day, very warm for the season. It was the kind of day you smell spring like a hint of what's coming. I'd gone for a long walk. I was warm and had dabbed my face with a handkerchief, when a gust of wind caught it and carried it to the water. I waded in after it. *Och!* It was so cold! That's where he happened upon me by chance."

Callum arched a brow. *By chance.*

She went on. "He was thirsty from walking and came to the burn for some water to drink. He was surprised to find me there."

With no warning, she glanced over at Callum and caught something in his expression. With a painful nod, she said, "I suppose that was a lie, too."

Callum imagined himself there, met with the sight of her wading—skirts up past her knees, legs wet and silken, turning a startled face toward him. Her chest heaving with a sigh of relief to find someone she loved. Eyes wide with trust, the brisk air drawing a blush to her cheeks. The thought alone stirred him. The sight would have tested his honor.

She continued. "I was chilled from the water. He opened his coat and wrapped it around me for warmth."

Callum looked away to conceal his disgust for the rogue.

Mari said, "It was a mistake to stay there alone with him. I should have gone home." She stopped talking, her troubled thoughts distant.

A wisp of hair brushed her jaw line. He wanted to slip it behind her ear, but then he would slide his fingers into her hair and touch his palm to the nape of her neck underneath it. All that thickness of hair seemed to cry out to him to be clutched in his hand while he kissed her. He resolved not to touch Mari's hair.

Her gaze hardened. "Afterward, he was furious with me."

A frown was only the surface of the anger now roiling within Callum. The man was a scoundrel, and a lucky one not to be here now.

"He said it was my fault. That I'd bewitched him." She lifted her eyes to meet his.

Callum dropped his chin with a sigh. "So when I said the same words... "

She nodded.

He had touched a raw nerve. How he wished he had known.

"He told me I was not fit for a godly man's wife."

Callum's jaw clenched. The only words that now came to mind were curses, so instead he quietly listened.

She swallowed her pain. "He never spoke to my father to ask for my hand."

"*Och*, lass." He was moved by her pain, which had only been deepened by her sweet, trusting nature.

"He had high ideals," she explained.

He scoffed, but then worked to suppress any further reaction. High ideals? The only thing high in this lout was in the front of his trews—that is, when he managed to keep it inside them. With restraint he said, "He was not worthy of you."

"He held quite the opposite view."

"Because he was a blackguard, or an *eejit*. Either way, he was worthless."

"He was married within a month."

"Then he was both."

"And I was a fool."

Callum's anger with the bairn's father doubled as he saw Mari's sorrow. Without thinking, he brushed a tear from her cheek, but his hand lingered there. She leaned into it slightly, enough to undo him. When she took in a soft breath, he touched his lips to her tear-moistened cheek. He told himself to stop there. But her face inclined toward his, and he gave her a kiss, soft and brief. But when it was over, neither pulled away as they should have. Instead their lips lingered, not touching, but near enough that a breath brought them nearer, and into a kiss. Callum lost himself to the taste of her lips and her mouth, the physical thrill of her body leaning against his, and her arms about his neck.

Mari's resolve came moments too late, as she pressed her hands to his chest and pushed him away. "Despite what you now ken and may think of me, your past kindness will purchase no more than my thanks."

"Purchase?" he said, eyes flashing in anger. "Mari ..."

"Marion." Her strong words came in a weak voice. "What gives you the right to be so familiar? Who are you to think you can call me what you want, and to do what you want?"

"What I want? It did not appear that I was alone in the wanting. Say what you want, lass, but your lips make you a liar." Callum shot a harsh look at her and then shook his head as he cast his eyes elsewhere. He had wanted that kiss; and, yes, she had kissed him back. He wished he could pause for a moment to contemplate that, but he had taken it knowing how fragile she was. With a good deal of trust, she had shared a deeply personal story, and it had moved him—enough, as it turned out, for him to lose control and scare her away. Again.

He looked earnestly at her. "I am not like the bairn's father. I'll admit that to kiss you like that was impulsive and selfish, but it was honest."

She considered his words for a moment, but abruptly said, "Ensign—"

"Callum."

"Ensign MacDonell." In vain, she tried to replace some formality between them, as though it could erase what they had shared.

"Mari," said Callum.

"Marion—Mistress McEwan." Color rushed to her cheeks, which made her look all the more lovely to Callum.

"Have we not progressed beyond formal address?" Callum asked her.

"No, we have not. We will not." She stammered, which drew a grin that he worked to conceal. She had feelings for him. No matter how reluctant they were, as long as he saw them he would not be dissuaded. She had touched his heart, and his heart once touched was tenacious.

She struggled to continue. "We met, and you saved me. I believe you are not—a bad man."

Callum did not lack modesty, but he thought he was a bit more than that. *Not a bad man.*

She went on. "But we—well, there is no we. We can be no more than... "

"Friends?" Callum said dryly.

"Friends? No. That isnae what we are."

With a knowing tilt of his head, he acknowledged her point.

"You have come on our land to force your religion upon us. We dinnae want you here. We are foes." She stopped, seemingly satisfied with her conclusion.

Her conclusion felt quite like a wall.

Her eyes darted about, seeking any sight but his troubling gaze. His silence made her feel as though she needed to explain herself further. "Royalists just killed my brother and my friend, both of whom I dearly loved."

"I'm sorry. I ken that your loss is a deep one."

"Aye," she said softly.

Gently, he said, "And you ken that my kinsmen suffered similar grief."

"Aye."

"But you and I have done nothing to hurt one another." He tenderly lifted her chin. Reluctantly, she shook her head as his fond look settled on her.

She said, "Tomorrow—or the next day—in battle, one of my people might kill your brother and your dear friend. Will you feel the same then?"

"Unless you hold the sword, I will view you as separate."

This troubled her. "I cannae view you the same way. You make me uneasy. You look like the others, and, given the chance, you will act like the others. You are one of them."

"I am." He could not refute it. "But am I not more than just that?"

"To us, you are one more thing the king has forced upon us."

"But what am I to you?"

Her agitation mounted. Her eyes darted to the door, but he stepped in her path.

Frustrated, she said, "You are someone I wish would stay out of my way."

"I willnae." He was quiet, but firm.

"Why?" she asked helplessly.

"Because I can protect you."

"From whom?" She leveled a look that convicted him, for in truth any danger ahead would most likely be at the hands of some royalist forces. How could he admit that there were Highlanders—not from his clan—but others who were taking property, sometimes women, on the lands that they occupied? His jaw clenched with the taste of his own hypocrisy.

She leveled a glare. "You are my enemy, and I am yours, Ensign MacDonell."

"Callum," he insisted, as though stripping himself of his rank might help her see him as a man apart from other Highland dragoons. "Mari, please dinnae judge me for things I have not done."

"Callum." She now turned his name on him like a weapon. Her contempt made it sound like a curse. "You are a strong man with deep convictions. I admire that. I do."

He knew he was going to wish she had stopped there.

She went on with a bluntness that disarmed him. "You have chosen to fight for your clan. I suppose that I must admire that, but it sets us at odds. Nothing can ever change that."

Her words stung, but he steeled his expression. "I am just Callum."

Her expression softened. "No, you are so much more than that." She lifted sorrowful eyes that searched his, looking lost.

Callum let that look wash over him until his lips parted.

"Good day, Callum." Mari turned and walked to her house.

MARI'S MOTHER called out from the kitchen. "Are you finished with the cows already?"

"Aye, Mum."

"And the chickens?"

"Aye, Mum."

"Mari?" Her mother came to a stop at the doorway. "Be wary around those Highlanders. They're not like us. If any of them talk to you, just act like you dinnae ken what they're saying and keep walking."

"Aye, Mum."

She ran into her room, shut the door and leaned on it. God help her, she hated him—and herself. She had spoken her true mind, but her true heart had been silent. She now breathed out what was on her heart in a whisper: "Callum MacDonell."

Chapter 9

The Dirk Oath

Callum stared at the night sky, unable to sleep. He believed in his reason for fighting. His people had been attacked first by the Covenanters. It was they who had come—four thousand of them—to his land, to his home. But they had not merely occupied homes as his people did now. Covenanters had destroyed homes and villages. Forty years had since passed, but Highland memories ran deep. To fight back was a matter of honor and loyalty to family and clan. Unlike that of the English, Highland strength was built not on owning land but on the number and loyalty of its people. Honor bound them together and gave them their might. This was his duty, and he would not waver.

Callum understood Mari's feelings. She thought she had lost her brother and friend at the hands of a rogue unit of soldiers who were using the law to justify their blood sport. He did not know them, but they fought for the crown, on the same side and for the same cause. The actions of one reflected upon the other, and so he was tainted in Mari's eyes. He knew that in battle not all men behaved honorably. It occurred on both sides. It was wrong. But all he could do was control himself and his men and ensure that they fought for their cause in a way that brought honor to their clan and the people back home.

He could not deny that he was glad to be here. Mari McEwan had changed him. She lingered on his mind, and his heart, and she gave him new purpose. He wanted to know her and win her heart over. Being here gave him time. In the meanwhile, he would keep her safe. It was a noble excuse for the truth, which was that she stirred longings in him, and this drove his desire to know her and watch over her.

His clansmen would protect her. He need only ask. They might have been full of whisky and mischief earlier, but they were good lads. He knew them, and trusted them with his life and with hers. He could not speak for the other Highlanders about them, though. While Mari might view him as an intruder, the truth was that by being there, he indeed protected her from the harm others might do. If his presence did that, he would not regret or apologize for it.

The next question was harder. If his honor were put to the test, which would win? If he had to choose between his desire for Mari or his honor to the crown for which he had sworn to fight loyally, what would he do?

Now who's the fool, Callum MacDonell? She hates you, and for good reason. Walk away. Let her grieve. You can only hurt her—and yourself in the bargain.

IN THE DAYS THAT FOLLOWED, Callum saw little of Mari. He forced himself to stay distant. Ignoring her came at a cost, but he did his best to respect her wishes. He had told her his feelings and she had rebuffed him. There was nothing to do but to wait. He hoped that she would change her mind, but days passed with no progress.

Daily patrols with his men gave him relief from the arduous task of concealing his feelings for Mari, but he became consequently ill-tempered, a state which did not escape the notice of his men. Alex made a snide remark about it—once. Nearly coming to blows, the subject was not brought up again, but seething looks were exchanged and a new unspoken rule was set: They would not discuss Mari.

He could avoid her, but he could not ignore her. When he did hide the yearning, it was close to the surface. At unavoidable moments, his eyes would meet hers and betray all. It was worth every pang of emotion to see that she worked just as hard to hide her own feelings for him. These infrequent glimpses into Mari's heart gave him hope and exhilarating torment.

No matter where their hearts led, she would not let him follow, for he was the enemy. She had lost too much to see past it, and soon she would lose more. When her desperate condition came to light, she would face the kirk's judgment. If she only would have him, Callum would spare her. But any attachment to a Highland dragoon would bring worse judgment upon her, perhaps worst of all from her own conscience.

And so they were apart, and would stay so. This made her clearly the wiser in his eyes, for her resolve was much stronger than his. He was afflicted with a ridiculous longing that drove him to watch her until he was sure he'd go daft from desire. She stayed close by her parents – smart girl – when Callum was in sight. For this reason, Callum grew increasingly fond of her mother for sending Mari outside to do chores and requiring her company for long spells outside doing needlework. Once he ventured too close and, catching his gaze, Mari's face flushed. He liked to think that her fingers had trembled, but he was not close enough to have seen.

On such a day, Callum returned with his men from a survey of the area, scouting for caves that peppered the moors, providing hidden shelter for Covenanter ringleaders.

As they led their horses into the byre, Alex said, "If I have to endure one more drowsy afternoon on the moors, I'll go daft."

Charlie said, "Shall I stir up a wee war—just to keep us from getting rusty?"

Callum smiled and said, "We're supposed to be rooting out trouble, not causing it." As he spoke, he caught sight of Mari, and his words trailed off.

Duncan followed Callum's gaze and said, "Aye."

Alex and Charlie quickly went on to talk about their next trip to Glasgow and how they would take Hughie to a nanny house. After Hughie endured some good-natured teasing, the lads were away, jabbing and chasing each other in the direction of the kitchen to see if they could cajole some food out of the cook.

That was, all except Callum, who lingered behind to brush his horse. Thoroughly—in hope it might afford him a glimpse of Mari. But with his task now complete, Callum stood in the shadow of the doorway and leaned with arms folded, while he wished for Mari to emerge with her near-sighted mother to work on her stitching.

By my sword! What a pitiful wretch I am!

Determined to shake off this mood, Callum walked to the doorway in time to see the minister and his son arrive on horseback. He stepped back into the shadow until they had entered the house. Knowing Charlie, he and the others would charm the news out of the kitchen help. It was a warm summer day. Windows were open. Callum sat down by the side of the house between bits of shrubbery and waited.

Spying was, it turned out, a dull endeavor, with rare bouts of peril thrown in to make it worthwhile. He was deeply involved with cleaning the grit from his fingernails with his dirk while he waited. Callum had, weeks before, determined the lay of the rooms in the house. He had concealed himself here while the guests had arrived and got settled. Now, horses in the stable and guests safely inside, he could go unobserved to the sitting room windows. Between meals, the dining room tended to go unvisited, so there was nothing to gain from lingering here any longer. He had decided to move on to the sitting room window when he heard a man's voice from inside. Of the two who'd arrived, this had to be the younger. It was a clear, youthful voice and, regrettably for the speaker, Callum thought, rather high. No doubt, this was the minister's son.

"Mari," said the young man in hushed tones.

Callum silently cursed him as he crouched beneath the window and listened.

"I have reason to believe that you are with child."

The lout. Callum listened intently as he thought how to spare Mari this painful conversation.

"Well, your reason fails you," she answered.

Good lass. Callum smiled.

"Does it?" The man would not be deterred.

His voice took on an edge that was sinister in its softness. Callum stood to the side of the open window and, risking detection, peered in through the crack between the hinges.

With a searing look, Thomas said, "'Tis a sin to lie, Mari."

"'Twas a sin to lie with *you.*" She lifted her chin and regarded him with bitter accusation, even as her trembling hand clutched the back of a chair for support. "And I regret it."

"Do you, Mari?" He stepped closer, until the fabric of their clothing touched. Thomas's eyes lit with fervor. In a quiet voice laced with menace, he said, "Just tell me that there is no bairn." Mari's eyes darted about, catching sight of a shadowy figure in the window beside her. Her eyes widened as she recognized Callum.

Thomas edged closer. "I willnae let you ruin me, Mari." With a sudden move that made Mari gasp, he pulled her against him and buried his face in her neck. His mouth slid up her neck to her ear.

"Not like you ruined her, you heap of swine slop!" Callum leapt through the window.

Thomas swung about to face him, holding Mari between them.

"Let her go," Callum said with a dark, restrained tone.

"What, and release her to the hands of a Highland barbarian?"

Callum leveled a calm but formidable look. "You stand before me forcing a woman to act as your shield, and you call me the barbarian?" Callum's mouth spread into a smile that was chilling.

As Thomas breathed in his anger, Mari sank her teeth into his hand. With a curse, he released her. Callum scooped her into his arms. "I'll be right there, lassie," he said, plopping her to the ground outside the window.

Thomas landed a blow to Callum's ribs just as Callum swung round and jabbed Thomas in the jaw, then the belly, knocking the wind out of him. Callum stood for a moment and studied the father of Mari's bairn, on his knees doubled over at his feet. He resisted the temptation to shove his boot in the lout's teeth. He could so easily finish him off in an instant, but Mari's family was in the next room. They were ignorant of any of this; and, for Mari's sake, it would be best to leave him, for now. Hoisting himself over the sill, Callum landed beside her.

"Fancy a ride?" he asked, grabbing her hand. Without waiting for an answer, he started to head for the byre. When she failed to follow he said, "Come, lass. We're in a bit of a hurry."

"Oh, aye," she said, her dazed mind catching up to the swiftly unfolding events. She ran with him. Callum saddled his horse within a minute.

"Mari?" Thomas called out with disturbing sangfroid as he approached the byre, having taken more than a few moments to recover from the force of Callum's fist before looking for them. He arrived in time to jump out of the way of Callum's horse as it stormed out of the byre and out onto the moor, leaving Thomas with little to do but glare as they rode off together.

Mari circled her arms about Callum's waist and clung dearly as they rode over the moors. Feeling her turn, Callum glanced back as well. "He didnae follow. I dinnae think he has the ba—em, inclination."

"He wouldnae stray so far from his daddy," she said bitterly.

They rode into a forest of green birches that grew from a violet blanket of bluebells. When they stopped, Callum circled Mari's waist with his arm and lowered her gently to the ground. Then he dismounted.

He left Storm to graze, tethered to a low hanging branch, while he took Mari's hand and led her into the forest. The air smelled of coming rain, while the birches rustled as if to whisper the same.

"You're cold," said Callum as he saw Mari shiver.

"I'm not sure if I'm cold or just shaken."

Callum unwrapped enough of his plaid to wrap around her. She dissolved into tears as she leaned her head on his chest. He held her, enveloped in his plaid and his arms. When her weeping subsided, she lifted her eyes. That one look did away with any resolve he had left. Her full lips parted only a bit. "Mari," came his voice, rough and aching.

Rain dropped from the shivering leaves. Mari looked up at Callum and wiped drops of rain from his face with soft hands.

"God's teeth, woman," he practically growled.

Mari shrank back, unsure of what had displeased him so.

Tenderly, he took her hands and held them in his as he took a step back to put space between them. His dark gaze bore through her. "If you touch me again, by my dirk, I shall kiss you."

Callum turned away and leaned his bent arm on the tree trunk. He breathed slowly and tamped down his emotions, as he had done so many times in battle. But these were far different emotions, and the battle was against a more formidable foe: his own heart. Bracing himself, he tried to focus his thoughts. The first thing he had to do was get out of these cursed woods, with their rich hues and soft shadows that soothed and seduced. "Fie on this rain. Will it ever stop?" He spat out the words.

Mari spoke in serene tones that worsened his struggle. "Dinnae curse the rain. It will stop in its time."

How could she be calm when he ached for her? It was unbearable. Callum glared at the tree trunks darkened by rain as the soft tapping of droplets on leaves failed to soothe him.

"Callum?" She touched her hand to his shoulder. He tensed.

"Is your dirk oath not good, then?"

Callum turned to face her with a puzzled expression. It took him a moment to recall his own words. *If you touch me again, by my dirk, I shall kiss you.*

She flew into his arms, and his mouth covered hers. She fit against him too well as he tightened his grip. The mist may as well have thickened about them, for it seemed as though nothing existed but them. He touched her hair, now drenched by the rain, and stroked the wet strands from her brow. Longing lit his eyes, and she returned his gaze with unbound emotion.

Callum yearned to take her right there. As he slid his

hands to her waist, he gently pushed her away. "Lass, I must take you back now."

Chapter 10

No Word from Callum

Alex was waiting for Callum when he came back to the farm. "Charlie's back. He brought this." Callum opened the letter. "We've been ordered to Stirling, where we'll receive further orders."

Alex nodded. "'Tis just as well. You and Hughie have enjoyed yourselves here, but it's been blindingly boring for Charlie and me."

Alex cocked an eyebrow. "From what I've observed, you and Charlie have managed to cope."

Alex grinned slyly. "Aye, well there was nought else to do, ken?"

"I've a feeling we'll have plenty to do by the end of tomorrow." Callum scanned the farm land and buildings as he thought of what waited. With a deep sigh, he shook his head. "I must go and tell Mari."

As he walked toward the house, a carriage pulled up. Thomas and two of the kirk elders got out. Sally, the maid, let them in. Callum's eyes narrowed. The two men had been under suspicion, but he had never been able to catch them attending a meeting, let alone conspiring against the monarchy. Callum's gut feeling told him something was afoot, but he had no proof. He walked toward the house. With no time to be subtle, he went to the door. Sally answered. He recognized her at once as the lass with a sweet spot for Hughie. As she did, a window closed and draperies were drawn closed. Well, that Thomas did have a brain, Callum thought. He had also seen Callum approaching. This would not be easy. He doubted Thomas would be fool enough to confront him, since Callum had the authority to clap him in irons—or worse. It was Mari he worried about. Whatever Callum did, she would pay. He would have to tread lightly.

"May I see your mistress—the younger?"

"Oh, sir, she's in bed burning with fever. You cannae see her right now."

"Shall I fetch a doctor?" asked Callum, inwardly kicking himself for having taken her out in the rain. And yet what choice had he been given?

"It's just a wee chill. Grizzal MacRorie is tending to her now." She answered Callum's questioning look. "She's the healer and midwife."

"Can I see her?"

"No." Sally glanced toward the footsteps approaching the stairs. She whispered, "If I can, I'll come fetch you later."

Callum nodded and left as she closed the door behind him.

GRIZZAL WALKED out into the dusk, which hung suspended in the air. Callum watched Grizzal leave, and then eased his way onto the porch, where, flanked by two of his men, he rapped at the door. Young Sally answered.

"Sir?"

He smiled, not intending to charm her, but he had such a smile. She cast furtive eyes back. Her mistress was not far behind.

She looked at him bashfully from beneath ginger curls, and then looked past him to Hughie. A blush spread into her freckled cheeks.

"Would you please tell your mistress that Ensign MacDonell would like to see her?"

"Aye, sir."

Callum glanced about, not having been in the house since the day they had arrived.

Mari's mother soon swept into the entrance. "Ensign MacDonell," said Margaret with measured grace.

"Good day, ma'am. We have orders to search the house."

"But why now? You have been here for weeks."

"There have been reports of Covenanters hiding out in homes in this area. We've been ordered to search all the houses."

"Indeed?" Margaret could not hide her disbelief. "But you've been here with us, watching us come and go. How could we possibly be hiding anyone here?"

"We have orders."

She reluctantly stepped aside while he and his men searched. His men kept Mrs. McEwan occupied downstairs while Callum went upstairs, straight to Mari's room. He found her asleep. Closing the door gently behind him, he sat down on the edge of her bed. Charlie had charmed Sally, the housemaid, into keeping him informed of Mari's condition. Her fever had soared for two days. No one knew of the bairn that she carried, and that worried him. He put his hand to her forehead. A deep sigh escaped. There was some lingering warmth from the fever, but she had clearly improved from what he had been told before.

"Mari, my love."

Her eyes opened and found his. She gave a weak smile. His jaw clenched and his eyes shone as he choked back a surge of emotion. "Mari, this was my fault. I shouldnae have kept you out in the rain. I was selfish." He lifted her hand to his lips. "You've worried me, lass. When I heard you were ill, I couldnae keep away."

She squeezed his hand weakly and whispered, "Are you through, Callum MacDonell?"

He smiled and said, "No, lass. I'm not." He touched the slim fingers he held in his hand as he pressed his lips to them. "I tried not to love you."

"And how did you fare?" she asked with shining eyes.

He lifted his eyes to hers. "Miserably."

A faint smile traced her lips. "Well then are we not a pitiful pair?"

His eyes shone with all that he had held in his heart. "Aye, love, that we are."

Mari's eyes gently closed. A soft smile curved her lips as she drifted to sleep.

THE NEXT DAY he was gone. He and his men had been called back to Stirling. Mari spent several feverish days in bed. Grizzal MacRorie came daily to tend to her with her teas and poultices. Once, in a fevered delirium, Mari threw off her quilt and sat up. Frantically she pulled at her shift, damp with sweat, desperate to cool herself. Grizzal found a clean shift to put on her. A seasoned midwife, Grizzal had suspected as much when she saw Mari get sick outside the byre at the Ferguson farm, but the telltale darkening nipples and thickened waist confirmed in her mind that Mari McEwan was pregnant.

Outside, the community was astir over a recent Covenanter victory over royalist soldiers at Drumclog. Some of the young men were off to Bothwell near Glasgow to join up with the mounting force of Covenanters. There was much debate over what should be done next, but no plans had been made.

Days passed, and Mari grew stronger. She started to busy herself about the house and the farm, but her thoughts were with Callum. No word came from him. One morning, she and Sally, the dairymaid, worked in the kitchen squeezing the milk out of butter. They formed the butter into small blocks and wrapped them in butterbur leaves. Mari set down the pitcher of buttermilk, and checked to make sure no one else was about.

"Sally?"

"Yes, Miss."

"I couldnae help but notice you spent some time with one of those soldiers—Hughie, was it not?"

"Aye, Miss." She went on with her work for a moment, but paused. "In truth, we went walkin' a wee bit." Sally smiled at the memory, but her mood shifted to fear as she added, "But we didnae do anything improper— I promise."

"*Och*—no! I didnae mean that. I just wondered if you had heard from him."

Sally lowered her eyes, and a small sigh slipped out. "Well no, Miss. But I didnae expect to, with him fighting."

"So he went off to fight?" Mari hid her alarm.

"Oh, aye, Miss."

Mari tried to quell the concern in her voice. "Do you ken where?"

"He wouldnae tell me, but—" Sally bit her lip, working hard to hold something back.

"What is it, Sally?"

"Oh, it's probably nothin'. Only I overheard one of the Highlanders sayin' somethin'."

With diminishing patience, Mari sternly said, "Sally."

"Loudon Hill," she blurted out. "That's all I ken."

"Loudon Hill?"

"Aye. There's to be a big conventicle there."

Mari mulled it over. It made sense. Other than looting some area homes, the Highlanders had accomplished very little since arriving. They would want to report some sort of progress. What easier target than a large gathering of families with their eyes closed in worship?

Sally continued, "And wi' our soldiers—well, not our soldiers, mind, but the ones who were biding here, ken— goin' off all a sudden... "

Mari nodded and said, as though trying to convince herself most of all, "Aye, well, it's hard to say for certain, is it not?" With a warm smile she said, "If you hear from Hughie, please tell me."

"Aye, Miss." Sally returned to her dusting, but cast a glance toward Mari as she walked away. "She's lanely for her ain soldier," she whispered to herself, shaking her head. "He's a braw man. I cannae blame her. An' I miss Hughie." The sound of footsteps drew her from her reverie and back to her vigorous dusting. "*Och*, weel, what cannae be helped must be put up with." Wiping her hands on her apron, she said, "*Och*, weel, I'd best go fetch some water before cook gets after me."

She was on her way to the well when she spied a rider coming over the hill. The grey horse and plaid marked him as a Highlander. He drew close. Sally stopped to watch, daring not hope. As she grew more certain it was Hughie, she dropped her pail and ran to him. Flinging himself from his horse, he took her into his arms and kissed her.

With cheeks flushed, Sally said, "*Och*, someone will see me."

"Aye, but I cannae let go," Hughie said, with a broad grin on his face. He kissed her, and kissed her again, until she backed away, blushing.

He stepped back, having come to his senses, but his smile would not fade. "Sally."

"Hugh." She smiled back. With a conspiratorial glance about, she said, "Put your horse in the byre. I'll meet you there, in the loft."

Without a word, he walked away smiling, while Sally went back to retrieve her water pail.

MINUTES LATER, Sally climbed up to the loft and looked about. As footsteps approached, she climbed up into the loft and hid, wondering what had happened to Hughie. As the footsteps drew nearer, an arm appeared from the hay and hooked her about the waist. As she gasped, a hand clamped over her mouth as the other arm pulled her loose.

"Shh," he whispered in her ear.

He let her turn enough to see who it was. Her eyes softened to see it was Hughie. He held her close while a worker took far too long at his duties in the byre. Hughie made use of the time with his hands, taking stock of her figure, which was rounded and soft in the places he wanted it to be.

"I was lonely for you," he said into her ear, when the farm hand had gone. "You havnae forgotten me, have you?"

She turned round eyes to meet his. "Aye, I have. I'm afraid you will have to remind me."

He answered her coy look with a broad, knowing grin. "Will I?"

She nodded and laughed as he rolled onto her.

Sometime later, they stood outside the kitchen doorway. Taking care not to touch, but forgetting their glowing expressions.

"I must go, but I'll come back when I'm able." He touched her chin, and she lifted it toward him.

"*Och*, lassie, dinnae tempt me." He looked about to make sure no one saw them, and then he kissed her one last time. "Now back to work with you." With a soft laugh, he moved closer and leaned on the doorframe, concealing his hand as he slipped it down and gave her backside a squeeze.

She put her palm to his chest and gently pushed back. "There's no work to be done with you here."

He feigned offense. "Oh, so you'd rather have me gone."

"I didn't say that," she said, pointing her finger.

He took it and touched it to his lips, and then kissed it. Sally went limp against him and breathed in the scent from his chest.

A noise startled them. They both turned, but saw nothing. With caution still in their eyes, they said their farewells.

Hughie started to leave, but turned back. "*Och*, I nearly forgot! Please give this to Mistress Mari."

She took a small, folded note from him and slipped it inside the cuff of her sleeve.

"Goodbye lassie." He touched her hand with the tips of his fingers.

She squeezed his hand, and then turned and went inside to the kitchen.

When, moments later, the door opened, Sally looked up with a smile, but it dissolved in an instant.

"Sally." Thomas sauntered in, taking the room in with quick glances. "It has been a long time, has it not?"

"Aye, sir, excuse me." She rubbed her hands on her apron and turned to leave, but Thomas rushed over and clamped his hand on her arm. "Please, sir." She cast a helpless look at his hand.

With a twist, he pulled her wrist close and probed inside her cuff with his finger. "What's this?"

"'Tis nothing , sir. Please let me go."

He released her so suddenly that she took a step to regain her balance. By the time she did so, he had slipped the note into his pocket.

"Please, sir. I was told to deliver that." She lowered her eyes.

With a smile, Thomas said, "I'll deliver it for you."

Before she could move away, he took a stride toward her and hooked his arm about her waist and pulled her against him, his face inches away. With his free hand, he grasped her face. "You'll say nothing of this, understand?"

Sally nervously nodded. "Aye, sir. Nothing."

"There's a good girl. You wouldnae want me to report you to the kirk elders for consorting with enemy high-landers."

"No, sir."

"You ken what would happen to a girl in that situation?"

Sally nodded slowly. "Please let me go, sir. I have work to do, and my mistress will wonder—"

"If you were to tell anyone, I would be forced to tell how you not only seduced several highland dragoons, but you'd brazenly tried to seduce me."

Her eyes flashed as she spoke in a hush. "Say what you will, sir. We both ken that's not true."

"But who will they believe?" he asked, grinning slyly.

Blood drained from her face. Seeing this, a look of pleasure crept into Thomas's face. "You'd be cast out. From town to town you would wander. With no reference from your kirk, no one would employ you. And then what would you do, pretty Sally? You'd be forced to go to the workhouse—or worse." He stroked her cheek and then forced a firm kiss on her mouth, muting her small moan of protest. "'Tis been a long time, has it not?"

He released her. Sally turned and reflexively touched her mouth to wipe of the feel of his lips touching hers.

"Not a word, ken?"

Sally nodded.

The cook called out, and came to the kitchen doorway. With a bold look, Thomas took a step back and met her questioning look with confident silence before walking away. Sally lowered her eyes and, still trembling, brushed past the cook and rushed into the kitchen.

ON A GRAY AFTERNOON, the cows rested under a tree as clouds rolled in and darkened the moor. With a sigh, Mari turned from the window and walked out of her room, where she bumped into Sally.

Mari dismissed the girl's apologies. "Not at all. It was my fault. She took a few steps before turning. "Sally."

Sally turned back. "Aye, Miss?"

"Have you had word from Hugh?"

Sally's eyes widened, but Mari reassured her. "I'll not tell anyone." She stepped closer. "You see, I've a similar secret. *Och*, now I've made you uneasy." Mari's face lost its poised look, and she faltered as she said, "If you heard anything of them, I would want you to feel free to tell me."

"Yes, Miss."

Sally glanced down at her armful of linens. Seeing this, Mari said, "Yes, well, thank you, Sally."

Mari continued on her way, pausing only to don and fasten her arisaid with a brooch.

She walked briskly, imagining reasons why Callum had not sent word to her in weeks. She was troubled by it more so than she cared to admit.

Before her, a horseman came over the hill and approached her. Her heart quickened, but she soon saw it was not Callum. The thrill changed to dread as the rider drew nearer. He tethered his horse to a tree branch.

"Thomas," she said, eyeing the minister's son with mistrust.

His admiring eyes drank her in. "Marion."

"Congratulations on your wedding," she said tersely as she went on her way.

"Marion, I ken that you're angry."

"Oh, you ken that, do you?" She turned away and shut her eyes for a moment. Losing her temper would just make things worse. She took a deep breath and calmed herself.

"You've no right to look down your nose at me, Marion McEwan."

"If you'd leave, Thomas Blackwell, I wouldnae have to look at you at all."

The chilling look darkened his eyes. "You drive men away with that temper of yours."

"Good. Then as angry as I am, you'll be on your way now."

He stepped closer. "I came to do you a favor, if you'd let me."

"I dinnae need favors from you."

"You need this one."

She looked at him with scorn, but he met it, undaunted, with a bold look of his own. "You're with child," he said bluntly.

Her eyes opened wide, but she turned her back to him to conceal any further reaction. "That's a lie. Go away. I'll not hear any more."

He lunged for her from behind and circled his arms about her waist. Even as she fought to be free, his hands felt their way over the front of her body before settling on the mound that proved his claim true. She jabbed her elbow back into his side and pulled free of him.

Thomas held his palms up as he tried to look harmless. "Grizzal told me. I wanted to see for myself. I'll not touch you again." He took a step backward.

Mari spied a piece of broken branch on the ground. She picked it up and gripped it in her hand, ready to thrust it at him. "See that you dinnae! Now go away. 'Tis no business of yours."

Thomas spoke in soothing tones. "Marion, listen. I'm trying to help you. The elders ken. Grizzal told them."

Mari started to ask how she knew, but then closed her eyes and let out a mournful sigh. Grizzal. When she was sick with a fever, Grizzal tended her. Tears filled her eyes. "No." The word caught in her throat. Soon they would bring her before the kirk to answer for her actions. She had thought she would have two or three months to plan what she would do. Now, all of a sudden, that day was before her.

"Marion, listen to me."

She shut her eyes, too mired in distress to contain her contempt.

He said, "I came here to help you."

"You've helped me enough, Thomas Blackwell. You can best help me now by just leaving me be." Mari started to leave, but he grasped her arm.

"Listen, Marion. When they call you before the kirk, they will want to ken who the father is."

Mari inwardly groaned in disgust. So that was it. He was afraid she would name him as the father.

"I've a new wife."

"So I've heard. Good for you."

"Marion, my father insisted. It was a superior match."

"Being the superior sort, then, I'm sure she willnae mind." She smiled to herself and tried to pull her arm free and go on her way.

"Dinnae jest."

"Oh, I promise you, I take all of this seriously."

"Listen to me. I've worked it all out. If there isnae a bairn, they cannae punish you."

"Brilliant plan, Thomas." Mari started to walk.

"It is. If they cannae prove there's a bairn, they will have to assume that Grizzal was mistaken—or lying."

Mari stopped short to regard him. "Are you daft? First of all, there is a bairn and they can prove it. And why would Grizzal lie?"

Thomas looked down. "Because she... seems to think that she and I—"

"*Och!* Have you nothing to fasten your breeches?" Mari strode off, but soon stopped as a wave of nausea came over her.

Thomas pulled out a vial. "I've brought something to help you."

"The only thing that will help me at present would be for you to leave me." Mari studied Thomas's face. He seemed almost wounded.

His eyes darted away. "Do you think I stopped caring for you?"

Mari looked at him coldly. "Aye. That particular thought came to mind on the day of your wedding."

"Mari. It was our parents who wanted the marriage. I couldnae go against my father."

"No. Only a man could do that."

"Aye, and no man keeps his manhood for long, around you." Thomas glared at her.

"Leave me alone."

"But I cannae." Still grasping her arm, he pulled her close and said in her ear, "I miss the feel of you."

She stepped out of reach. "You have your wife now for that."

His breathing grew heavy. "Her bed is a cold one. I need more."

"No." Mari put her hand up to stop him. She glanced about. Only cows looked back. She would have to fetch them later. She would make some excuse. With a sigh of exasperation, Mari left.

He ran after her and caught her by the arm. "Feelings like ours dinnae just end."

Mari heaved a sigh and looked plainly at him. "Yes, they do."

He appeared outwardly chastened, and yet showed little remorse. "I deserved that."

"Thomas," she said, feeling calmer for having spoken her mind. "Go home to your wife."

He nodded, and pressed the vial into her hand. "Drink this. It's savin. It will make it go away."

Mari knew what savin did. Women snickered about babies being born under the savin tree. It made pregnancies end. She had thought about taking it, and she had come close. But as she looked at Thomas, she knew she could not be so desperate as he, so she pushed his hand back.

"No, Thomas. We made a mistake, and since I am to pay for it one way or the other, I'll be the one to decide how."

"Marion, think what you're saying. It will be like it never happened."

"But it did happen," said Mari.

Thomas said, "When they bring you before the kirk elders, you'll just tell them it's not true, and they'll have no proof against you."

The thought did appeal to her. She did wish that it never had happened.

Thomas said softly, "And no father need ever be named."

Mari's eyes shot up to his. "Dinnae worry. I wouldnae stoop to give you the credit."

His eyes flashed with anger. "If you willnae cooperate, I'll be forced to ruin you, Marion."

Bitterness darkened her eyes. "Haven't you done that already?"

He pulled a paper from his pocket. "I've a note here from your Highland lover professing his love."

"Forging a note? Is nothing beneath you?"

Thomas said, "'Tis real enough."

"You're wrong. He has never written to me."

Thomas smiled. "Oh, but he has. You just never received it."

Mari reached for it, but he held it out of her reach. "There's enough here to ruin your life. But I'm not so vindictive. You're still dear to me, Mari. Let's take the easier path. I've been to the midwife. This savin will put an end to the pregnancy."

Mari looked squarely at him. "I'll not do it."

Grasping her shoulders, he said, "Everything could be as it was."

"I cannae do it. How could you ask that of me?"

"If you don't, I will have to tell them that he forced himself on you."

"I'd deny it."

"He's a Highlander. The bairn is proof enough. If you deny that he forced you, you'll bring judgment upon you."

Mari looked straight into eyes so cold they burned through her, and said, "So be it."

She turned to leave, but he grabbed her and swung her into his arms. "Mari, don't you see? I still love you. I cannae watch you go through that." He kissed her and tightened his arms about her as she struggled. Down to the ground he pulled her until he sat straddling her.

Thinking he meant to force himself on her, she said, "Thomas, no. You cannae want me like this."

He looked at her, stunned. "Marion, how can you think such a thing?" His eyes swept over her face. He said softly, "Remember the first time? How I loved you! You're all I ever wanted. It was my father who forced me to marry. But we can still be together like we were before. No one can spoil what we have."

He looked at her with the warmth she once saw in his eyes, but the sight only proved what a fool she had been. "Thomas, we will never be like that again."

Her words pained him. "Oh, Marion, I wish you hadnae said that." Although Mari fought him, he pinned her arms under his knees, and pulled a vial from his pocket. With one hand, he cupped her chin and squeezed tightly, forcing open her jaw. Mari tried to turn her head, but he yanked it back. She bit the hand holding her chin, but he cursed through clenched teeth. Lifting the vial, he pulled the cork out with his teeth and spat it out to the side. He then poured the vial's contents down her throat. Tossing the vial, he forced her mouth closed and tilted her head back until she choked and involuntarily swallowed. A drop escaped and slipped down her cheek. With his finger, he tenderly smoothed it to her lips, then he bent down and kissed her. "Good lass. Drank it all down."

With a free arm, Mari felt about the ground frantically and seized hold of a rock. As Thomas got up, Mari struck him in the groin. He cried out, holding himself. In too much pain to control his balance, Mari pushed him over and scrambled free.

Thomas lay on his side, knees bent, moaning and cursing. As she ran away, he cried out, "I'll make you regret that!"

Chapter 11

A Wild Wind from the Moor

The next morning was a Sunday. Despite Mari's pleas to stay home, her father insisted that she go with them to kirk. It was the first time in weeks since they had worshipped as they chose, in a secret kirk service called a conventicle. While the Highland soldiers had stayed there, Mari's family had gone to the local kirk services, which were now under control of Episcopal curates. Every curate had a list of parishioners. Anyone absent was fined. Should they be suspected of harboring Covenanter sympathies, they could be questioned, forced to take oaths renouncing their faith, and even tortured or executed. Mari had resented being forced to attend the king's kirk, but complied with her parents' wishes and attended them every Sunday. Jamie's death had worn down their spirit. They were weary, and felt they had given enough. She would not trouble them over this.

However, once the soldiers were gone, the secret meetings resumed. Convinced they were no longer under suspicion, the McEwan family set out for their first secret kirk meeting one Sunday before the sunset. It would be at the Ferguson farm, Ellen's home.

Mari had awoken to uncomfortable cramping. Thomas's vial had taken effect. She told her parents she was feeling ill and would not be able to go to the conventicle planned for the evening. But her father said she looked well enough and insisted. Mari could not defy him.

When the McEwans arrived for the service, they were met with awkward greetings and stares that made Mari's parents uneasy. By now Mari was in too much pain to notice. Not only did she have to endure stabbing pain, she also had to hide it from anyone watching. As one wave of contractions subsided, Mari caught sight of Grizzal MacRorie standing outside of the byre, eyeing her slyly. No, it could not be today. The agony was too much, but to endure it in public? She could not. As much as Mari had tried to prepare herself for this moment, her heart hammered in her chest. She was too sick now to think clearly.

One of the elders approached Mari and led her away from her now troubled parents. Agnes Blackwell, Thomas's new wife, joined the elder who led Mari to the back of the byre.

"Mistress McEwan," said the elder.

She looked plainly at him, but did not reply.

"We know that you are with child," he stated, waiting for her to refute it. Mari could not meet his cold stare. Thomas Blackwell stood off to the side. Her eyes drifted toward him, but he shifted his weight to avoid looking at her. Her heart pounded so much she thought everyone could hear it. The elder gave a nod to the women and left them alone to attend to Mari.

She did not resist as they stripped her off her shoes, stockings, and skirts—all but her shift. There was little point in protesting, unless she wished to be forever cast out from the church and her friends. Nor could she run away and start fresh somewhere else. In order to settle in a new town, a person needed a testimonial from the previous church attesting to their good character. Without this, the person would not only be barred from the new kirk, but would be further unable to obtain work. Left with no choice but to comply, Mari set her mind on one goal: She would find a way to persevere. She said not a word and did her best to hide any emotion that might give her accusers satisfaction. If she could impress them with her repentance, they might spare her the rest of the punishment. Often the sentence included being chained to the Mercat Cross with a paper crown upon which was written the offense. They did not usually shave the heads of first offenders, but Reverend Blackwell was an unyielding man.

The pains were now coming more often. A light-headed sensation dulled Mari's fear as she clutched the side of the byre for support.

The women escorted her into the byre, which would serve as a kirk for this meeting. The elder prodded her forward to begin her solitary walk to the stool of repentance. A sharp pain shot through her abdomen, making her pause, but she steeled herself and kept walking along the dirt aisle. Now dizzy, she hesitated between steps and breathed deeply. Things came back into focus. As she resumed walking, she began to feel as though she were watching herself from a distance. At last, she arrived at the stool. There was talking. She heard words, but the pain soon returned and distracted her from their meaning. She bent over, but then gripped the edge of the stool and willed herself to sit up and face them. Only once did she let herself glance at Thomas Blackwell. She drew strength from the fear in his eyes. *Agnes can have you and all of your lies. Wee one or not, I'll not name you as the father and be yoked to you for the rest of my life.*

Another stab of pain seized her. Her ears rang and she felt herself slipping away. A muffled voice spoke from what seemed like a distance. "Are you so shameless and prideful to think you can raise this wee one with no father and no kirk? Would you wallow in your blasphemous ways rather than swallow your pride? Confess now and be delivered from—"

A bold, kilted figure eclipsed the light from the doorway. Wild wind from the moor tossed the hair of the fearsome Highland warrior.

He had come back.

Chapter 12

The Battle

Across the moor and up into the hills they rode, to a cave Callum had found on patrol. Here Callum made a pallet for Mari and covered her with his plaid. He stepped outside long enough to send the other dragoons on to Hamilton. It was not far, just southeast of Glasgow, but Mari could travel no farther. He and Mari would stay here for now and catch up to them later.

She lay on her side, curled up in pain. "I ken it's not cold, but I cannae stop shaking," she said through chattering teeth.

He sat leaning back against the cave wall and gently pulled her back against him, and enfolded her in his arms. She leaned back into the warmth of his body and trembled. As a sharp pain shot through her, she gripped his arms as she called out his name.

"Aye, lass?"

"I'm sorry."

"God's teeth, love, what for?"

She winced and drew a sharp breath. "For all of the trouble I've caused you."

"*Och, whisht.*" Callum put his hand on her moist forehead and rested his cheek against her hair.

Mari tried not to cry out, but tears streamed down her face as she clung to him.

In his deep, soothing voice, he said, "We'll get through this, my love. We'll get through this together."

THE NEXT DAY, ribbons of midday sun shone in through the branches that covered the cave opening. Mari opened her eyes.

"Callum?" She barely recognized her own voice in the raspy sound that came out. "Callum!" She tried to sit up, but she lacked the strength.

Pushing the branches aside, Callum ducked into the cave. "I'm here, lass." Concern and fatigue etched his brow and darkened his eyes. He sat down beside her and stroked her hair. During the long night, he had feared he might lose her. But morning came, bringing sleep.

Mari whispered, "Have you buried it?"

"Aye. I found a wee place under a tree. It looks out over the moors."

She gave a slight nod and rolled onto her side. A tear rolled down her cheek.

Callum lay down beside her and held her.

THE NEXT MORNING, Mari walked outside, leaning on Callum's arm. "Go slowly, lass, you lost a good deal of blood."

"Dinnae worry about me. It's a short ride to Hamilton. I can rest when we get there.

He laid a thickly folded plaid over the saddle, and cradled her in his arms as they rode slowly along. She did not complain, but he knew that the ride caused her pain. Mari had insisted on leaving. He was overdue back at camp, and he would not leave her alone here. With the promise of rest when they arrived, they rode. They spoke little. The sun warmed and soothed them, and they were together. Grief had a way of distilling one's life to a moment, and another, each hanging in air thick with spent emotions.

After a time, Mari said, "How did you ken to come get me?"

"Young Sally."

"Sally Hay?"

"Aye. It seems that she and Hughie were keeping company. He snuck over there to see her one night. She had heard the girls gossiping. The dairymaid—"

"Grizzal MacRorie."

"Aye. Grizzal was quite proud, the old cow, telling stories about how she tended you when you were sick with the fever. It was then that she discovered your condition."

"I think she knew even before that. I got sick by the byre one day. When I looked up, she was watching me. I was afraid then she'd guessed."

"Aye. When she was certain, she told a kirk elder."

Mari was too worn out to react. "I'd hoped to hide it a

few sennights more. But what difference would that have made? The damage was done."

"Shh... " He looked at her sternly. "We'll not wonder about the past anymore. We're here now, and I'll not let anyone hurt you again."

THE ENCAMPMENT in Hamilton was humming with activity. In the morning they were to march on Bothwell Brigg, where some four thousand Covenanters had established their camp. Hughie met them and took Callum's horse.

"We dinnae have as much time as I'd thought. Wait here." Callum ducked into his tent, then came out moments later, extending a flask of water to Mari. While she drank thirstily, he said, "We'll go find you someplace to bide."

"Can I not stay here?"

He leveled a look. "Mari, my love, there is nothing more I would like than to offer this to you. But, first, it's not proper."

"Not proper? Last night we slept in a cave."

"That was different. We had no choice then. And there was no one to see us."

She looked at him plainly. "And what shame could there be left for me now?" Sadness crept into her expression as she looked away with moist eyes.

Sudden concern came over him. "Lass, you're weary." He led her to a log to sit down on. "I'm sorry not to have something more comfortable." Although she had not complained, she sighed with relief to sit down.

Callum knelt down and took her hands in his. His eyes softened. "This is not what I wanted for you."

"What you or I want is no longer important." She took a breath and straightened her posture in a manner that was both brave and false.

"Aye, lassie, it is." He kissed her hand and tenderly placed it back on her knee. With firm hands on his knees, he leaned forward and stood up. "I'll go find you a place to stay now."

She touched his arm, and he stopped to look down at her. Warmth filled his eyes.

Mari said, "I dinnae mind staying here. I dinnae care if it's proper."

"No, lass. I stay here with my men. While I'm sure they would not mind, I would." He raised a brow and, with a most charming grin, let her reflect on the prospect.

Suppressing a weak smile, she looked up through her lashes. "Well then, where will I stay?"

After she had rested, he took her to the area of the encampment where the followers stayed. Soldiers' families, sometimes children included, would follow during the mild seasons. Wealthy officers brought their servants. Washerwomen, cooks, barbers, and surgeons were all needed to support troops. Many troops would not have joined on or remained as long as they had without their families in trail. For the men without families, there were women who followed to meet other needs.

Callum led the way to a tent, where he glanced about and soon spied a matronly woman hanging clothes on a line. Sneaking up from behind, he bent down to circle his arms about her plump waist and planted a kiss on her cheek.

"*Och!*" Startled, she whirled around, ready to swing a fist. But her fists soon landed on each hip. "Callum MacDonell! You gave me a fright!" But she stretched out her arms and embraced him. She then spied Mari and looked inquisitively back at Callum.

He took Mari's hand and drew her closer. "Nellie McKinnon, I would like to introduce Mari McEwan." Nellie greeted her warmly and offered her a folding stool and some tea.

"Nellie's from Glengarry too. You ken her sons, Charlie and Hughie."

"Aye." With a broad smile, Mari said, "Such braw men!"

While Nellie grinned with pride, Callum said, "Nellie, Mari needs someplace to bide while we're here."

"Aye, the lads told me."

Mari looked away as she thought of how much they had told her. Before shame could begin to take hold, Nellie gave Mari's arm a comforting squeeze. "Of course you'll stay here."

Mari looked at her with a hint of surprise that was mixed with relief.

Nellie said, turning to Callum, "I'll make a pallet to use, until you can find us a cot."

"I'll help you," he said, bounding up. "Stay here, Mari." She started to rise, but he gave her a warning look to sit back down and rest.

Inside the tent, he spoke softly. "She's been very sick, Nellie. I'm worried about her. She'll not let on, but she needs to lie down and rest."

Nellie finished smoothing out the pallet and fluffing the pillow she'd pulled from her bed. That done, she put her hands on her hips and asked bluntly, "Callum, what is she to you?"

He looked squarely at her. "Everything."

THE NEXT MORNING the Sabbath dawned, and the Duke of Monmouth led fifteen thousand royalist forces to the north side of the bridge. Filling the width of the bridge, the troops were followed by eleven square formations of men with firearms bearing six unfurled banners, and two cavalry units. They looked over Bothwell Bridge to the south, where five thousand rebel Covenanters collected in an unorganized mass. A contingent of rebels came forward to meet with the duke. They set forth their demands, to which the duke listened, but he would do nothing until they laid down their arms. The rebels were unwilling or unable amongst themselves to agree, so the royalists began firing their field artillery. When the rebels fired back, some of Monmouth's men bolted, abandoning their weapons. Callum drew his men forward and rallied others to follow before the Covenanters could take advantage of the royalists' moment of weakness.

They broke rank and retreated. Advancing again, cannons fired. Bodies lay strewn across the bridge. Still they advanced into cannon fire.

Monmouth was moving his artillery forward, but before he could fill in a breach to his right, rebels fired on the Highlanders. Royalist cannon fire soon deterred them as once more the dragoons advanced.

After two hours of fighting, the ammunition ran out on the Covenanters' side. Rebel cavalry fled, leaving the

Covenanter foot soldiers at Monmouth's mercy as the royalists crossed over the bridge en masse and defeated those who had not died or fled. Monmouth ordered the fighting to stop, but as soon as he left, some rogue royalists chased the surrendering men through the town of Hamilton. By the end of the day, four hundred were dead, and twelve hundred more were taken prisoner. Three hours from when it had begun, the Battle of Bothwell Brigg was over and the Clyde River ran red.

MARI AWOKE to the chaos of men coming back from the battle. She bolted up. How could she have slept? It was Nellie who had insisted that she lie down. To appease her, Mari lay awake in the tent as the sounds of battle filled most of the morning. She was weak from the loss of her baby only two days before, and the ordeal in kirk before that; but Callum was out there somewhere, and she needed to find him. Nellie was gone. Mari got up and combed her fingers through her hair, then went outside to find a plate of oatcakes covered with cloth, which Nellie had left for her. Mari went to the bucket and splashed water on her face and wiped down her neck; then she drank half a cup of the ale just to stave off a weak, trembling sensation.

Soldiers walked past and talked of the battle. Mari walked through camp, searching for Callum. With each passing dragoon, she felt more and more lost. Without knowing whether Callum was safe, time moved slowly. She did not know how the camp was laid out, where the barbers or surgeons might be, so she headed in the direction from which all the soldiers were coming. Some were bloodied and wounded, while others looked oddly unscathed.

She stopped soldiers as they passed. "Please, sir, I'm looking for Callum MacDonell."

Soldier after soldier shook his head.

"Callum MacDonell! Has anyone seen him?" she cried out, walking more briskly.

She found her way to Bothwell Bridge. Mari stopped and looked out over hundreds of bodies strewn over the landscape. "Callum." His name caught in her throat.

People wandered through the field and searched bodies for items worth taking. Prisoners were taken and ordered to lie on the ground without moving. One Covenanter turned over and was shot. Dead soldiers were stripped of any uniform garments that might be reused. They were then loaded onto handcarts and taken to a large pit in which bodies were collected. A dragoon sprinkled quicklime over them, layer by layer. Mari watched blankly.

"Madam, this is no place for you." When she did not respond, a gentle hand touched her shoulder.

"I'm looking for someone," she said without taking her eyes from the scene.

"Come away, madam."

When she finally looked back, Mari saw before her an English officer of some rank, judging from his uniform decoration. He led her to a stool outside one of the tents. "Please, do sit down for a moment," he told her. She looked at him with the blank stare of a woman in shock, but allowed him to guide her. He introduced himself as Captain Lumsden. As they exchanged introductions,

Mari thought it so strange that they could be so civilized amid all of the carnage about them.

In answer to his inquiry, she explained, "I am looking for someone. He might be hurt, and I dinnae ken how to find him."

He handed her a pint of ale and said, "Tell me about him. Perhaps I can help."

She told him Callum's name, with which clan he was fighting. "He's a cavalry officer. An ensign."

"I will make inquiries. In the meanwhile, go back to your camp. He or his men will know to find you there. They're probably looking for you now."

Mari stood, ready to leave. "What if he's out there?" She looked across the moor littered with bodies all broken and bloody.

He looked squarely at her, and did not mince words. "If he's out there, it is better that you didn't see him. He would not want it, I promise you that. Go back to your camp and wait there."

"Thank you. You've been very kind." Mari left, headed toward Nellie's tent. "Excuse me, can you tell me where the surgery is?" she asked a passing soldier.

"Oh, madam," said the soldier, "You dinnae want to go there."

"Yes, I do, and I want you to tell me." She looked frantically at him. "Please, I've got to find someone."

He reluctantly nodded his head toward the surgery, and watched with concern as she walked away.

Mari found it and the discarded limbs. She took in a sharp breath. Acrid odors assaulted her senses. She turned away, shutting her eyes to the sights until she could numb her memory of what she had seen as well. When she could move, she began to walk without thought or direction. She passed by men. Well or wounded, she looked long enough at each to see whether it was Callum. If not, she walked on like an impassive observer until she was sure she had seen every man there. Drying tears streaked her expressionless face as she found her way back to Callum's tent. It was empty.

She went on to Nellie's in hope that someone might have returned there. The sounds of battle, long abated, had been replaced by sounds of grief mixed with the sounds of men drinking to ease their minds of the visions of war. Nellie was gone. Mari stood staring, weighed down by aching dread. She sank down on a stool, buried her face in her hands, but she could no longer cry.

"Mari."

"Aye?" Without thinking, she answered and then jerked her head up to find Callum standing before her.

"Mari, love, if it's not a bother, could you give me some help?" He was smiling.

Only then did she notice him leaning on a crutch fashioned out of a tree branch with a uniform jacket wrapped around the end under his arm.

"Aye! Put your arm around me."

"If you insist," he said, grinning, then wincing from pain.

He hobbled over to the cot in the tent. Mari propped him up on pillows. "What happened? How bad is it? Have you seen a surgeon? I'll go find someone." She got up, but he grasped her wrist.

"Sit here by me."

"But you're hurt."

He pressed his fingers to her lips until she was quiet,

and then took both of her hands in his. "It's not bad. I took a musket ball to the leg. Shh, love. It only grazed me. Yes, I've seen a surgeon. There, have I answered your questions?" Her concern made him smile.

Relieved to find Callum, Mari took in the sight of him. Suddenly she thought of his men. "Where are they?"

"They're a wee bit scraped up, but we suffered no losses. We're a fierce lot, you ken."

Mari studied the hands that held hers. A tear fell on Callum's hand.

"What's this?" he asked as he wiped tears from her cheeks.

Alex strode in with his arm bandaged up. "*Och*, Mari! Look at you—wasting your tears on that one, when I've got real wounds that need tending. See here? I've got this wee scratch on my arm!"

Nellie was next to return with Hughie and Charlie on each side. "It's a good day. My lads are all safe."

"But where is Duncan?" Mari asked.

Nellie suppressed disapproval. "He had plans. I've learned not to ask that lad anything."

The rest of them shared a meal and some laughter. While Mari and Nellie were cleaning up from supper, Callum called Hughie over and sent him off on an errand. When he returned, Nellie took his arm and the two of them went for a walk.

"What is it?" asked Mari, fully aware they had not been left alone by mere chance.

"Come sit by me, Mari," he said, as he reached out his hand. She pulled a stool close beside the cot in which he sat propped up, with his injured leg stretched out straight.

He clasped her hand and pressed it to his lips. "Have you thought of what we will do after this?"

"I've not had time to think, yet."

"Well, I have," Callum said.

"Have you now? I thought you seemed a wee bit busy today," she said, smiling.

While he smiled back, it soon faded. Mari watched him, concerned.

"Lass, I ruined you—taking you away as I did." Before she could protest, he said, "Perhaps not in fact, but in people's eyes."

"Callum, if you'll recall, I was ruined already."

He went on without giving credence to what she had said. "I have taken you from your home and the people who love you. And the people you love."

"Aye, and from the kirk and the people who hurt me." Without thinking, her hand went to her abdomen. She lowered her eyes.

Callum took note but said nothing. His jaw clenched through his hardened expression. Rage roiled inside every time he thought of the minister's son. What a sorry excuse for a man he was! Callum tamped down his anger and grasped Mari's hand. She brought warmth to his soul and heat to his body. The dark thoughts washed away as her gentle spirit filled him so full of love that it ached. Smiling, he told her, "You ought to be married."

She lifted her eyes to meet his intense gaze. "And who would I marry, when no one has asked me?"

A frown creased his brow as he tilted his head and looked off to the distance. "*Och*, I'd not thought about that." His eyes glimmered under his furrowed brow.

"Aye, well, you'll have time to think later, and no one

to bother your thinking." Mari started to rise to leave him, but he would not let her hand go.

A smile spread from his brightening eyes to the crooked curve of his mouth as he said, "You bother my thinking, Miss Mari McEwan."

She could not resist the smile that his words drew from her.

He went on, "And there's no help for it."

She shook her head and feigned a sympathetic look. "Poor lad."

"Aye, no help," he went on, "unless you marry me."

His words warmed her heart as tears shone in her eyes. "And why would I do that?" she said softly.

He tenderly turned her hand over and traced his thumb up the back of her wrist to the crook of her arm. Lifting his eyes to find hers fixed on him, he dropped all guard. "I dinnae ken why you would."

She could not look away. Her lips parted to take in an unsteady breath. "Because I love you."

He smiled to hear the words, then a sudden frown creased his brow as he studied her. "Mari." Combing his fingers into the hair at the nape of her neck, he drew her closer. As their lips brushed together he whispered, "Do you ken how I love you?"

"Aye," she whispered, and he kissed her.

THEY WERE in the midst of a kiss when Nellie and Hughie returned. Nellie cleared her throat.

Playfully giving Mari a tight squeeze, Callum said, "I've asked Hughie to find someone to marry us."

Turning to the others, Callum smiled broadly and said, "That priest had best get here soon. The lass looks a bit shaky."

Mari went still. "A priest?" She looked away.

Seeing her reaction, Callum exhaled, only now realizing how Mari would feel. "I'm sorry, lass. But we're short of Presbyterian clergy on this side of the bridge."

She looked at him as though realizing for the first time. "An Episcopal priest?"

"Aye."

"But you're not even… "

"No, lass. I'm Catholic."

"Aye. Well, there's no difference, is there?" she said, making little effort to conceal her sarcasm.

"Mari, we have no choice. In this camp, all we will find is an Episcopal priest.

"So I'm to be married by a papist?"

"And to one." Callum watched her, concerned.

"I hadn't thought. I suppose I just saw us together, in love and married. I didnae think how we might get to that point."

"My love, I want you as my wife. It's that simple. I dinnae care who does it, as long as we're married."

Mari spoke as though thinking aloud. "I knew you were not Presbyterian. Of course you were not. But I hadnae thought of our marriage—a Presbyterian and a Catholic."

"Lass, we're just us, Mari and Callum."

She heard him, but could not ignore her heart and her conscience. "But we're not, don't you see? We cannae be. Jamie and Ellen died for their right to worship our way. To turn from that would be to scoff at their memory."

"Mari, love, what happened to them was wrong, and I grieve for your loss. But this is our time. We cannae let this stand in our way."

"But it is in our way." When at last she looked at him, her eyes were distant and troubled.

"Mari." He took hold of her shoulders, eyes burning into hers. "There is only one God. Do you think he cares whether we go to your kirk or mine? He knows your heart, and he knows mine. And God knows I'd do anything to be with you."

She met his gaze with wavering certainty.

He gripped her shoulders a little too tightly. "Tell me you would do the same."

"I... cannae. I dinnae ken."

He looked like a man wounded in battle who does not quite know it yet.

She shook her head slightly. "I need to think. I cannae think here." Turning, she walked with quickening pace down the path through the tents.

Callum took a step to follow, but cursed as he put weight on his wounded leg. He reached for his makeshift crutch, but Nellie stopped him with a hand on his arm. "Give her time to think, lad."

Without taking his eyes off of Mari, he said, "Hughie, follow her. Dinnae let her see you, but make sure that she's safe."

Hughie sprang into action as Callum stood watching. "I've lost her, Nellie."

Chapter 13

The Promise

Once out of sight, Mari slowed to a walk. Going past some young dragoons, she watched them passing a bottle around and laughing. Past sermons on the wickedness of strong drink echoed in her mind. A tent glowed with the light from an oil lamp as an officer sat on a cot quietly writing. Outside, a handful of soldiers spoke in quiet grim words. Distant strains of a fiddle drifted through the camp. From the hospital tent, a young soldier wept softly in pain, while farther on children ran about playing, unfazed by their surroundings. Soldiers waited their turn outside tents where the camp followers entertained in their beds. The whole human condition seemed housed in this camp, and Mari felt smaller with each step she took.

She arrived at a hill overlooking the camp and the bridge, and the wild moor beyond. The moon cast its dim light over the men and their battleground, while a grand sky specked with stars stretched above. From which side of the bridge did God watch over them? For the heavens stretched over both sides of the battle.

"Where do I fit here?" Mari wondered. Poised amid living and dying, she felt lost and alone. Things that were once so clear and true now tangled themselves with new thoughts that confounded her logic. Men had fought and died on the field before her because their way was right, and they staked their lives on it. Both sides believed fiercely, but both could not be right. Whose religion was the right one, then? As she looked at the field strewn with lifeless bodies, she wondered if either was right anymore. For who had the right to impose their church on the other? But if neither was right, how could two lovers form a union of wrongs? Even if one was right, wasn't it wrong to mix right with wrong? So she had always been taught. And there was the problem. To be with Callum would be to give up her beliefs—everything she had known to be true. Could she set it aside for this man whom she loved? If she did, of what value was everything else she believed? She could find no middle ground in the world she had grown to believe in, and the sorrow of this cut her deeply. Their hearts would forever be drawn together, while their minds would inevitably pull them apart.

Soft weeping interrupted Mari's thoughts. A young man lay dead on the ground, while his love wept over him. It was like watching her earlier fears played out, and she wondered. Had she found Callum dying, would she hold him in her arms and feel sure that to leave him would be the right choice? Deprived of the warmth of his sturdy arms around her, how sure would she be of her principles then? Were it she leaning over the man who completed her heart, she would weep for the loss of his body against hers, for the sight of his eyes sweeping down to her lips just before he kissed her. She would miss his strong hands and how gently they touched her. She would desperately treasure the feel of his heart joined to hers. This was the loss from which she would never recover.

Callum was of the wrong faith according to whom? Men made these judgments, and men could be wrong. How could God be housed in her church and her church alone? He could not; nor was he solely at Callum's. And yet, both sides believed that God was with them. If God had found them, he would find Mari, too. And she knew just where that would be.

Mari turned about and walked with increasing speed back to camp. Still weak, she did not try to run until she saw Callum. He glanced up to see Mari approaching, but braced for the news that his logic told him was coming. He waited, in no hurry to hear it. But as she drew closer and started to run toward him, he wished that his leg did not keep him from running to her.

She flew into his arms. "Take me wherever you go."

Callum put his hands on her shoulders and held her at arm's length as he tightened the loose fabric of her sleeve into his fists. She searched his intense gaze with eyes open with trust.

"Mari, I will not take you in tow like a camp follower."

"How will you take me then?" Her mouth spread to a smile.

"I'm serious, Mari." He was, and fiercely so.

"Serious enough to marry me?"

Dark eyes met hers. "Aye, lass. You ken that I am."

"Well then let's find a priest, or a minister or a blacksmith." She laughed. "I dinnae care! I just want to be married to you."

She threw her arms about his neck and they clung to one another.

HUGHIE CLEARED HIS THROAT. "CALLUM?" He stood awkwardly, searching for words.

"What is it, Hughie?" Reluctantly, the two lovers pulled apart to stand arm-in-arm.

"About the priest."

Callum smiled and nodded. "Aye, run and fetch him."

"I did," Hughie said, looking troubled. "Could we talk alone?"

"Aye."

"No," said Mari. "If it concerns me, I will hear it."

Callum glanced at Mari, and then nodded to Hughie.

Nellie joined them just as Hughie said, "The priest willnae do it."

"Why not?" asked Callum, but already knew the answer.

"He got angry when I offered him money to forget about crying the banns. And then he asked for a letter of testimony from both of your kirks."

Mari said, "My kirk will not write such a letter for me."

"They would not recognize a letter from a Presbyterian kirk if you had one." Callum cursed. "Has the Church of England not got one greedy priest?"

"Not in this camp, nor in this town," answered Hughie.

Nellie said, "Laddie, I'm sorry."

Mari felt more than disappointment. How could she

have thought she could have a future with Callum? In every way, they were from opposite sides.

Nellie produced a bottle of scotch. "Have a wee dram. I brought it from home. I was hoping we could celebrate with it, but it's best not to waste it."

It was Mari who broke the long silence that followed. "He's only one priest. If he will not marry us, then we'll find someone in Edinburgh."

"And in the meanwhile?" asked Callum.

"In the meanwhile, I'm not going anywhere."

Callum said, "I will not have others looking at you like you're...not my wife. I will not have that for you."

Mari lifted her chin. "Would you send me away, then?"

"*Och*, lass! Come here." He put his solid arm about her. "I'll not cast you out, you daft woman. But neither can I ask you to lower yourself to be with me."

"You can ask or not. I will do what I want."

Nellie spoke hesitantly. "You both ken...you dinnae always need a priest to get married."

Callum said, "Mari deserves a proper marriage— recognized by the kirk."

Nellie nodded. "I'll no speak for the kirk, but I do ken of a marriage the government will recognize. The solicitors call it an irregular marriage."

Nellie looked at Callum. "If you declared it before two witnesses, you'd be married."

"In the eyes of God?" Mari asked.

Callum held her chin gently. "Would the eyes of the law do for now? It may be all we can manage for a while."

"I want to be married to you."

"Are you sure, Mari?"

Mari smiled. "I am."

Turning to Nellie, he said, "How is it you ken so much about this?"

"Cover your lugs, Hughie."

"I'm seventeen, Ma."

She leaned forward toward Callum and Mari, and smiled. "I ken someone who was married like that." Her eyes moistened. "Till the day he died, no twa were more married than my man and I."

MINUTES LATER, Nellie stood beside Hughie with tears in her eyes, watching the couple, who stood facing one another. There was no kirk or fine clothing as Callum leaned on his crutch facing Mari. The lads from Glengarry stood by with broad smiles. Duncan was the last to arrive. Trying not to draw attention, he pressed something into Mari's hand, and in a gruff voice muttered, "It's white heather for luck."

Pleased and surprised by the gesture, Mari thanked him.

He made a guttural, dismissive sound as he joined the rest of the men.

Callum took her hand and drew her attention to him. "I, Callum, take you, Mari, as my wife. I will love you as long as my heart beats."

The words caught in her throat. "I, Mari... "

"*Och*, lass," he said, wiping tears from Mari's flushed cheeks. He shook his head, and lifted her chin. "This weeping is not a good omen."

She laughed in spite of her tears. "They're tears of joy."

"Aye, joy." He nodded and grinned, as if he did not believe her. "Go on, then."

Their smiles faded. "I, Mari, take you, Callum, as my husband, because I cannae imagine not being with you. And because I love you, and will till I die."

Callum pulled Mari close and kissed her so thoroughly that she blushed as he released her. Callum followed Mari's gaze to Nellie and Hughie, who were both unaware that their mouths were agape. The other men made encouraging noises. With raised brow, Callum said, "Haud yer wheesht! We're married now."

"As married as *twa* people can be!" Nellie glowed from the obvious joy, and perhaps just a bit from the whisky. She filled all the glasses and they toasted again, while a few of his men played the fiddle, pipes, and bodhrán, and everyone danced—except Callum and Mari.

Tired of watching the others, Callum stood with the help of his crutch. "Come, lass. We're going to dance."

Mari looked at him, stunned. "No, I could not. It's wicked."

"So is marrying a Catholic. So you're making great strides today."

With a grin, he pulled her to her feet. The lads played a slow song. What they did was as close to a dance as Callum's injured leg would allow. As he held her fully against him, Mari protested no further.

As the late summer darkness came, Callum sent his men off to continue the celebration on their own. Nellie made herself scarce, having made arrangements to sleep elsewhere for the night. This left Callum and Mari to spend their wedding night on a cot in the tent.

Mari became very busy tidying up.

"Mari." His eyes shone as his unsettling gaze bore through. "Turn down the light—else we'll make a grand silhouette outside the tent."

With a small gasp, her eyes rounded. She quickly extinguished the lamp. A full moon lit them in soft shadows. He held out his hand, which she took and came closer. She hesitated, looking uncertain. "Your leg... how can we...?"

Callum assumed a brave, noble tone. "Aye, well, lass. We must." He shook his head, frowning. "There's one wee problem with common law marriage. It's not legal until it is consummated." He looked into her eyes with a satisfied smile. "Aye. So, you see, wound or not—it's my duty."

"*Och!*" Mari released his hand with a playful shove. "I can see this is not going to be easy," she said, rolling her eyes.

"Aye, well, the cot will make things awkward, but we'll manage."

"I meant being married to you!"

Outside soldiers were drinking and singing, releasing the burdens of battle. But inside the tent it grew still. Callum touched Mari's skirt and gathered the cloth in his fist, pulling her to the edge of the cot, where he sat. In a low voice, he said, "Come closer, lass." He slid his palms up the front of her bodice and slipped his fingertips over the edge. Mari inhaled sharply. Slowly he unlaced her bodice and set loose her breasts, holding them in his palms. Mari's breathing grew shallow and uneven. Callum slid his hands down to her hips and guided her, until she straddled him. When he winced she began to get up, but he shifted her weight from his wounded thigh.

She resisted. "What if I hurt you?"

"I ache already from wanting you, Mari."

He caressed her until her back arched and she clung to the folds of his discarded plaid. He grasped her and fitted her to him. She responded to him, eliciting a guttural sound from his throat. Mari panted and whispered his name as he held her hips for a final thrust, and exhaled. She leaned over to kiss him, and then carefully lay down against him.

"What's this?" he asked, touching her cheek, moist with tears.

"Nothing."

With sudden concern, he said, "Mari, have I hurt you?"

"No!" She kissed his neck and whispered, "No. It's just that I love you so."

"My love." He gathered her close, pressing his lips to her forehead, as she rested her head in the curve of his neck.

After moments had passed, he said, "Lass, about these tears of yours—there have been so many today, I cannae keep track. These are the happy ones, aye?"

Even in the darkness, he heard the smile in her voice. "Yes, my beloved daft Callum. Very happy ones."

THEY AWOKE to the sounds of the troops breaking camp. Callum emerged from the tent to find Nellie beginning to pack up her cooking utensils. She rested her hands on her hips. "I must bid you farewell, lad."

"Farewell?" Mari ducked out of the tent and stood beside Callum.

Nellie said, "A few of the lads who were injured are going back to Glengarry." This much was not news to Callum. With a resigned air, she said, "I'm going back with them. They need a good cook, and they'll see me home safely."

"But do Hughie and Charlie have leave to go with you?" asked Mari.

"No, but these bones are too old for this sort of life. Hughie's a man now, and Charlie can take care of himself. They've no need of me, and I need to go home."

Callum had noticed Nellie moving more stiffly. This could not have been easy for her, so he had to agree that she ought to go home.

Nellie stepped close to him, taking his hands in hers. "Laddie, will you look after Hughie? Charlie's a bit too— Charlie." She grinned and Callum nodded with a laugh.

"Aye, of course I will."

Nellie peered into his eyes. "Bring them home to me safely. Promise me."

"Nellie. I'll do my best. You have my word."

Tears filled her eyes. "*Och*, Callum, you're a good lad." Through her tears she added, "And you have a good wife." She turned to Mari and hugged her, and then Callum. Before an hour had passed, they were waving to Nellie as she rode her pony and cart out of camp.

Callum was granted two weeks' leave to recuperate, which he welcomed as a chance to be with his bride. He had offered to take her home to make things right with her family, but Mari sadly said no. She had already publicly disgraced them. Even if they were to accept a marriage outside of the Presbyterian Church, which in itself was out of the question, it would fan the flames of her scandal and make her parents' life unbearable. She would not do that to them—assuming they would welcome her home, given this final blow, which Mari was sure they would not. In truth, they could not, if they were to stay in the good graces of the church. Callum had to agree. There was no question that her parents would oppose the marriage on principle alone. With him as the groom, it was worse. He was the stranger who had practically kidnapped their daughter in the middle of a kirk service. How could they not be reluctant to see that man bring home their daughter as his wife? But he saw that she was homesick. Callum did not like beginning their life together under a cloud of estrangement from her parents. For now, though, he agreed with Mari to leave things as they were. So they set out with the rest of the dragoons for Edinburgh. When Callum was better, he thought they might journey on to St. Andrews, for a few weeks alone by the sea. But for now, his leg pained him and he needed rest.

Barely able to mount his horse, Callum did not ride with ease, but the aching was dulled by the feel of Mari's body before him, softly molded to his.

On the way out of camp, they passed the twelve hundred prisoners taken in battle. They were tied, two-by-two, in a seemingly endless procession.

"Where will they take them?"

"Edinburgh," answered Callum.

"But where can they put that many men?"

"I'm not sure. The Tollbooth cannae hold all of these men. There was talk of Greyfriars Kirkyard." He stopped as Mari stared over at one particular prisoner, and the young man stared back with an accusatory gaze. As quickly as their eyes had met, the young man gave his head a subtle cautionary shake and looked away.

"Jamie," she whispered. She took a breath and was about to call out to him more loudly.

An English officer rode within earshot. Callum suddenly took hold of Mari's shoulder and chin and pivoted her about for a kiss. Mari struggled to speak, but he held her firmly in place until the officer had passed them. As he released her from his kiss, he murmured, "Quiet, lass."

"But Callum," she whispered, "I thought I saw Jamie."

"If you did, you cannae speak to him now without putting yourself in grave danger."

"From speaking to Jamie?"

Callum turned her to face forward again and spoke in low tones in her ear. "They think he might have been one of the lads who murdered Archbishop Sharp."

"My brother? That's nonsense."

When Callum did not readily agree, Mari said over her shoulder, "Well, it is. Jamie would never—Callum, how do you ken this?" Mari's eyes widened as she studied Callum. "You knew he was alive."

Callum did not speak or alter his expression.

She turned away. "But you chose not to tell me."

"Lass, this is not the place to discuss this."

Mari could not hide her dismay.

He leaned close to her. "Smile, lass," he said quietly through a feigned smile. "People are watching."

Mari looked about. There were soldiers all about them.

Callum spoke quietly. "I knew that he might be alive, but I had to be certain. It would have hurt you too much if it turned out not to be true."

"And you think losing my faith in you doesnae hurt me?"

Mari's words wounded. "Lass, in truth I could not tell you without revealing that he was a suspect."

Mari stiffened as the truth hit her. "And that you were sent to my farm to find him?"

"Aye."

"And do what?"

Callum said nothing.

"What were you going to do when you found him?"

Callum lifted his head and kept his eyes on the road straight ahead. "I cannae say."

"You mean that you willnae say."

His eyes hardened. "I said what I mean. I cannae say what I would do without knowing how I might have found him. Whether he had a gun pointed at me, or..."

"Or you at him."

Callum tilted his head to acknowledge the possibility without voicing it.

"You let me fall in love with you, and all the while you were planning to kill my brother."

Callum said, "Capture."

Mari nodded bitterly. "Oh, capture—so that someone else might kill him."

"Lass, you knew I was there on the side of the crown."

"Aye, but I didnae ken you were after my brother, or that he was alive."

"Might have been alive."

"*Och!* And that's different, is it?" Mari shifted her weight but, riding together as they were, she had nowhere to go. "You lied to me."

"Withheld the truth."

"I dinnae ken you. You're a stranger to me."

Callum took her bitter words with clenched jaw. "I am your husband, and you are my wife. I will not trade your safety for his."

"Well, I would. And I'm glad he did not come home and fall into your trap."

"*Och*, lass, you should wish that he had. When they ken who he is, what I say or do will not matter."

WHEN THEY STOPPED AT MIDDAY, Mari slipped from the saddle. They had ridden together without words. Mari now seized this first chance to be free of the man she had married, and went walking alone. The prisoners were not far ahead, chained and seated. Keeping a distance lest she arouse suspicion, Mari walked along the line of the six hundred pairs of prisoners.

"Stay back with the other camp followers, Miss," said a stern voice.

Startled, Mari turned to face a dragoon guard. "I was just walking."

"Back with the others, Miss."

Heading back, she spied Callum struggling toward her with his crutch, looking furious.

When he reached her, he took hold of her elbow and said in a hushed growl, "Take my arm and walk nicely, wife. I'll not ask what you're doing." He guided her firmly along. Angry as she was, Mari could not bring herself to struggle against him, for the pain each step caused him was clear.

"Husband," she said with near loathing, "I will find my brother."

Her eyes caught the attention of one particular prisoner who held her gaze for several moments, and then looked away as a guard drew closer.

Callum gripped her elbow and tugged her away. He quietly scolded, "Think what you're doing, lass! Do you want to wind up marching with them?" With reluctance, she walked on. "It was Jamie."

When they were well past the prisoners, Callum paused to lean against a tree. Although he did not complain, his leg hurt him badly.

Mari said, "What if I had not seen him? Would you ever have told me?"

"Not until I kent it for sure. There was only suspicion that he was alive."

"Which you did not share with me." She stopped walking. "What else have you not told me? Is anything true, or were you just using me to find Jamie?"

"I married you, lass. Is that not proof enough?"

"No. After all, it's not even a real marriage."

She took a step, but Callum grabbed her and spun her around with her back to the tree. Callum cursed his leg as he shifted his weight and leaned against her, with one arm on the tree. If Mari thought she had seen the anger of Callum MacDonell before, she was wrong. For this was an anger that quietly seared. Mari took in a fearful breath, worried by what he might do in this state.

He bent down. Pinned to the tree as she was, Mari flinched and looked off to the side, but he took her face and held it so she was forced to look into his eyes. She willed herself not to cry, and faced him with defiance. And with that, Callum kissed her. His thighs pressed against her. When her resolve softened, her lips followed suit. Callum's hand slid from its hold on her face and slipped beneath her arm. He kissed her deeply and well past the point when her arms circled his neck and a small moan escaped from her throat. His hand slid down the sides of her breasts to her waist, and she arched into him. As his arm circled her waist, he pulled her against him until their two forms molded together. Before his own knees went weak, he gently pulled away, leaving Mari's lips helplessly parted and breathless. She watched him with round, helpless eyes, unable to form words.

Callum's fierce eyes glimmered with anger. "If this is not a real marriage, then that was not a real kiss."

Chapter 14

At Home in Edinburgh

For two days the prisoners marched until they arrived in Edinburgh. Jamie was imprisoned, along with the bulk of the Covenanters, at Greyfriars Kirkyard. There was no shelter there, but the Highlanders thought little of it. No Highlander reached manhood without having slept out in the open air. Snow and freezing temperatures made no difference. They would wet down their plaids, which would freeze and block out the wind. Having heard tales of this, Mari dreaded finding out what her Edinburgh accommodations might be. But Callum surprised her by bringing her to some rooms he had rented on the third floor of a merchant's land on High Street.

"Oh, Callum!" she exclaimed as she rushed from one room to another. Large windows looked out over the street. The last room she found sported an iron bed with a thick mattress. She sat on it and sank into bliss.

"Eiderdown! Callum, it's grand!"

The door latched with a click, and the mattress shifted as Callum stretched out next to her. He leaned on one elbow beside her and stroked the edge of her bodice. "Since we've been married, we've not had a proper bed to lie in."

She looked into his eyes, which had a mischievous glint. "Aye."

Callum sat up and seemed to be preparing to leave, much to Mari's surprise.

"Well, I'm glad you clarified that fine fact," said Mari, confused by his sudden inattention. She had not seen him removing his hose and shoes.

Callum turned and leaned over Mari's feet. First he slipped off one shoe, and then the other, then one finger's length at a time he slid her hose down until they lay pooled at her ankles and soon after slipped to the floor. Mari helped him unwind his plaid and let it fall in folds. Wearing only his leine, he knelt straddling her, taking care to favor his wounded leg. Mari took up the hem of his leine in her hands while Callum slid his palms up the length of her thighs. She drew deep breaths as she held onto his muscular shoulders, and clutched at his back while he touched her and fed her longing. The need to be one drove them together. And after their passion was spent they lay entwined, having gasped and whispered their passion until all that remained was to breathe in like cadence. In the midst of the hush that settled upon them their love bound them to one another. No matter what might befall them, that love would bide well and forever with them.

MARI TRIED daily to visit her brother, but no visitors were allowed. She left food for him each time, but suspected that he got very little of it. Callum's clansmen were among those assigned to guard the inmates of Covenanter's Prison. With Callum at home, they came often to visit. Mari soon made a habit of entrusting them with food and supplies to take back to her brother. She welcomed their visits, not only for what they could do for her brother, but for the way Callum's spirits improved in their company—not only from the wee dram or two that they shared, but also for the laughter they gave him. Sometimes they brought news from home. Nellie had returned safely home to the Highlands, and all was well there. When they shared stories of other dragoons, Callum grew restless and eager to get back among them. Mari insisted he wait, for his leg was not healing. His pallid skin and the dark circles under his eyes confirmed Mari's fears that it was getting worse. Even Callum could not argue the point, for he could not hide the pain that he suffered.

Ten days had passed since they had arrived in Edinburgh, and the lads were over for supper with news. The Privy Council had issued an order offering liberty to prisoners if they would sign a bond promising not to take up arms against His Majesty again. When she heard it, Mari jumped with glee and threw her arms about Hughie.

"Does Jamie ken yet?"

"Aye," said Hughie, smiling. "Duncan told him not an hour ago."

Then Mari threw her arms about Duncan and kissed his cheek. Callum sat across the room with his feet propped up and watched, laughing as Duncan took

Mari's elbows and gently stepped back an arm's length from her.

"Jamie's going to be free!"

Duncan said, "Not yet, Mari. He's not yet agreed to sign it."

"Well, I'll just have to convince him." She looked at Duncan frankly.

"He didnae seem very likely to do it when I saw him."

Mari would hear none of it. "He just needs time to consider it. He'll see it's the right thing to do."

Hughie pulled out his fiddle. "This calls for a ceilidh!"

Duncan gave him a dark look.

"For Mari," said Hughie.

Charlie swept Mari into a dance while Alex played the *bodhrán*. Soon he begged off, claiming fatigue, but Mari saw through him. He wanted a drink. With gentlemanly flourish, he offered Mari back to her husband, but he declined.

"Oh, Callum, dance with me!" said Mari.

"No, lass, my leg's not up to it." He noticed Duncan leaning on the mantle, a drink in his hand. "Duncan, this fine lass needs a partner." Callum held out Mari's hand. Mari's smile faded to see Duncan's reluctance.

"Callum, no," Mari said, her eyes darting toward the frowning Duncan.

Duncan surprised her by coming over and taking her hand. Mari smiled, and his frown nearly dissolved. They danced about the room. To Mari's surprise, Duncan was a fine dancing partner. Whatever had troubled him was gone now. Mari's joy seemed to spread to everyone present. Charlie took a turn dancing with Mari. In the midst of the song, Callum set down his whisky. It landed too hard, causing the music and dancing to stop. All turned toward him in silent expectation.

"Sorry," said Callum as he took pains to slowly stand up. "I'm going to bed." His balance faltered.

"Steady, lad." Charlie laughed.

Alex chimed in, "Whisky willnae cure your leg, but it fails more agreeably than most."

Everyone laughed except Callum, who stared with a look of confusion and then sank to the floor.

Charlie was closest. Still laughing, he knelt down to pat Callum's cheek and drag him up by the armpits. His broad grin changed to alarm. "It's not drink that ails him. It's a fever."

Alex and Duncan helped carry him to bed. As they set him down, his plaid folded over, exposing the putrid bandage covering his leg wound.

"Mari!" Duncan called out, but she was already on her way into the room. "How long has it been like this?"

Tears filled her eyes. "Over a week. The doctor said there's no more we can do but keep it covered and wait for it to get better."

"Or worse," Duncan muttered. He left, and returned an hour later with a professor from the University's College of Medicine. How Duncan had found him and got him to come so quickly, no one knew or dared ask. A dirk poised at the poor man's back would not have surprised anyone there, but there was none. He, in fact, seemed to have come quite willingly, which impressed Mari even more with Duncan's skills for persuasion.

The surgeon applied a mixture of egg yolk, oil of roses, and turpentine to the wound. "I'll be back tomorrow to check on his progress," he told them.

Duncan showed him to the door and pressed something —money, Mari presumed—into his hand. Closing the door, Duncan turned to find Mari before him.

"Thank you," she said, looking weary.

His reply was brusque. "What else would I do?" His mood changed as he looked intently at her. "I'll be back in the morning." He abruptly left, closing the door behind him.

Callum remained feverish, barely talking—and then only in fits of delirium. The doctor came back daily; at what cost, Duncan would not say. Duncan, in fact, said very little, which did not go unnoticed by Mari. The one time he spoke at any length to her was the day after Callum fell ill.

"I've been guarding the inmates at Greyfriars Kirkyard."

"Have you seen Jamie?"

"Aye. Sit down, Mari."

This prompted immediate alarm. "Tell me." She searched his eyes as she placed her hand on his arm. He looked down at her hand in annoyance. Remembering herself, she removed it at once.

"He'll not sign," Duncan told her. "I have talked to him, Mari. He willnae change his mind."

Mari looked up, and then closed her eyes. "*Och*, why must he be so stubborn? He could be free."

"He said he wouldnae sell his conscience for comfort. He's one of the few. Your brother has strong convictions," Duncan said with respect.

Mari buried her face in her hands. "First Callum. Now Jamie. It's too much." She wept as Duncan sat silently by. When she had calmed down enough to speak, she said, "How many are left?"

"Lass?"

"How many prisoners are left?"

"Of the twelve hundred, barely more than three hundred remain."

"What will they do to him?"

"I dinnae ken. It's best not to think of it until we know for certain."

Mari looked at him gravely. "They could hang him."

Duncan was reluctant to agree, but he would not lie. "Aye. Or transport him."

"And what good will his conscience be then?"

"He did ask me to give you a message."

"What is it?"

"He asks that you not tell your parents. It would be better for them to go on believing he is dead than to suffer another death, should it come to that."

"There is no chance of my telling them anything. I have written to them. They sent me one letter, their last. I'm not to write to them again."

He scrutinized her as she looked away. Tears filled her eyes and one trailed down her cheek, and another. His hand twitched as though he might reach up and wipe them away, but he did not.

Her voice wavered as she tried to hold back her emotions. "I'm losing everyone I hold dear."

"Not everyone, lass."

As she wiped tears, she said, "If I lose Jamie, I'll have lost my whole family."

Duncan said, "You're one of us now. We're your family."

Moved by his words, she reached out and gripped his arm as she turned away and covered her face and her now uncontrollable sobbing.

"*Och*," he murmured as he touched his hand to the base of her neck. She spun around and buried her sobs in his chest. Duncan held her in his arms until she was cried out.

Mari lifted her chin and looked into his eyes. "You're a good friend."

His expression grew grim, and he looked away. "Aye." He gave her shoulder a squeeze as he took a step back. "Goodbye, Mari."

He turned from her and left without looking back.

THE LADS STOPPED by increasingly often, so that someone was always there with her. It worried her that they felt Callum was so ill that they could not leave her alone for fear something might happen. Duncan came with one or more of them daily to check in on Callum, after which he would slouch in a chair by the window and wait for the others.

On one such day, Alex once caught Mari studying Duncan. "Dinnae worry about him. He's in a dark mood, is all. It will pass."

But the dark moods continued. One day, after Mari saw Callum's doctor to the door, she closed it gently and turned to face Duncan. "What have I done?" His expression was dark and unreadable.

"You are Callum's friend. He thinks highly of you and

of your opinion. And I see that something's changed, but I dinnae ken why."

He held her gaze long enough to scowl and say, "I dinnae ken what you mean." He turned away and walked to the window.

"I think that you do." Mari waited. "Duncan, I love Callum. He is my life. I will never hurt him. Why won't you trust that?"

Impatiently, he glared at her. "Have you not got enough to worry about without bothering with me?"

Hurt but persistent, Mari walked over behind where he stood at the window. "No."

Duncan bristled.

Growing desperate, Mari said, "I can see you no longer approve of me, or perhaps you never did."

"Dinnae be daft, woman."

She said, "Callum's friends should be my friends. Am I daft to want that?" When he did not respond, Mari put a gentle hand on his shoulder. "Duncan? Look at me."

He whirled about. He grabbed hold of her shoulders and glared. His look frightened her. "Mari, just leave it alone!"

Callum called out from his bed. Duncan released her, and they both rushed to the bedroom. Callum was fully awake for the first time in days. His fever had broken. Duncan watched from the doorway as Mari smiled and brushed Callum's hair from his forehead. A moment later, the door closed and the latch clicked behind him.

Chapter 15

The Price of Freedom

In the lingering light of a summer evening, the MacDonell lads arrived to see Callum. They brought armloads of food, which was their habit. For Mari, they brought the surprise of a new shift, jacket, collar, and petticoats.

When she tried to refuse them, Alex said, "You were looking a wee bit tattered there, lassie."

Charlie added with a wince, "We could not take any more of it, dearie, as we were the ones forced to look at you!"

Feigning offense, Mari said, "Oh, I see! Well, all right then. If I must, I'll accept these—but only to spare the likes of you sorry lot." She looked up into his mischievous eyes with a smile as she took the parcels of clothes and started toward the bedroom.

Hughie called after her, "It had nothing to do with two shop girls they followed—or with needing an excuse to go into their shop and make their acquaintance."

"*Och*, hold your tongue, Hughie!" said Alex as he swatted Hughie's head.

"Dinnae listen to him, dearie!" said Charlie. We were only thinking of you."

Several minutes later the men sat talking and laughing with Callum, whom they had brought to the sitting room and propped up on pillows. The laughter stopped as one by one they saw Mari, just arrived in the room and enjoying the sight of them laughing with Callum. They were pleased by the sight of her too, as she stood in fresh clothing with a warm glow about her. Callum clasped her hand and smiled. His eyes swept over his Mari as the men showered admiration on her. She accepted their words with grace, even though she had not been raised to receive such attention. Her eyes settled on Duncan, who had been silent. Their eyes met. He seemed almost to smile. It was not much, but Mari took it as a semblance of acceptance.

DAYS FOLLOWED in which Callum grew stronger. He and Mari went on walks. By summer's end, Mari could no longer keep up with him. He was climbing the steep closes and wynds at a near running pace. He would wait at the top and scoop Mari into his arms and steal kisses in shadows.

The lads were over for supper one night, teasing Mari about Callum's renewed vigor while she cleaned up after supper.

"Mari, lass, that broom will do you no good now that your man can outrun you," said Alex.

"Aye, then I'd better put it in your more capable

hands. And dinnae miss that corner over there," she said as she placed the broom in his hand.

Callum circled Mari's waist from behind and said, "A man would be mad to run away from this bonnie lass." He planted a kiss on her neck.

Charlie clapped his hands over Hughie's eyes. "Dinnae look, laddie. 'Tis no sight for young eyes to see."

Hughie ducked and swatted his older brother away.

With no warning, Duncan announced, "I'll be leaving."

Everyone stopped to stare.

With a dismissive shrug, Duncan said, "I've signed on with a merchant ship."

No one seemed quite able to find words, except Mari. "But why?"

He glanced about, but without making eye contact with anyone in the room. Gruffly, he said, "Adventure. New scenery."

Hughie and Charlie exchanged looks of disbelief. Alex studied Duncan intently.

"Duncan, do you ken what you're doing?" asked Callum.

Duncan shot a look of annoyance at him. "Aye. I ken well what I'm doing."

Mari softly said, "Forgive us, but it's a wee bit sudden."

Duncan stood abruptly. "Sudden or not, it's my decision to make, is it not?" The subject was closed. "Thank you for a fine supper, Mari. Callum." With barely a nod, he was gone.

Callum stared at the door. He had known Duncan since

they were boys. When something was wrong, the other one knew it, whether or not they spoke of it. This was different. Something was wrong, and he had not a clue what it was.

Alex rose and went over to Mari and took both of her hands. With a light peck on her cheek, he said, "Thank you, lass. Dinnae worry about Duncan." Charlie and Hughie started to get up, but Alex waved a hand, urging them to sit down. "Stay, lads. I'll go find him."

The next day, still drunk and head pounding, Duncan walked along the Leith docks to a ship bound for Poland. He boarded and did not look back.

Callum took Mari walking that day. The first falling leaves of the season swirled about their feet, looking as restless as Mari now felt.

"I want him to be happy," said Mari.

"I've kent Duncan a long time. He's a tough man, even by Highlander standards. He will work out what's bothering him." Callum gave Mari's hand a pat where it lay on his arm, and they walked on, enjoying the day.

EDINBURGH'S STONE buildings cast shadows over the narrow streets as the bare trees stretched up to the darkening sky. It was a November evening, already dark when Callum came with news. Since Duncan had gone weeks before, Callum had taken his place guarding the prisoners housed in Greyfriars Kirkyard.

"Come, Mari. We're going to visit your brother."

"Jamie? Oh, Callum!" She threw her arms about his neck. "Truly?"

"Aye, lass, but we must make haste, and be quiet when we get there. I'm breaking the rules, ken."

Mari bundled up what was left of a loaf of bread and some bannocks. "I wish I had kent. I'd have cooked for him."

"Dinnae worry. I've seen that he's gotten the food that you've sent. He's better off than many." Mari stopped at the door. "He'll need another plaid." She rushed to the bedroom and returned with a plaid.

A nearly full moon lit their way through the dark night as they wended their way through the kirkyard. Skulls and crossbones carved into gravestones and mausoleums peered at them as they passed by, while skeletons seemed to stop in the midst of grotesque dancing to watch them.

"*Och!* 'Tis a dismal place!" whispered Mari.

Callum looked at her patiently. "It is a graveyard, Mari."

"Aye, but to make good men bide here alive is not right."

"It's a bad business for all of us."

They arrived at the gate, where a guard stood concealed by the grotesque shadows from tree limbs overhead.

"Hughie?"

"Aye, Callum." Hughie opened the gate, let them in and then closed the gate quietly behind them.

Callum told Mari, "Wait here with Hughie."

Mari nodded, bright-eyed with excitement. It had been over seven months since she'd seen Jamie.

Callum gave her shoulders a squeeze and, with a steadying gaze, released her and went in through the gate.

He walked down a stone path, leaving Mari behind under the shadowy limbs of an old oak. She shivered, more from nerves than the cold. Yet she could not shake off the uneasy feeling that someone was watching. A sudden flutter of wings taking flight overhead jarred her senses. When the sound of footsteps drew near, she stood still.

"Marion?" came the familiar whisper.

"Jamie!" She threw her arms about him. "*Och!* You're so thin!" She took a step back and stood holding his hands.

"Marion, I've missed you!" His smile looked weak in the shadowed moonlight.

"Is it very bad, Jamie?"

He lied. "Not as bad as it was. There are only three hundred of us left, so it isnae so crowded."

"Good." Mari looked at him, knowing their time would be short, yet finding it difficult to broach that which loomed largest between them.

"Jamie, it's so good to see you."

"Aye." As he gazed at her, memories returned of their last time together, and his eyes shone with the tears he choked back.

"*Och*, Jamie. How could you let us believe you were dead? We grieved for you so."

The roar of shouting rose up from the prison. "Stay here with Mari," Callum told Hughie as he ran. The sounds of fighting grew louder–a brawl had erupted.

Jamie grasped Mari's hands and pulled her farther from Hughie and spoke in a hush. "Listen, you must help me get out of here."

"I'm trying, Jamie. But you gave up your best chance."

"What? To sign their bond an oath saying that we were wrong to fight back? Never. You can live with your choices, but I'm no turncoat. Not after what they did to Ellen. She never backed down. Nor will I."

Mari flinched, but overlooked the affront. "But Jamie, it's only paper. You'd be free! Ellen would want that."

"I'd liefer spit on her grave."

"Jamie!"

"Nor will I sign an oath saying that Archbishop Sharp's death was a murder. It was justice."

"You dinnae ken that."

"Aye, I do."

The moonlight caught the cold pride in his face, and it made Mari shudder.

The sounds of scuffling grew louder as a brawl escalated around the corner. Hughie said, "I'd best see what that is." He headed down the short path and around the corner.

Mari studied her brother, now a stranger before her with a look so hard that she wanted to turn from him. "Jamie, they're hanging five men for the murder of Archbishop Sharp."

"I ken that. And I ken that they've got the wrong men."

Fearing the answer, Mari said, "How do you ken?"

"Those men were not there. I was."

Her hand flew to her mouth. "*Och*, Jamie, what have you done?"

"*Whisht*." He glanced down the path toward Hughie, and pulled her closer.

Mari shook her head slowly, not wanting to believe him, but she knew he was speaking the truth.

He said, "Those five accused men are innocent—and the royalists ken it." He glanced down the path again and lowered his voice. "They're just hanging them to make a point. It does not matter to them if they hang the right men, do you not see? They will punish the cause even more this way. Faint-hearted men will give up —signing oaths—out of fear that they could be next. But what they dinnae grasp is that they will just make the rest of us stronger. Those who cannae be moved by ideas alone will be moved by their own moral outrage. The more martyrs there are, the more people will join us."

"But they're innocent men. They did not choose to be martyrs. You must do something."

"What? Give myself up?"

Mari did not like that choice either. "It's wrong to let innocent men hang."

Jamie said, "So not only would you have me die, but you'd have me betray those who were with me?"

"Is there no way to let the authorities ken that they've got the wrong men without turning yourself in?"

"Marion, dinnae be daft. Forbye, it would weaken our side, and we cannae have that. No, it's better this way. We must get back our freedom to worship—whatever the cost."

A brilliant light shone in his eyes, and its harshness frightened her. "Jamie, you're weary. You're not thinking clearly."

"I wouldnae expect you to understand. You're one of them now. But you're still my sister. If you love me, you'll help me get away from here now. There's still a chance that someone could come forward and say I was there. If that happens, I cannae be here. They would kill me for certain."

Mari did not know what she wanted herself. If she urged him to sign the oath, he would run from his duty to those innocent men who would die for his crime. But in saving their lives, he could die. He was her brother, she could not wish for that.

He grabbed hold of her shoulders with a bruising grip. "Help me, Marion. You must."

"How can I?" Mari wished Callum would come back. She was frightened. This was not her Jamie.

"That guard of yours."

"Callum?"

"Make him let me go."

"Make him? I cannae make him do anything."

"Oh, Marion. You could. You could talk him into it."

"No, Jamie. I wouldnae use him like that."

Jamie sneered. "And why not? He's one of them."

"Because I love him."

"*Och*, wake up! He's just using you, Marion. And when he moves on, he'll leave you. You're just one more dragoon's whore in his eyes."

Mari slapped him. He reflexively reached for her wrist and took hold with a grip that brought tears to her eyes. But more shocking than that was his hardened expression. Gone was her dear brother, replaced by a stranger.

He glared. "Dinnae be a fool, Marion. He's one of them. They dinnae think like we do. They are brutal. They murdered my Ellen! How can you not see that? And by sleeping with them, you're no better." He released her wrist in disgust.

"Sleeping with them? He's my husband!" She

wrapped her fingers around her wrist, still white from the imprint of his fingers. "I don't know you anymore."

"Oh, aye?" He paced about, glancing back down the row of cells. "Well, I ken myself better. I'll no longer cower under the fist of the crown. I've put my faith into action." He moved closer until he was inches from her. "And what about you? You've turned from God—and for what? One of them—to amuse him between murdering decent people like Ellen."

Bitter tears streamed down Mari's cheeks as Jamie went on. "You're no better than a royalist camp follower. And the sooner you're rid of him, the better."

Two hands clamped down on Jamie's shoulders and hurled him to the ground. "You'll not speak to her like that."

"This is a family matter and none of your business."

Hughie reached down and lifted Jamie off the ground by the collar. "She's my kin, too—Clan MacDonell. And I will not allow it."

Jamie spat in Hughie's face.

His full anger now at the surface, Hughie landed his fist in Jamie's jaw. With a glance back, he said, "Sorry, Mari, but I'll not let him talk to you like that."

In that moment's distraction, Jamie pushed back and regained his advantage. He kneed Hughie in the groin, and landed a blow to his jaw that sent Hughie back to the ground. With a dull thud, his head hit a stone and he lost consciousness.

Chapter 16

An Honorable Act

"Jamie, what have you done?" Mari looked up to see light glint from the blade in Jamie's hand. It was Hughie's dirk; he must have taken it during the struggle. Jamie turned over the dirk in his hand. Certain that he was ready to use it, Mari cried out and lunged. Startled, Jamie turned too fast and lost his balance. He fell with a grunt, and lay still. Mari went to him and saw the dirk stuck in his side. "Oh, Jamie!" She called out for Callum, but the brawl, though subsiding, was too loud for anyone to hear her. She turned him over to look at the wound. The blade had not gone in far, and his breathing was steady.

"Callum!"

A grunt drew her attention to Hughie. He stirred, but then went still. She reached over to check him. He moved when she touched him.

"Mari?" murmured Hughie.

"I'm sorry, Hughie, but Jamie is worse. I must tend to him." Turning to her brother, Mari tore a wide strip from her shift and then wrapped one end around her hand. She took a deep breath, braced herself, and then pulled out the dirk and pressed the wadded bundle of cloth to his wound. As blood seeped through the fabric, she wrapped the bandage tightly about Jamie's abdomen. As she pulled the ends into a knot, he moaned. "Are you trying to kill me?" He opened his eyes, and groaned as he put his hand on the bandage. "What happened?"

Mari's eyes swept over his face. Even in the moonlight Jamie looked pale. "You fell on the dirk. It's not very deep."

A quiet moan drew Mari's attention to Hughie. Wiping the blood from her hands, she felt his head to determine how badly he was hurt. With a loud groan, he swatted her hand from the large lump on the back of his head.

"I'm sorry," she hastened to tell him.

As she leaned over Hughie, she was pushed to the side with a force that took her breath for a moment. She looked up to see Jamie step on Hughie's slumped body and struggle to boost himself over the wall. "Jamie, no!" With a grunt, he landed on the other side, on the ground. Gasping for air, he pulled himself to his feet and staggered away until his uneven footsteps grew faint in the distance.

Hughie fell unconscious as Mari cried out for help.

THE NEXT DAY, Hughie sat, with a headache to match the large lump on his head, beside Callum, Charlie, Alex, and three other guards who had been on duty the previous night. Before them was Captain of the Guards. Having heard their account of the prisoner's escape,

Captain Lumsden completed his examination of the other three guards. There seemed to be little doubt that the prison brawl had been staged to provide a distraction so Jamie could escape. He looked first at Callum, and then studied Hughie. "The events seem to hinge upon you two men. I now read from the Order of the Privy Council, under which we serve here:

... And that for that end they shall put them into the inner Greyfriars churchyard, with convenient guards to wait upon them, who are to have at least twenty-four sentries in the night time, and eight in the day time; of which sentries the officers shall keep a particular list, that if any of the prisoners escape, the sentries may assure themselves to cast the dice, and answer body for body for the fugitives, without any exception; and the officers are to answer for the sentries, and the town of Edinburgh for the officers. And if any of the prisoners escape, the Council will require a particular account, and make them answerable for them.

"Private?" Captain Lumsden said to Hughie.

"Aye, sir."

"Tell me again how the prisoner came to be so close to the wall that he was able to climb over."

"He climbed over my unconscious body, sir."

"And how did you come to be unconscious?"

"There was a fight. McEwan got away and I chased him." He glanced at Callum, and continued. "We fought and he struck me. I'm told that my head hit a rock. That's all I can remember." Hughie's face reddened. He could feel Callum's eyes on him.

Captain Lumsden raised an eyebrow. "And how do you know that he climbed onto you?"

"I could feel it."

"While you were unconscious?"

"No, after."

"And the blood that we found on the ground?"

"Oh, that. Well, I... I must have stabbed him. I— forgot to mention that."

"You forgot to mention a trifling detail like stabbing the prisoner?" He peered skeptically at Hughie.

Hughie's brow furrowed. "Aye."

Captain Lumsden studied him for a moment, and then continued. "And what of this piece of torn cloth. Where did this come from?"

Hughie looked at the cloth. "I dinnae ken."

The captain leaned over the table between them. "This is the kind of cloth one might find under a woman's skirt, is it not?"

"It might be." Hughie was too honest a man to lie well. He shifted in his chair and looked up at the captain.

"The nights can get quiet and long in that dismal kirk-yard, I imagine."

"Aye, they can."

"So you brought in a little visitor."

Hughie's eyes widened. "No!" Callum inwardly groaned. Hughie did not see that a plausible explanation was being unwittingly served up on a platter.

"Thought you'd have a little slap and tickle to pass the time, eh?" Captain Lumsden smiled. "Things got a bit rough, did they?"

Hughie leapt to his feet. "No! She's not like that!"

Callum slowly blinked, and then focused his gaze to the floor.

"And does she have a name?"

Hughie frowned and shook his head. After a quick glance toward Callum, he sat down and was mute.

"Ensign MacDonell?"

Callum clenched his jaw, and met the captain's pointed look.

"Your lad Hughie here seems to have slept through a good portion of the incident. Shame that he missed the part where the woman's undergarments were torn off."

Hughie straightened and leaned forward in protest, but one look from Callum settled him back into place.

The officer continued. "So we're left with a situation in which we have no witness."

Callum gave a cautious nod.

Captain Lumsden said, "I met your wife once."

Callum's eyes widened, but he quickly recovered and made it look more like interest than surprise. Captain Lumsden looked down with a hint of a smile from the memory. "We shared a pint on the day of Bothwell Brigg."

Callum studied Captain Lumsden, not quite able to read him. Mari had never mentioned meeting the captain. As he studied Lumsden's expression, he could not gauge in which direction this story might lead, but he was fairly certain he was not going to like it.

"Your wife has a relative here, has she not? Or rather, had a relative here. That is, until he escaped."

Callum said nothing.

"If we were to send men to your house, would they find a torn shift to match this cloth I am holding?"

He met the captain's gaze plainly, and said, "What they'd find, if they tried to look under my wife's skirts, is my fist in their faces."

The captain's mouth curved up a bit at the corner. "If

we found such a torn shift, we would have to arrest your wife as an accessory to treason."

Callum steeled himself. "Aye, sir. You do have that power."

With a steady look, the captain said bluntly, "Did your wife conspire to help the prisoner, her brother, escape?"

"No," Callum said with no hesitation.

"He is her brother, after all."

"Aye, he is that. But she would not have done it." He leveled a cool look at the captain. "If she had been there."

"Why not?"

"Because she would never hurt me."

Captain Lumsden looked Callum straight in the eye. "And you honestly think she would choose you over her own flesh and blood?"

Without hesitation, Callum said, " I am certain she would never hurt me."

Lumsden held Callum's gaze for long moment. "So am I."

He sat down in the chair across from Callum and leaned back. "I found her after the Battle of Bothwell Brigg combing the camp looking for you. I was of the impression that she was prepared to take on the whole English Army if it stood in the way of her finding you."

Callum smiled to himself at the thought and, in doing so, failed to notice Captain Lumsden doing the same. His mood shifted, as if he were turning something over in his mind. "What cause had she to think you would be put in danger if her brother escaped? What had you to do with it, after all?"

Callum cursed at himself as his thoughts raced through each word he had said. "I had nothing to do with it. Nor did my wife. But she would ken well enough, as do you, that what happens on my watch is my responsibility, regardless of who is to blame. I dinnae take it lightly." Captain Lumsden scrutinized Callum. Moments later, he stood and walked to the door and beckoned for someone. In came his assistant to record his report.

"There were no witnesses, but the evidence shows that the prisoner overpowered the guard, knocking him unconscious. He then used the guard's body as a sort of human stile to climb over the wall."

Hughie's expression and breathing relaxed at the news that Mari would not be charged with a crime. Callum did the same inwardly, but refused to reveal it. He felt quite certain that Lumsden suspected Mari of helping her brother. And yet, he had chosen not to involve her. Although Mari was smart, Captain Lumsden was clever and skilled. He would have drawn the truth from her. He said he had met her. Whatever had transpired in that meeting, Callum felt sure it now prompted the captain to protect her.

Captain Lumsden said, "The unfortunate matter remains. The Privy Council orders, under which we serve here, call for the guards to answer body for body for every escaped prisoner. So to pay for the loss of the prisoner, someone must take his place."

So that was it, thought Callum. Lumsden did not want to put Mari in prison. He seemed to think she was guilty, and yet he was choosing to spare her. Callum said, "Sir, may I speak?"

"Ensign," he said with a nod.

"The other guards were nowhere near the incident."

"Except for Hugh MacDonell."

"But I am the officer. Therefore I am the one you should hold to account. I accept my responsibility for the incident, as well as the consequences."

Charlie and Alex protested. Alex said, "The order says to cast dice. We will not be denied."

"Aye," Charlie said in firm agreement.

Lumsden's mouth quirked at the corner. "Your men think very highly of you."

Charlie said, "Aye, and we'll prove it. Just hand us the dice."

Lumsden assessed Callum's resolve, and then stood and went to the window to consider for several moments in silence.

Callum watched and wondered at what drove the captain's decision. If he had had any suspicions of Mari, he had either ruled them out or chosen to protect her. So he now had a choice, and Callum intended to make it an easy one.

"I need only one man to take the prisoner's place. If I have a volunteer, there's no need to cast dice. Have I a volunteer?" He looked at Callum for confirmation, before making his decision final.

Callum met his eyes squarely. "You do."

It was an honorable act on Callum's part, and it was met with respect. Captain Lumsden gave Callum a nod, and then walked to the door and called for the guards.

"No, Callum!" cried Hughie. He sprang to his feet, refusing to let Callum take his place.

Callum leaned over to Charlie and Alex. "First see to the lad, and then look after Mari." He gave them a grave stare, which they returned with solemn nods.

Hughie said, "Callum, I will not let you do this!"

To Hughie he said, "I made a promise to Nellie to keep you safe, lad."

The guards each took an arm and led him away, leaving Hughie crying out in futile protest. Charlie and Alex went to Hughie, and each gripped an arm and held him back until Callum was gone.

"No!" cried Mari. "You did not let him do it!"

"It was Callum's decision," said Charlie, in his warm soothing way that charmed all women but Mari, at this moment. No one defied Callum; they respected him too much for that.

"I dinnae care a whit about Callum's decision. He should not have done it."

Charlie looked somberly at her. "Would you rather have Hughie in prison?"

His words struck their blow. Mari shook her head and tamped down her frustration.

"We'll look out for him, lass," added Alex.

"I'm sorry, Mari. I didnae want to. These two held me back," Hughie said, as he sat down in Duncan's old chair by the window and sulked.

"It's not your fault, Hughie," she said, watching him. She sighed and looked at Charlie and Alex, who both returned the same helpless stare. She shook her head in resignation. Softly, she said, "It was the right thing to do, but I hate that it had to be done. I should never have gone there to visit my brother. It's my fault."

Charlie took Mari's elbow. "Sit down, lassie." She gave a nod, and he took her hand and led her to a chair in the sitting room. But first, with her hands on her hips, she said, "Hughie, come here."

Hughie lifted his heartsick eyes to meet hers. She took his hand and pulled him into a hug. "There's no point in trying to argue with Callum when he wants his way." She touched his cheek and combed back his hair as though he were a child—a very tall one—and then sat down.

Alex brought her a glass. "Here, Mari; doctor's orders."

"With you as my doctor, I'm in even more trouble than I thought." She laughed, but tears soon filled her eyes.

"*Och*, lass," said Alex as he put his arm about her and let her cry on his shoulder. When she ran out of tears, Alex said, "There, now, lass." He lifted her chin. "Dinnae tell anyone about this. We dinnae want word to get around that I've got feelings."

Mari tried to smile, but she could not be distracted. "Why could Jamie not have just signed that oath?"

"I suppose you've got to admire his sense of honor," said Charlie.

Mari shook her head. "There was no honor in this. It was pride."

Alex said gently, "He has principles, lass. That is not a bad thing."

Mari shook her head. "Pride or principles, I wish he'd have swallowed them, and signed the pledge. Then he would have been free. But instead he escaped, forcing Callum to take his place."

Charlie leaned closer to Mari and put his hand on hers. "We'll get Callum out. Dinnae worry about it."

Mari's glanced absently at him. "If I didnae ken better,

I'd think Jamie planned it this way. He doesn't approve of my marriage to a papist Highlander. It would give him great pleasure to see Callum out of my life."

Alex said, "But he couldnae have known. I saw your brother in there day after day. There's one thing on his mind. He's lost his true love, and he's bitter about it. How can we ken what that does to a man unless we've been through it?"

"I pray that I'll never learn what it does to a woman," said Mari. "One thing I do ken is that if anything happens to Callum, I will hold Jamie to blame."

In the early hours of the morning, Mari fell asleep, exhausted, in a sitting room chair. Alex carried her to bed while Hughie laid a quilt over her. After they had all crept out, Charlie gently closed the door to the bedroom. As no one was willing to leave her alone, the three slept on the sitting room floor.

CALLUM WAS PUT in a cell with the men he had once guarded. He had been fair with the prisoners, but guards did not win friends, so he counted himself lucky to be left alone. Each guard there knew that he might have been in Callum's place, so they kept an eye out for him. But the prison was an open-air structure—little more than stone pens for men, as if they were animals. The effect was the same, except animals were far better sheltered in byres than he was in this kirkyard. The winter wind blew over the hill. Callum wrapped his plaid about himself and settled back against the stone wall. If he could not sleep outside in the cold, he was not much of a Highlander. But he thought about Mari at home in their bed, soft and warm, and he missed her. The lads would take care of her, of that he was certain. But when he would see her, he did not know. Visits had never been allowed, and the one he had arranged had gotten him in here. His clansmen had taken care not to report Mari's presence at the time of the escape, but a few of the other guards knew she had been there. While Callum had their respect and their silence, it served as a warning. While they did not suspect Mari of wrongdoing, they would not allow Mari—or anyone else —to make an unauthorized visit again. Callum was now paying for the first mistake. They would not join him with a second.

Chapter 17

The Crown of London

Captain Teddico sat in his crumpled coat and waistcoat across the desk of a young and prosperous merchant. If William Paterson had vision and purse for grand schemes, it was Teddico who had the sea legs to get the job done without being hindered by questions, excuses or scruples. He knew this well as he faced the fine merchant in his fine velvet clothes, sitting in his fine carpeted office. His hands never got dirty. But Teddico did not mind. Men like Paterson needed the likes of him, and they paid a fine price.

"These prisoners in Greyfriars will require transportation to English plantations in the Colonies," said Paterson.

"Aye," said the captain with a confident nod. He had carried human cargo many times before. African, Scottish, Irish or English, it made little difference to him.

Paterson told him, "I've chartered a ship, the *Crown of London*."

"The *Crown*." Teddico nodded. "For how many?"

"Two hundred and fifty-seven."

"And when would we sail?"

"By December."

Teddico's bushy brows met in the middle as he considered it. "December? You ken that there's rough seas in December."

Paterson acknowledged the fact with barely a nod, barely bothering to make eye contact.

"It takes longer that time of year, with the weather and such."

"But you can do it," said Paterson, cutting to the point.

"Aye," said Teddico, drawing out the word as he feigned deeper thought. "But there's added danger, and a much longer journey. That will mean more supplies, and more pay for the men."

Paterson held his gaze. "The usual price. That is what I am offering."

Teddico lowered his head, disappointed, but lifted his eyes to offer his continued, begrudging attention.

Paterson seemed not to notice, and continued. "Each prisoner will pay a charge of five pounds sterling transportation for each adult; for children under twelve years of age fifty shillings; and forty shillings per one ton of goods. Those unable to pay for their passage will be promised twenty-five acres of land and a new suit of clothes upon the completion of four years of service. Of that, Captain, you will receive two pounds per prisoner carried and delivered at your own proper cost and charge, reimbursement for costs incurred for those who die, and no payment for those who escape."

Teddico's eyes narrowed. As though factoring the

costs in his head, he said, "At this time of the year, we'll have six hours of light, storms and delays due to weather, which means more supplies, more expenses." He paused. "I think a fair share would be two pounds fifty per man." He had no work lined up for the next few months, but he was not about to reveal that, nor how much he wanted the work.

"The offer is two pounds per man, as I've stated."

Teddico sat silently staring down at his hands as he nervously rubbed his fingers.

Paterson eyed him, and allowed him several long moments to squirm. When Teddico started to shift his position, Paterson placed his palms on his desk and pushed his chair back. "If it's a problem... "

"Now, I didnae say that." The captain reached a weathered hand out to stop him. He winced, as though Paterson's terms were a hardship. "I suppose I could do it."

With an unimpressed but satisfied nod, Paterson said, "Good. I'll have the papers drawn up."

With minimal pleasantries, Paterson shook Captain Teddico's hand and showed him to the door. Teddico walked down the stairs to the street, slyly smiling as he summed up in his head how he would increase his profit by purchasing supplies from certain merchants who, for a share of the difference, would bill him on paper for more than he paid, thus increasing the costs he could charge for the prisoners' transport. After all, he was a businessman too. He would transport the prisoners. They might not arrive quite as healthy, but cargo was cargo. Sick and hungry still put two pounds per head in his pocket. He would lose a few prisoners on the way, to be sure, but he would make up the loss in the costs saved on food and medical supplies. Captain Teddico grinned to himself. And, unlike common criminals, these Covenanters most likely came from good homes—and good homes had money. With that money, before they pulled into port, they could pay for the added expenses incurred on the trip —that is, if they still had money by then. In two months at sea, things could happen. Sometimes money was lost on the way—gambled, washed overboard, or pinched by some common thief in the hold. You just couldnae trust your fellow prisoners these days. Crying shame, but that was their problem, not his. He had a business to run. Just for good measure, he took out insurance. If he could not make profit enough from the men, the insurance would cover far more than the value of both ship and cargo. He heaved a satisfied sigh. This might turn out to be a most lucrative journey. Teddico smiled and pulled a cigar from his coat as he walked into a tavern for a pint and a meal.

A FORTNIGHT LATER THE PRISONERS' fate was announced to the guards of Greyfriars. Alex, Hughie and Charlie brought the news to Callum shortly after.

"We're still looking for Jamie, the wee bastard," Alex assured him.

Charlie chimed in, "Aye, and when we find him, he'll wish somebody else had."

Alex said, "We'll keep him alive, but only so he can take your place."

"We'll not let them take you onto that ship," added Hughie.

Callum forced a weak smile. "We're a wee bit short on time." Although no one would say it, there was no escaping the truth. If they could not find Jamie, Callum would be put on the *Crown* and transported across the sea. Even if he survived the journey, they might never find him.

Alex turned to practical matters. "We'll get the money to pay for your passage. You'll not be sold as an indentured servant."

"Pay the captain yourself," said Callum, "and make sure he signs for it—twice. Keep a copy and give one to me."

"Aye." They both knew Alex was too smart to trust the captain, but it bore repeating. "He may give me his word, but I'll trust in the paper."

"We'll get money for you to book passage from wherever you land back to Ireland. Hide it well. That captain and crew will do all they can to relieve you of it before you reach shore."

Charlie said, "We'll find a place in Ulster and wait there with Mari."

Callum nodded and clenched his jaw as he tamped down his emotions. "You're good lads." He forced a stoic smile. "It's Mari I worry about."

"We'll look after Mari," said Alex.

Charlie said, "We'll not leave her alone."

Callum lifted a brow. "Aye, that's one of my worries."

Charlie balked. "Callum, she's like a sister... a very pretty sister, but still... "

Callum gave Hughie an arch look. "Keep an eye on those two."

Hughie grinned.

Charlie laughed. "*Och*. With us for company, she might not notice you're gone until spring."

"I dinnae ken about that," said Alex. "One day with Charlie and the poor lass will dive off the docks and start swimming for the colonies."

Callum smiled at the thought of her meeting him there, but the humor faded. "I dinnae want her to wait for me too long. If anything happens, I want her to move on and find someone else."

"Good God, Callum!" said Charlie. "You'll buy back your freedom and be on the next ship bound for Scotland. In six months, you'll be home with your Mari."

"Aye, well it had to be said. Just take care of my Mari." Although the others did not want to admit it to him, Callum knew—they all did—there were dangers in any sea voyage. No matter how strong the man, the sea was stronger and more brutal than any warrior in battle. For those being transported as prisoners, the dangers were worse: lack of food and water, disease, and cramped quarters. If he did arrive safely, he would be a slave for the term of his indentured servitude. Despite paying off the Captain, something could go wrong after he arrived at the plantation. There was always a chance he would not be set free, as arranged.

Callum could not speak of it in front of Hughie, but he worried that the burden of this would be too much for Mari to bear. It weighed heavily on him. He had done the right thing in taking Hughie's place in prison. How could he have gone home to face Nellie if he'd let Hughie suffer this fate? But now the fate was his, and it would keep him from Mari. Mere weeks before, he had vowed to protect her, and now he could not. This would change her, and it would change them as a couple, assuming they ever got back together again.

Alex gripped Callum's shoulder and looked in his eyes. "She's one of us now. We look after our own."

Callum met his direct gaze with a troubled but grateful nod.

"A FORTNIGHT?" Mari looked into Charlie's eyes as though he could make the truth change. "And I'll not see him before he sails?"

He shook his head. "I'm sorry, lass." As she dissolved into tears, Charlie gripped Mari's shoulders and looked into her eyes. "Mari. You must listen to me. We're here. And we're not going anywhere without you."

Stepping closer beside her, Hughie took her hand in his. Mari met his adoring eyes with a weak smile.

Alex leaned back, arms folded, against the wall nearby. "And Mari, I promise—if these *glaikit eejits* ever let go of you, I'll be there too. You'll not be alone—even though, after this, you'll be wishing you were." He brandished his most charming grin and was rewarded with a smile.

Mari said, "What on earth did Callum threaten you with to make you behave like this?"

"Like what?" said Charlie, looking defensive.

Hughie said, quite sincerely, "We're here because we want to be."

Charlie held Mari's chin gently and gave her the deep blue-eyed gaze that made ladies' hearts flutter. "What gave us away, lass?"

He was rewarded with a genuine laugh through her tears.

"*Och*, you've wrung the truth out of us. The original plan was to leave you to the workhouse, but Callum twisted our arms till we promised care for you." Charlie winked and planted a kiss on her forehead.

Mari put her hand on his chest and playfully pushed him away. "*Och*, Charlie! How could you play with my emotions like that?"

"All the lassies say that," Alex said dryly.

"And you!" Mari turned to Alex, her hands on her hips.

He stopped leaning on the wall and stood straight. "Me? What have I done?"

"You're no better than your friends here." Mari took his hand in both of hers, and then turned toward the others. "I love Callum for putting you up to this."

"Callum?" Charlie rolled his eyes. "How is it that Callum never fails to get all of the credit? And here we are, doing all of the work."

With an endearing grin, Mari said, "And I ken that you'd be here whether or not he asked you. And I love you all for it." Tears unexpectedly pooled in her eyes and rendered them helpless. "Would you please excuse me?" Without waiting for an answer, she escaped to her bedroom and closed the door.

The three men stared after her, and then at each other. Alex said, "Well, that's grand. You try to be nice, and what do you get?"

"Tears," said Charlie.

"How much can a man endure?" said Alex, moving not one muscle to escape.

"For Mari?" said Hughie with a wistful look. "A good deal."

Several minutes later they exchanged helpless glances, paced, stood at the window, and sat restlessly. "Well, you lads can sit there. I cannae take any more of this," said Charlie. He went to the bedroom door and knocked.

Mari opened the door, her eyes red from weeping. Upon seeing Charlie's concern, she said, "I was just trying to spare you all this," waving her hands toward her tear-streaked face.

With a wave, he dismissed it. "*Och*, that. I've seen women cry before."

Alex appeared. "Aye! With Charlie, they all cry sooner or later. Most often sooner."

Mari laughed through her tears.

Alex went on, "'Tis so! I've the shoulder to prove it. They all wind up here. *Och*, the wailin' and cryin'! My poor shoulder would surely have melted by now, were it not for the powerful muscles."

Hughie smirked. "I'm feeling sick all of a sudden."

Alex shrugged. "'Tis merely the truth. I've the perfect shoulder for crying here, hen. I am at your disposal."

Mari looked from Alex, to Charlie, to Hughie, and shook her head, smiling. "You're all daft."

They grinned as though this were not news to them.

"But I'm lucky to have you!"

Hughie took Mari's hand and led her to the sitting room. They all sat in their usual seats, leaving Callum's and Duncan's chairs empty. The settled into quiet talk about what they could do to help Callum. There was little. Jamie's name came up but, concealing their disdain, the men took care to change the subject. They turned their attention to deciding which provisions Callum could take on the voyage, even though they all knew the chances of him keeping such things to himself would be slim. As they talked, a knock sounded. Alarmed, Mari rose, but before she could go to the door, Alex protectively pulled her behind him and opened the door himself.

Charlie led Mari away from the door and was now in the process of defending himself against Mari, who insisted that he was being far too protective. He soon stepped aside.

"Duncan, you're home!" Relief flooded her heart as she held out her arms and took hold of his hands. She took in the sight of him. He returned her gaze, but his was dark and distant. Her pleasure at seeing him faded as Callum's plight came to the fore. "Duncan, so much has happened."

"Aye, I've been to see Callum."

Mari felt a pang of jealousy. She wished it had been she who had seen him. She missed Callum so. But Duncan was his close friend. "He must have been so glad to see you."

"Aye, he was that—as was I to see him." Duncan's face revealed his concern and other emotions, which he soon checked as he looked back at Mari. "I wish there were more I could do, darlin'."

His concern touched her deeply. After being away for so long, it was good to see him. His concern comforted her. Without warning, the tears came and she crumbled into his arms. Duncan held to his chest as she wept and the others looked on. An uncharacteristically subdued mood settled over Alex as he studied them both, but with particular attention to Duncan. With a sudden sweep of his arm, he circled Mari's waist and spun her about. "I ken just what you need, hen. Wait here." He led her to a chair and gave her shoulders a steadying squeeze. Then he left and returned moments later with a bottle and some glasses. "There's no problem that a wee dram cannae help."

For the rest of the evening, they kept Mari's glass full and cheered her with lively stories. Even Duncan joined in with some stories of his travels, as eager as any for the distraction. But although thoughts of Callum's plight went unvoiced, he remained foremost on everyone's mind.

MARI STOOD at the window and gazed absently down to the street. A fortnight had passed with no sign of a pardon for Callum, and no sign of Jamie. The *Crown* was to set sail on the morrow. She picked up her pen and wrote.

My Callum,

My heart has been yours. You ken the moment it happened. Since then you have kept my heart safe. You are in my soul. I feel strong with you there. The double-hearted charm I pin into this letter is a trinket I bought from a luckenbooth near St. Giles. It has little value, so no one will take it from you on your journey. The value it holds is but this: It rests against my heart as I write.

When you feel this against you, feel my heart there as
well.
      Your Mari

MARI FOLDED the letter and held it to her chest. *And*
like it, I am broken without you. Mari wept until strong
hands grasped her shoulders. She looked up, startled.

"Come with me," said Duncan.

"Duncan, I cannae."

His gaze bore through the deep sadness in her eyes.
"You can, and you must."

Something in his intense look cut through her sorrow.
"What is it?"

"Someone owed me a favor."

"Callum?"

Duncan nodded.

Duncan left out the part about how he had been out
half the night playing cards with the guards at Greyfriars
until his chance came. Well, technically it was not purely
chance. He had learned a few things out at sea, one of
which was how to play cards, and—he learned this the
hard way—how to lose to a cheater. After one such game,
having pulled his sgian dubh from his sock, Duncan
offered the winner a choice: one involved the sharp edge
of his sgian dubh; the other was to show him his card
tricks.

At the time, it was not in Duncan's mind to cheat
others, but instead to detect when others tried to cheat
him. When he came home and saw Mari, he could see no
way around it. Callum could not have visitors—unless a

guard looked the other way. But why would he? After what had happened to Callum, no one was willing to do any favors—unless they were forced. To that end, he could have scaled the wall and leapt down, sword in hand, interrupting their card game. Or he could join them and win. The only problem was that he had worked there with most of those lads, and he liked them. Except for that one Mackenzie. Cheating was the least a MacDonell could do to a Mackenzie. A deck of cards, a few drams, and a few hours later Mackenzie came up short. Duncan let him pay off his debt with a visit. He would go home, get some sleep, and return the next night when Mackenzie was on duty again.

MARI RAN TO THE BEDROOM. She dipped a cloth into the water basin and pressed the damp cloth to her eyes. "Och! I look awful."

"You look bonnie."

She lifted her eyes to catch a soft smile of approval from Duncan. His gaze lingered only a moment before he offered his arm.

Mari took it, but released it with a gasp. "Wait!" She rushed to the window and retrieved her letter with the heart inside.

Duncan stood watching her, smiling. How long had it been since he had seen her so happy? He was glad to have done this for her. She donned her cloak and came close to him, lifting her eyes to meet his. The love shone from her eyes. Love for Callum.

"Duncan!" She smiled, amused by his distraction.

Slipping her hand into his, she said, "Dinnae just stand there! Let's go!" She headed for the door, tugging him along with her.

Chapter 18

Farewell

Dark clouds overhead matched the dismal gray stones of Greyfriars Kirkyard and kept it hidden from the sun and its warmth. The damp clung to the weather-streaked walls as though tears had been etched in the stone. Oak trees now bare for the winter waved misshapen limbs over frost-covered grass. A cruel wind that whipped up the hill from the sea caught Mari's cloak. Duncan circled his arm about her, holding her close to shield her from the bitter wind's bite. Along a curved path they hastened, past the dank gravestones and ominous mausoleums. At a tall iron gate, they came to a stop.

Mari looked up to Duncan as he gave the guard on duty a nod. The guard walked down a path between the open-air cells, past shadowy faces that peered out from the dark. Minutes later, at the far end of the walk, a prisoner rounded the corner and walked toward her.

She dared not hope it was Callum, and then as he drew near a small part of her wished it were not. His gait was too weary and uneven, and his back was bent over, made weaker by hunger and cold. He hurried as well as he could and reached through the bars. Unable to embrace, they grasped onto as much as the iron bars would allow. Duncan walked a ways down the sloped path to the street. There he leaned his shoulder against the thick trunk of an oak.

Callum touched Mari's face and pressed his lips to her mouth. He kissed her, and kissed her again. When he stopped, he took in every feature, desperate to sear her into his memory. Callum rested his forehead against hers. His voice broke as he said, "My love. I cannae hold you like I would."

Mari touched his beard. He inhaled as she trailed fingers down his strong neck to his collar. "You're so cold."

Callum lifted her chin with stiff and trembling fingers. "Mari." His eyes swept over her face and he kissed her. His lips barely moved from her mouth as he whispered, "I've dreamt of your skin." He slipped his hands inside her cloak to the warmth and the softness. "But for these bars, I would take you right here."

"I would let you," she whispered into his neck.

Brushing his mouth on her cheek, he circled her waist until the bars stopped him. Mari leaned her whole body against the cold iron bars, but he could not reach around. Instead, he slid his hands from her waist up her sides until he felt every curve with his palm. Mari sighed. Callum buried his face in her neck and moaned. She leaned her head down against his and said softly, "I'll be here waiting until you come back."

His head shot up, as he fiercely said, "No." He took her face in his hands and looked sternly into her eyes. "If

I'm not back in a year, you must go on without me. I will not have you waste your life waiting for me."

"You can say what you will, Callum MacDonell, but I'll do as I please."

"*Och*, Mari. If I have breath in me, I will come back to you. But if I dinnae—"

She put her fingers over his lips as she fought back her tears. "I'll not hear it. Now you listen to me, we'll talk no more of that." Her tone softened. "I've brought you something." She pulled the letter from beneath her neckline, where it had been pressed to her warm breast. Callum took the folded paper and held it to his lips. Mari watched and smiled warmly. "Dinnae read it now. Save it for later."

"Mari." He looked into her eyes, trying to memorize their softness and light. He would also remember their sorrow, and its weight on his heart.

Mari held his gaze as though she might hold onto him if she looked hard enough. "You cannae be rid of me, so dinnae think that you can. If you will not come back to me, I will come find you." She tried to sound strong, but she faltered.

She buried her face in his neck as he held her head gently. "I will come back. And I'll take you home to the Highlands. We'll drift in a boat across Loch Oich, while I look at your bonnie face. Then we'll climb into a thicket of trees, where we'll kiss until our knees buckle. And then I will touch every inch of your body with my hands and my mouth." He gave her a deliberately piercing gaze that he knew would affect her, and then he grinned when it did, looking almost as though life were normal. Mari attempted a smile, but could not, so she hid her face in his chest. She could no longer hold back the tears.

He let her weep for a bit, and then in a deep voice that caught in his throat, he said, "Look at me, Mari. I want to memorize you."

She lifted her face and studied him, too. "You'll see me again in the daylight. I'll be at the dock."

"No, Mari. Not there."

"I have to see you every moment I can."

He spoke with his officer's tone. "You will not go there."

She answered in soft tones, touching his face. "Callum, I must see you again."

He clenched his jaw to think of how low he had come, and angry for having to make it so plain. "I will not have your last memory of me be that of a weakened wretch walking in chains to a ship."

The tears in her eyes caught the moonlight as she held his face until he looked into her eyes. "A braw warrior once found me when I was brought low, and he loved me in spite of it. And again, he came to me and lifted me up when I could not go on, and he carried me off on his horse. I will be with you every moment I'm able. And if you are low, I will lift you."

"And carry me off on your horse? I would like to see that."

"If I could, my fine Callum, I would, and you ken it."

"Aye, Mari, I do."

They shared a smile and a kiss, and then she wiped her eyes. Flashing a brave smile that was nearly convincing, she said, "I'm very strong, ken? And I do have some help. Those lads never leave me alone." With a crooked grin, she said under her breath, "They're a bit of a nuisance, aye?" They smiled, knowing the truth of how much those men meant to them both.

The guard gripped Callum's shoulder.

"No." Mari's soft plea came out in a whimper.

Callum held Mari close one last time as she gripped his coat collar. She took off her cloak and pushed it through the bars. He tried to resist, but she insisted. "You're no good to me sick."

Duncan put a supportive hand on Mari's back. Callum exchanged glances with Duncan, and gave him a nod. Duncan stood behind Mari, holding her shoulders as Callum stepped back. Soon all Callum held was her hand, which Mari gripped tightly. Lifting her hand, he kissed her palm gently and released it as he turned away from her and walked away.

Mari whispered his name as she gripped the iron bars. He stopped once to look back before turning the corner.

Mari's legs gave out beneath her. As she grasped Duncan's arm, he scooped her up and carried her out to the street.

Mari awoke in the carriage, with Duncan's strong arms shielding her from the cold and the sorrow.

When she stirred in his arms, Duncan said, "I'm taking you home."

MARI AWOKE in the dark to find Duncan still sitting in a chair by her bed, where he had been since bringing her home. He had given her a cup of whisky to calm and warm her, which, with her exhaustion, brought her a few hours of sleep. When she opened her eyes, Duncan was sitting beside her, watching her closely. "I'm leaving now, darlin'."

"Leaving? Where? What time is it?"

His brow creased for an instant, but he went on with little emotion. "It's early. I'm shipping out to sea."

"No, Duncan. Not now, please. We need you here."

His gaze softened. "I've taken a job on the *Crown*."

It took a moment for Mari to grasp it. "The *Crown*? Callum's ship?"

"Aye. It wasnae hard to find a guard willing to let me take his place guarding the prisoners."

"Oh, Duncan!" She threw her arms about him. "Thank you! You're a true friend to Callum."

"Aye, well, he's been a good friend to me."

"Take care of him, Duncan." Mari leaned against him.

Duncan felt the soft breath of her words at the base of his neck. He inhaled the scent of her hair as he held her and stroked the silk strands at her shoulders, too aware of the thin cotton fabric between his coarse hands and her skin. "Aye, lass, I will." He gripped her shoulders and pressed her away. With a kiss on the cheek and a brusqueness that startled her, he murmured, "Goodbye, Mari." Turning his back to her wounded expression, he left without a glance backward.

Too stunned to reply, Mari watched with troubled eyes as he walked through the doorway. The latch clicked into place. "Goodbye, Duncan," she whispered.

MIST CLUNG like a shroud to the ships at the Leith Docks. The sun hid behind ashen clouds. Flanked by Alex and Charlie, Mari leaned against a building as the men huddled closely to shield her from the brutal North Sea wind. Menacing gusts brought smells of bilge water, fish and mildew as waves frothed and crashed on the docks.

Mari glanced at Hughie. He had been aloof all morning, riddled with guilt, thinking he should have been in Callum's place. Mari had tried to convince him that she did not blame him, but he blamed himself just the same. She in turn blamed her brother, whom she had trusted and risked all to help. In return, he had escaped, putting himself above those whom she loved. She reminded herself that he could not have foreseen the results of his actions, but that did not help Callum. He was being sent away on a slave ship and might never come back.

Hughie swallowed hard as he stared at the ship. Mari hooked her arm into Hughie's and pulled him close to her side. He kept his eyes fixed on the ship. "Hughie, this is what Callum wants. You cannae go against him."

His emotions flooded to the surface. He could not face her. "Mari, I'm sorry."

"Dinnae blame yourself. I do not. Neither does Callum." Mari leaned her head sideways to rest on Hughie's shoulder. They clung together for several moments until Mari fought to rein in her feelings. She was determined to be strong for Callum.

"Mari. I cannae watch him board that ship knowing it should have been me."

She gripped his arm as she steeled her gaze. "Yes, you can. You will do it for Callum."

Alex was first to notice how upset Hughie was, and

the toll it was taking on Mari. He gave Charlie a nudge, and they watched for a moment. Charlie clapped a brotherly arm on Hughie's shoulder. "Lad, do you think we could find a pub on these docks?" After dodging an old man pushing a handcart, he led Hughie away on their quest, leaving Mari with Alex.

Mari settled into melancholic silence, which Alex allowed for a while. But as fears for Callum darkened her eyes, Alex tried to distract her.

"I saw Duncan this morning. He asked me to tell you goodbye. He had something to do before boarding the ship."

"Aye." Mari was not surprised, but she was disappointed. "When Callum is gone, so is Duncan. You'll think me a fool, but I wonder sometimes if Duncan dislikes me."

"*Och*, Mari. He does not dislike you."

"Are you certain?"

"Aye." He shrugged. "Duncan is...Duncan. If he's troubled, he goes away by himself, like a wounded hound."

"Well, he certainly makes himself scarce."

"Pay him no heed."

With a weak smile, Mari said, "I suppose you're right. I've enough real problems. I dinnae need to invent more." She clutched Alex's arm and tried to grin. "I'm lucky to have you here to keep me from thinking too much."

In an effort to cheer her, Alex said, "Oh, I keep you from thinking, do I? I dinnae ken what you mean. I'm a thinker. I'll have you know that I'm thinking right now."

"And a fine job you're doing," she said, trying to smile. "But it's no use. I'll not be cheered up."

The sound of the leg irons and chains announced their approach as the prisoners ended their march from Greyfriars. Callum had told her not to come, but she needed to see him. It might make him angry at first to have his wishes disregarded, but Callum was in no position to argue the point. Mari hoped he would be glad, after all, for one last chance to see her.

The two hundred and fifty-seven prisoners marched in two lines, chained together in pairs. If one stopped it pulled on the other men's chains, and grated the leg and neck irons against the others' raw skin.

Mari rushed to Callum's side. "Lass, I did not want you to see me like this."

"I could not stay away."

His eyes swept over her, committing to memory every feature and curve until the chains yanked him along.

She walked beside him until ordered by one of the guards to step back. Solid hands took hold of her shoulders and held her as Callum walked on.

"Be strong for him, hen," Alex told her.

Mari gripped his hand, never once taking her eyes from Callum's back as he walked on toward the water. Charlie and Hughie were standing with her, but she paid them no heed. They all watched as the prisoners boarded the small boats that would ferry them out to the ship in the harbor.

"I trust Duncan with my life," said Alex. "So does Callum."

Chapter 19

A Wind from the North

Hours after darkness had fallen, the *Crown* approached the tip of Deer Sound in Orkney as the waves pounded the deck. The wind, usually from the west, now came from the arctic north, and with it the snow—not falling, but blowing in icy shards, coating every surface with slick slush that the men's frozen hands could barely hold onto. Duncan held tight to the rigging as he worked his way to the hatch to go below the main deck.

Countless times since they'd left nearly a fortnight ago, he had not been able to make sense of the captain's choice of a northerly route in the midst of December. Why had they not headed south along England? The North Sea was rough even in milder months. In fair weather, the choppy water would have slowed their progress. Their provisions looked as though they might last for two months, for a journey that could take twice that in bad weather. An experienced captain would have known better than to come so ill-prepared. But to chart such a course through the rough seas of winter, when bad weather loomed, was unforgivable folly.

Hours before, Duncan had cautioned the captain to take shelter while they were still able. Waves pounded the ship and heaved the prisoners about. The blizzard winds wailed and the waves were relentless, pounding and tossing the ship toward shore. The prisoners had begged and the sailors complained, but the captain heard none of it. On he pressed. It was not until the ship nearly capsized and seemed almost to groan in protest that the captain finally sought shelter.

He ran the ship into Deer Sound and drew close to the shore. Duncan and the other sailors struggled to furl the sails and prepare to wait out the storm. As they dropped anchor, lightning flashed to reveal jagged rocks jutting out from the land. Icy waves shot up like mighty arms from the watery mass to wield power over the ship, whipping it to and fro in its foam. The freezing salt mist blinded Duncan as he made his way back to the hatch.

Once below deck he knelt down and leaned over the chained and locked hatch to the hold of the ship.

"Callum!" he yelled, but his only answers were despairing cries from below, nearly lost in the din of the storm. He knew, packed as they were, with no room even to lie down for sleep, these rough waters could hurl them about to their deaths. Duncan muttered a curse to the captain as he searched the darkness below.

A violent lurch threw the ship with a deafening crack. Duncan climbed to the main deck.

"The anchor chain snapped," cried a sailor.

The captain ordered his men to cut down the mainmast. They were going to use it as a bridge to the shore.

The prisoners were in a death trap. Callum would die. In that instant, Duncan thought about Mari. And then the thought crept out from some dark part of his soul.

Callum's death would free Mari to love someone else.

"GIVE ME THE KEY!" hollered Duncan over the din of the storm.

The captain glanced toward Duncan, but then pivoted back to the work at hand. Duncan grabbed hold of his shoulders. "The key! Give me the key to the hold!"

"Why?"

"Those men will die if we leave them there!"

"I'll be paid for my costs if they die. If they escape, I get nothing." The captain looked away. Just as Duncan was swinging a punch, one of his mates caught his arm and pulled him away. "Do you want to find yourself down there in irons? You're no good to anyone there."

The mainmast was coming down. Every hand on deck guided it as well as they could until its weight brought it crashing to the rocky shore. As the men began crawling along the length of the icy mast toward the shore, Duncan picked up a discarded axe and went down to the hold as the crack in the ship widened. He heaved the axe on the chains and the lock until they broke, then opened the hatch and began pulling men out. He yelled down to Callum as he grasped one man after the other.

"Duncan, is that you?"

"Callum!"

"Aye!" Below, Callum was hoisting the prisoners up to Duncan. Someone found the ladder that had been thrown across the hold. It was missing some rungs, but it sped up their progress.

Above deck, the prisoners tried to cross the mast to the shore, but the captain and his crew kicked them from the mast and pushed them back down the rocks while they themselves scrambled up the steep cliff. The lucky ones fell back to the sea, while the others fell to their death on the jagged shoreline below.

Callum and Duncan helped dozens of men from the hold before the ship groaned and cracked. Duncan grasped Callum's arm and pulled him up out of the hold as the sea hurled the *Crown* to the rocks.

MARI WALKED along the high street with a full basket of food from the market. Fresh snow dusted the cobblestone street and the buildings, making everything look nearly clean. She took a deep breath. It was brisk, but she warmed herself with thoughts of a cup of hot tea at home before starting to cook. The lads would be home soon for supper. After Callum's ship sailed, one of them had been with her each moment for a week, until she finally sent them away for the day. She smiled now to think of how much of a family they had become. With Callum gone, they made sure that she lacked for nothing. In turn, she gave them the things she knew best to provide: a home to come to with good food to eat. She tamped down her longing for Callum. With Callum's passage paid, he could leave the ship and catch another returning for Ireland or Holland. He might return to her within a year. But that year was so far away.

Her thoughts were drawn back to the present as the droning sounds of a piper and drummer drew a crowd to the Mercat Cross. Mari joined the outskirts of the crowd to hear the town crier call out the news.

"The *Crown of London* sank off the coast of Deerness, Orkney."

What had the man said? One week ago?

"Over two hundred of the Covenanter passengers dead."

Callum dead? She pressed forward into the crowd, but the crier was already telling others that a few may have survived, but they have not been able to determine the number of dead. Bodies continue to wash onto the shore.

Mari walked numbly into St. Giles Cathedral. Was this her punishment for leaving the church of her childhood? Was it not enough to lose her family, her home— her wee bairn? But that had been Thomas's fault. She could not blame God for that. But why must she pay and not Thomas? And now Callum may well have paid with his life. It was not fair, and yet how perfect a judgment, Mari thought. What worse torment could there be? In exchange for leaving her church and her family, all she held dear was gone. Nothing could have hurt her more. She leaned against a stone column and looked up at the tall arches that seemed as though they could go on forever. So would her despair.

She walked out of the church. A soft snow fell. Had it grown colder in the moments since she had learned of the news? And yet how much colder was it for Callum as the ship sank and the freezing water overtook him? But Duncan was there. He would not have let Callum perish.

Mari stopped. Unless he perished, too. Only then did she realize that she had lost Duncan as well.

Mari walked into the apartment and set down her basket. This was her home with Callum. She went to the chair where Callum used to sit. She leaned back and tried to feel him there with her.

It was dark when the pounding woke her. She had fallen asleep in Callum's chair, hoping to dream of him. Now she remembered. Her Callum was gone.

Mari opened the door to find Alex, his chest heaving from running.

With one look at her, he said, "You've heard."

She looked absently at him and said, "Aye."

Mari started to turn to go back to Callum's chair, but Alex grasped her shoulders. "Mari." He looked deeply into her eyes, and she seemed to awaken. "I'm sorry."

Mari looked at the tears welling in Alex's eyes. "No, we dinnae ken it for certain. He might have survived."

"He's gone, lass. They're both gone."

"No." The word stuck in her throat. Alex pulled her into his arms and held her to his chest.

For the first time, she wept.

Chapter 20

The Shadowy Wynd

The funeral service was simple. With no burial, they had only to go to the kirkyard where Callum had spent his last days. When they arrived at the gate of Greyfriars, Mari stopped outside. As a woman, this was as far as she would be permitted to go. But no women were there to wait with her. There were only soldiers. They filed through the gate —dozens of them. In her short time in Edinburgh, Mari's life had been caught up in Callum's. She had no women friends to stand with her or go back to prepare food for the dredgy, when the men would come back to feast and drink and remember. She longed for her childhood friend, Ellen. But she was gone, too. As the men filed in, a hand slipped into hers. Hughie stood beside Mari and listened with her as the pipes played for Callum and Duncan. Alex and Charlie spoke briefly, then the piper played one last tune. As the last tune neared its end, the piper walked away playing, and with him the music faded away.

At home, the dredgy was lively with drinking and dancing. Mari found herself comforted by the presence of so many of Callum's friends. They told stories and laughed, and she felt closer to him for it. It was a boisterous affair until, many hours later, the door closed and sudden quiet draped itself over them. Mari could not give into the stillness, for pain would soon follow. She busied herself cleaning up.

"*Och*, we've left the old milk and butter in here, and the onions!" she said as she gathered them all. "Tis no good to keep them in the house."

"Why?" asked Hughie.

"The spirit might enter and never find rest." But as she echoed the words she had heard as a child, she now wondered if Callum's spirit might find its way to her from so far away, and she started to hope that it would. She set down the onions and gave in to the thought.

"Mari."

She whirled around toward the voice from the door.

Duncan stood quietly watching as Mari stared, numb for a moment. "Is it you?" She drew closer and touched a tentative hand to his chest, making sure he was real.

Her words drew a worried expression from Duncan. "Are you not well, Mari?" He then looked about at the stunned expressions. "What is it?"

"Well, Duncan," said Charlie, as he grasped Duncan's shoulder, "we've just had your funeral." He laughed, only now absorbing the truth that Duncan was alive.

"An' you did not invite me?" He gave Charlie a smirk.

Mari gripped Duncan's arms. "Where is Callum? Please, Duncan. Tell me. Where's Callum?"

He exchanged glances with Charlie, then Alex, whose grave looks confirmed his fears. "I was hoping that he might be here."

Mari's eyes drifted down, unaware that her hands fell to her sides. She could not speak, for the only words that would form in her mind she would never say. Why was it not Callum who had lived?

Duncan seemed almost to know her thoughts as he said, "I'm sorry."

Alex interjected, "Come in. I'll get you a glass so you can drink to yourself."

LATER THEY SAT STARING into the fire as Duncan took another in a series of drinks. "I had him in my grasp. We held onto each other with all the might we possessed, but the ship tore apart, and the waves were too wild."

"But did you look for him? He might have washed up alive and needed help." Without meaning to, Mari's tone accused, and Duncan had had too much to drink to ignore it.

"Aye, I looked. I looked all over the whole bloody island. I bloody walked, and I bloody looked everywhere for your bloody Callum!"

Charlie cleared his throat. "Em, Duncan, you're not talking to sailors. It's Mari."

Duncan shot a glare at Charlie that chilled him to silence. "I ken that it's Mari. It's always been Mari. I combed every inch of that shoreline for Mari."

"For Callum," Alex quietly corrected.

Mari sat still, watching Duncan with wide-open eyes.

"Aye, for Callum. Who else would I look for?" Duncan poured another and drank it down. "I knocked on doors, asked around at the docks of Stromness to see if he might have escaped on a ship. You see, I wasnae the only one looking. They wanted their prisoners back." Duncan's eyes grew glassy with tears, but he closed his eyes and willed them away with clenched jaw. He set down his glass with a resonant whack, and then picked up a bottle and took a long drink. He wiped his sleeve across his mouth and said, "Bodies washed up for days and for miles. And I looked at each bloated, drowned carcass." He leaned back with a hollow-eyed stare. "The sea just swallowed him up."

As if Mari had spoken to him, Duncan looked at her with bitter sorrow. "I ken what you think—that you wish it were me—and I'm sorry. For to come back to see you looking like that at me now—I'd liefer be under the water getting smashed to the rocks than for Callum to—"

Mari got up and left the room. Hughie rushed after her.

"I'm sure that was a comfort," Charlie told Duncan dryly. Before Duncan could react, Alex leapt up and led Duncan outside with a promise of pubs and loose women.

Charlie considered for a moment and, with the tilt of his head and a shrug, rose up to follow. He stopped to give Mari a kiss on the forehead. "I'm away, dearie. I'll be back in the morning." He gave a Hughie a questioning look, which Hughie answered with a nod. He would stay there with Mari.

ALEX WAS first to awaken that morning. He lifted a woman's arm from his chest and set it down gently so as not to wake her. Donning his plaid and brogues, he went across the hall and gave the door a light knock. "Charlie," he said in a loud, raspy whisper. After some jostling about on the other side, he heard a quiet, "Aye, dearie," from Charlie. After a cajoling whine and a woman's soft laugh, Charlie emerged with a lingering trace of a grin.

Next was Duncan. The two rapped on the door, and were answered with curses. Alex burst through the door and hoisted Duncan up by the shoulders. "Come on, lad. We're away to see Mari and tell her you're sorry."

Duncan cursed and leaned over the basin to splash water on his face. A woman rolled over in bed, then went back to sleep, snoring. He looked up and said, "Sorry?"

"Do you not remember last night?"

Duncan buckled the belt about his plaid, and frowned as he thought for a moment and shrugged. "No."

Charlie said, "It's probably best that you not, until your head ceases pounding." Then he looked closer at Duncan. "It is pounding, is it not?"

"*Och, aye,* it is that," he said in a gravelly voice.

"Good," said Alex. "You deserve it."

Duncan gripped his forehead. "Bloody hell."

"That's what you said to Mari last night."

Duncan's eyes lifted painfully to meet Alex's direct look.

"Aye."

Still groggy, Duncan said, "I cursed her?"

"*Och*, no. You didnae curse her," Alex said.

Duncan relaxed.

Alex went on. "You just cursed at her."

Duncan shut his eyes and moaned, and then looked up. "Why?"

Charlie chimed in. "We stopped asking that about you long ago."

Alex clapped a heavy hand onto Duncan's shoulder. "Come. We'll go have some breakfast while you sober up."

Duncan squinted in pain as they stepped out into the bright morning sunlight.

Charlie said, "I can just taste some porridge with cream and some fresh brown bread slathered with butter."

"And salmon!" said Alex with mounting enthusiasm. "And oatcakes."

"And cold sheep's head," added Charlie.

"Excuse me, lads," said Duncan, as he ducked into a close and heaved the contents of his stomach.

MARI ANSWERED the door and eyed Duncan with quiet reserve. She stepped aside to allow them to enter. Alex and Charlie let Duncan go first, while exchanging a look upon seeing Duncan's humble expression and bonnet in hand. Few others ever saw this side of Duncan.

Mari took a step toward the sitting room. "Come in and sit down."

"Mari, forgive me," blurted Duncan.

She stopped, but did not turn to look at him.

He went on. "I dinnae recall very much. But I ken I was—"

Mari interrupted. "Drunk. Vulgar. Rude."

"Aye. All that and more." He absorbed all of her hurt and resentment, for he knew he deserved it. In a deep, quiet voice, he said, "I'm sorry, Mari."

"I am too, Duncan." She stunned all of them by

turning to rest a softened expression on Duncan. "I practically accused you of not caring enough to look for him. I ken that you did." She laid her tender hand upon Duncan's. "Last night I was overwhelmed by the grief of it all. I'm fearing I let you feel as though I was not happy to see you alive. And for that, I am truly sorry."

Duncan swallowed and put a hand over hers. "There's no need."

Tears fell as she looked up at him. "Duncan, I am so glad to see you." With that, she put her arms about him, and he held her there.

Charlie eyed them with growing amusement. "I'm glad to see you too, Duncan. Gie us a hug." He held his arms out, grinning broadly. He was repaid with a quick fist to his gut, which he dodged, but just barely. He doubled over, but from laughter.

Mari looked from one to the other. "You're a troublesome lot, but I'm glad that you're here."

The late afternoon darkness of winter was falling on Edinburgh, casting the closes and wynds in deep shadows. Across the street, a shadow clung to the wall of the wynd. Its kilted silhouette caught Alex's attention.

"What is it?" asked Mari.

"Em, nothing." Alex turned around, forcing a grin.

"Is there a fair lassie out there that you fancy?" asked Charlie.

Alex's face brightened. "Aye, that was it. But not so pretty as the lassie right here." He gave Mari a wink. He turned his attention to Charlie. "Come help me pour some ale."

"Are you so weak that you cannae manage alone?"

"Aye," Alex said, as he walked by him and gave him a subtle kick in the ankle.

They served everyone ale, and then Charlie and Alex leaned against the window frame. Soon the others were engaged in lively conversation and Alex spoke to Charlie under his breath. "Look across at the wynd. There's a figure there in the shadows. Do you see it?"

Charlie said, "I think I saw something move. I cannae be sure."

Alex looked again. "He's gone now."

"He's probably waiting for a friend."

Alex stared down at the wynd. "Aye, that's what I thought yesterday when I saw him."

"I'll tell the others to keep an eye on that wynd."

"But there's no need to frighten Mari."

Charlie gave a nod as he turned from the window. "There are a dozen or more others who bide in this building. Even if he is watching this building, it could be for them."

"Aye." Alex frowned. "But still, I dinnae like leaving Mari alone."

"We can take turns staying here." Charlie sighed. "It'll be hard for the lassies—not being with me."

Alex winced. "Oh, indeed? The lassies tell me it's not hard without you or with you."

Alex dodged Charlie's fist and escaped to the safety of Mari's company. "I'll take that tray for you, Mari, lass."

"Why thank you, Alex."

Alex took the tray, and tossed a mischievous smile back at Charlie.

Chapter 21

Escape from the Finfolk

Callum opened his eyes to see an old woman sitting beside a peat fire and knitting. Wiry gray curls sprang from her cap, framing her plump face.

"Thou art awake!" The old woman came over and felt his forehead. "I'm fair blide to see thee feeling better." She studied him with kind eyes, and then rose abruptly. "Here's some soup for thee. A rookle o' bones thou wert when we found thee."

Callum looked at her, puzzled, as she brought him a bowl of soup.

"Beuy? Dost thou ken where thou art?"

He looked away as he tried to remember. "The ship sank... "

"Aye, the finfolk nearly got thee." Seeing Callum's questioning look, she said, "The finfolk rise from the depths of the sea and take men to serve as their slaves."

Callum gave little heed to her story. He could think only of how his head hurt, and how he needed to get back to Mari. "Where are we?"

"Scarva Taing."

"Orkney?"

"Aye."

"Duncan pulled me out of the hull." He looked about the cottage. "Where's Duncan?"

"Thou hast been asking for Duncan. An' Mari, as well. I've no idea where they've geen."

"Mari wasnae on the ship. But Duncan was."

The old woman settled into troubled silence at the question of where Duncan might be.

"Thou maun sleep now. And when thou art awake, a grand talk we will have," she said, tucking a blanket over his shoulders and smoothing his hair back as though he were a child. Feeling already weary, Callum drifted to sleep.

"BEUY." Someone pushed his shoulder.

It was dark, except for the light of a candle on the table.

"Beuy, wake up."

Callum opened his eyes and bolted up, ready to lunge at his attacker, when he saw that it was the old woman. "Sorry," he said, withdrawing his arms and then putting a gentle hand on her forearm. "Have I hurt you?"

She spoke between deep breaths. "No. Faird of thee I was, but I kent thou did not mean it. Thou wert dreaming. Listen, beuy, men art about looking for folk frae the ship."

Callum tried to get up, but she held him steady.

"Some men—friends of mine—will come get thee and take thee to Stromness."

"Stromness?"

"Aye. Thou cannae stay here. There is no place to hide. If they find thee, it's to the plantations for thee, and to jail for me."

Callum sat on the edge of the bed. "I'm sorry. I dinnae want to put you at risk."

She shook her head. "Dinnae be sorry. It was my choice to bring thee here. No one forced me.

"When thou get to Stromness, my friend Angus will hide thee until thee can board a ship to go hame."

The old woman put some clothes on the bed. "Here, put these on."

"Where's my plaid?"

"Lost in this storm."

"And my leine?"

She shook her head and suppressed a grin. "Thou arrived lightly dressed." She went to the cupboard and pulled something out of a jar. "This was next to thine hand when they found thee." She handed him the double-hearted charm Mari had given him. Seeing the faraway look on his face, she smiled gently and went back to her cooking. With her back to Callum, she busied herself while he put on a shirt, breeches, waistcoat, and coat. As she stirred a steaming pot, the old woman said, "Those belonged to one of my bairns. He was a strapping lad, but not quite so tall as thee."

"You had a son?"

She smiled. "Three bairns I had. Lost at sea were they, and their father as well."

"I'm sorry." Callum thought of the loved ones he had

lost, and he imagined how unbearable a loss Mari would be. She must think him dead now, and be grieving his loss. It made his heart ache.

When he was dressed, Callum sat at the small wooden table, feeling weary from the exertion of just getting dressed. His weakness frustrated him.

The old woman smiled to see him. "Aye, that will do. Thou could pass for an islander now.

"When it's dark, they will come for thee. Here, eat this." She put a large bowl of porridge before him at the table.

"Thank you... I'm sorry, I dinnae ken your name. Mine is Callum."

"I am Phoebe. Phoebe Flett."

"Thank you, Phoebe."

She smiled and went to retrieve something. "This will help keep thee warm on thy journey," she said as she poured a tot of whisky into his porridge.

While he ate, Phoebe bundled together some knitting. Its patterns were more intricate than any he had seen done by the women at home. When she saw Callum watching, she said, "The beuys look after me. When they go out to sea, they always take some of my knitting to sell in the ports down south. I grew up on Shetland, and learned the lace knitting from my mother, and she from her mother. It puts food on my table and keeps me busy. In spring and summer I fetch what I need for the dyes. I scrape moss off the rocks, collect seaweed, and gather heather, bloodroot, meadowsweet and dock. Could you help me with something?"

"Aye, Phoebe. What is it?" Callum was glad for the chance to help her. She had done so much for him.

Although what help he could be in this weakened state was doubtful.

Phoebe looked at him frankly. "When the need arises, you could leave me some piss in that barrel outside the door. I use it for the dyeing."

Callum laughed. "That should not be a problem. I've been told I'm quite full of it."

"I thought as much," Phoebe said with a grin. "Once I have all of my moss and flowers and roots, I can dye the wool, and then spin and knit through the winter. The beuys tell me it fetches a fine price, but I sometimes wonder if they dinnae add a bit of their own money to it. Folk here are like that. You cannae trust them to tell you the truth." Phoebe tossed a knowing look with a twinkling eye.

Dark came in late afternoon. Callum was finishing his porridge when two farmers arrived with a plow horse for Callum to ride.

Seeing the horse, Phoebe said, "Good. I told them that you were not ready to walk for four hours to Stromness."

While the men tied her bundle of knitting to the horse, she pressed a knitted cap into Callum's hands. He put it on, and grasped her hands in his. "Phoebe, you've saved my life, fed me and clothed me, and I have nothing for you."

Her warm nature shone through her eyes. "What thou will do is get home to thy Mari." She smiled with glistening eyes, and gave Callum a hug.

A SMOKY GRAY light faintly outlined the edges of buildings as the men walked down the flagstone street of Stromness to the dock. Around the corner, the sound of a lone pair of gritty footsteps grew fainter. It was the desolate time before dawn, when the water lapped up against boats in the harbor as a reminder that there was something beyond the gray mist.

"This is Angus," said one of the farmers. "It's with him thou wilt go now."

Callum's head started to swim, and his knees buckled. Angus grabbed him under the arm and pulled the other arm over his shoulder and held it. "We'll look like we've been out for a dram. Easy, we're not in a hurry."

As weak as he felt, Callum had no trouble making his feet roll and stagger like a ship with three sails to the wind.

The first stirrings of dock life were beginning. Steady footsteps approached.

Angus cautioned under his breath. "Act too drunk to talk, elsewise he'll ken thee are not from here and ask questions."

"Whit like the day?" called out the newcomer.

"Not bad at all," answered Angus. As they drew closer, he hoisted Callum up by the armpits. Callum looked like a proper loose-jointed drunk.

"Angus, is that thee?"

"Aye."

"Who's that with thee?"

"It's my friend Robbie."

"Come in to port frae the weather?"

"Aye. It's to whaling we're off in the morn. Come, Robbie, a peedie more it is."

The constable chuckled and walked on down the pier.

They boarded a small rowing boat and went out to a whaler. "This will take thee south."

"To the mainland?" asked Callum.

Angus looked at him, puzzled.

A long while passed, until Callum looked away, thinking no answer was coming.

Angus said, "We've just been on the mainland. It's to the south this will take thee."

Seeing Callum's puzzled expression, he added, "To Scotland."

Chapter 22

Highland Vengeance

Mari set down her basket of food from the market and opened the door. It was a lonely house now without Callum in it. The MacDonell lads were about every day, trying to distract her from her grief. She could not be distracted, but she no longer cried in front of them. She busied herself putting food away and tidying up. With that done, she picked up her needlework and sat down by the window.

A faint rap at the door pulled her back from her daydream of Callum. With a sigh, she rose. Those lads would not give her a moment of peace, but she loved them for it.

Mari opened the door. There stood a ragged wretch of a man. She was thinking of how to protect herself from him, when he spoke her name. Only then, from the sound of his voice, did she know him.

"Jamie?"

He collapsed in a heap at her feet. Mari pulled him

inside far enough to close the door. She knelt down beside him, touching his face. "Jamie."

He moaned. His eyes fluttered, trying to open, and then he was still. Mari rushed to the basin of water and brought back a damp cloth, which she pressed to his face and parched lips. Then she laid the cloth across his forehead. With trembling hands, she struggled to start a fire. "Blasted flint!"

At last she set the kettle on the hook over the fire and returned to her brother with a cup of water. She squeezed drops of water into his mouth. "Jamie. Jamie, wake up."

When at last he opened his eyes, he smiled up at her.

"Drink this," she told him. It revived him enough to be helped up, leaning on Mari, guided to the bed. There he lay propped up on pillows. Mari brought him the broth and a thick slice of bread, which he eagerly took.

"Dinnae fash. I just fainted. I've not eaten in a sennight. Have you any more bread?"

"Aye. Jamie, why are you here?"

"I'm sorry, Marion."

"You should be," she said. "Do you ken what you've done?"

"What? Oh, the escape. But surely you were not held to blame."

Mari's face flushed with anger. "No, but Callum was!"

"Was he?" said Jamie, barely looking up as he ate.

"He took your place."

Jamie sopped up the last of the broth with his bread. "Serves him right, the Highland Royalist scum."

Mari slapped his face. "He was my husband, and he died in your place!"

Jamie gave her a look nearly devoid of emotion. "I am sorry."

Mari stared in disbelief.

He said, "But the truth is, the cause is better served with me alive and one less Royalist to oppress us."

"I never knew you to be cruel."

"Marion, we are engaged in a battle for God. We cannae let our own feelings get in the way."

"Feelings? Like your feelings for Ellen?"

Jamie's harsh look started to crumble, but he forced back the emotions that caught in his throat.

Mari said, "You have caused such a loss for me. Can you not see that?"

"I couldnae turn from my calling." He spoke gently, but it hurt just the same.

She quietly said, "Your calling?"

"Aye. I will do all that I can to defeat papist tyranny."

"And just what have you done that was worth Callum's life?"

"I've been fighting for freedom. Do you not recall how we were forced to sneak around just to worship?"

Mari exhaled wearily. "Jamie. All of this fighting, and nothing has changed—except Callum is dead."

"That isnae my fault."

"It's your fault that he's gone, and I miss him."

"Just as I miss Ellen. Do you not see it's the same?"

Mari looked at him with eyes full of sorrow. "I miss Ellen, too. She was my dearest friend. What happened to her was a terrible thing. But my husband didnae cause it, nor does his death pay for it."

"I didnae put him on that ship. It was his own people that did that."

"But you had to have known it would happen."

Jamie scoffed. "How? It was a shipwreck. How could I have known that would happen?"

Mari's eyes darted about as anger welled up within her. "Someone had to take your place, and you knew it."

"Marion." He waited for her to meet his fixed gaze. "I didnae ken about that. How could I?"

"It was in the written order from the Privy Council."

"With a bitter chuckle, Jamie said, "Do you think they sat us all down and read it to us like a story? *Och*, no. They herded us into pens as if we were cattle. All I did was to escape. I didnae ken it would hurt you."

Mari's anger turned to heartache, for she knew that her brother was telling the truth. She put her hand on his, and he grasped it and hugged her. Before her emotions overwhelmed her, Mari took hold of his shoulders and smiled. "Look at you. You look like you've crawled out of a byre."

"I've been in hiding until the time's right to take action."

Mari shook her head weakly. "More fighting."

"If we cannae worship as we choose, then what are our lives worth? I will fight and, if need be, I will die for freedom."

"I believe that you will. And then I'll have no one left."

A loud rap at the door startled them both. "Dinnae answer it," Jamie whispered.

"Why?"

"Someone's following me. Bolt the door." Jamie got up and looked out the window.

"*Och*, Jamie! What have you brought to my home?"

Before he could answer, another loud rapping sounded. Mari carefully stepped toward the door. After Jamie fainted, she had left it unbolted to tend to him. Now she would have to do it without making a sound. Halfway to the door, the wooden floor creaked; she froze. Any of the lads would have called out her name. It was quiet. Had they gone? Mari took another step, and another.

With a booming crash, the door opened. Mari flinched as her eyes locked on the piercing gaze of Lieutenant Kilgour. In a flash, she relived it—the dark moor, the crack of the gunfire as Jamie and Ellen were shot, and Kilgour on top of her. She stepped back and stumbled against the table. Spying a kettle of broth in the kitchen, Mari seized it and hurled it at him, but it had been off the fire for too long for the liquid to scald him. He deflected the kettle with the palm of his hand as he sneered.

"I see you've not lost your charm, minx. Come, gie us a kiss." He grabbed her arms and slammed her back against the wall. Then he ground his stiff groin against hers. Mari fought against his overpowering strength as he clamped his hand about her chin and cheeks and forced his mouth over hers. She tried to keep her mind focused on how to escape. He leaned his forehead against hers and said softly, "Now why dinnae you tell me where he is?"

"My husband has stepped out—but he's coming back any moment," she added, hoping the lie would persuade him to leave.

"Husband, is it? And which one would that be?" He grinned with cold eyes. "I've been watching you, minx. You're a busy girl. You've got so many dragoons coming in and out that I'm hard pressed to find you alone. But I'm a patient man. I knew he would show up sooner or later, and then I'd have my turn with you."

Before she could respond, he spied the closed door to the bedroom. With the swipe of an arm, he hurled her aside. She crashed into the table, and clutched a chair to right herself. With desperate haste, she said, "Why bother with the bedroom? You can take me here," she said, hoping to buy Jamie time.

He flashed a chilling smile. "Dinnae worry. I will." Then he kicked in the bedroom door and strode in.

Mari followed. The bedroom was empty, but the curtains billowed from the open window. Kilgour chuckled, knowing they were too high up for Jamie to jump. He strode to the window and cautiously looked out, ready to seize Jamie from the ledge. Mari waited, heart pounding. Kilgour stuck his head out the window, but found nothing.

Relieved, Mari guessed that Jamie must have leapt down to the lamp jutting out from the building, then dropped to the ground and escaped down the close. But in doing so, he had left her alone with Kilgour. She inched quietly back toward the door as he pulled his head back inside and spun around to face her. She looked about for something to strike him with. Her eyes swept past pillows and quilts to the fireplace poker. It was too far away. She bolted for the door, but he lunged at her. Hooking his arm about her waist, he yanked her against him. No match for his strength, she could not pry herself loose.

"I should use that on you," he snarled, nodding toward the fireplace poker. He smiled slyly. He was toying with her. He allowed her enough freedom to struggle, and grinned to see her fear mounting.

With a sharp pull, she was flat against him. He took hold of her hair and pulled her face against his. His hot breath in her ear made her shiver. He chuckled.

"Well, now, what will we do now that your brother has left us alone?"

"Who do you mean? No one was here. You saw that for yourself, so now you can leave," she said, hoping to distract him.

"I'll just have to come back, for we both know your brother will. Just one thing before I go." He pulled her into his bruising embrace and pushed her face down onto the bed. Mari screamed and thrashed about, but he pressed her face into the mattress. She fought to breathe. "One more sound, minx, and I'll leave your face down there, ken?" He pulled her up by the hair.

Mari nodded, frantic for air.

He turned her flushed face, and pressed her ear to the bed while he dug his knee into her back. With his other hand, he pulled her skirts up to her waist.

Mari stared at the wall.

The rough wool of Kilgour's plaid brushed against her bare skin as he pulled it out of his way. A clamor of footsteps broke through the ringing in her ears. Kilgour was suddenly gone. Mari barely heard the dull pounding of fists and the grunt as a body fell to the floor. She lay trembling. Gently, her skirt was pulled down to cover her. A hand touched her shoulder. "Mari?"

She looked up to find Charlie staring at her. She felt strangely detached until she saw the tender concern in his eyes, but she could not respond with words or emotion.

"Come here, Mari." He helped her to sit up and put his arms about her. She caught a glimpse of Alex and

Hughie dragging a well-pummeled Kilgour through the doorway.

"Shh, dearie. It's over. He'll not hurt you again."

She sat still, content to be numb. When she started to feel more herself, Mari said, "Charlie, please take me out of this room." She could still smell and taste Kilgour, and the sight of the room made it worse.

"Aye, we'll go sit by the fire."

Alex and Hughie had gone, and Kilgour with them.

"Now, Mari, I ken you're a good Presbyterian lass, but right now you need one of Dr. Charlie's medicinal draughts." He rounded the corner from the kitchen with a well-poured glass of whisky, which he then pressed into her hands. Mari took it and sipped without question.

After stoking the fire, Charlie pulled a chair close beside Mari. The two of them stared at the flames.

It was Mari who first broke the silence. "Charlie, I cannae properly thank you." Tears pooled in her eyes, and she could not continue.

"*Whisht.*" He gave her that same confident smile that left a trail of melted hearts in his wake, but it faded. He spoke in a quiet voice, thick with emotion: "I'm sorry we were not here sooner."

"*Whisht* yourself, Charlie." Her sad gaze settled on him. "How could you have known?"

"I promise you this, we'll not leave you alone again."

For a long while, the two quietly talked. Mari told him about Kilgour. Charlie took it all in without sharing his newly formed fear for her safety. Charlie soon distracted her with stories of Glengarry, and the home she would find there when they left for the Highlands.

Alex and Hughie returned some time later. Alex said

proudly, "I had to pull Hugh off before he killed the haggis-brained sack o' muck. Not that I wouldnae enjoy the sight of his sorry dead arse. But we had the cursed luck to have a constable happen along. We couldnae have our Hugh here in jail for killing a Royal Dragoon." Alex clapped a firm hand on Hughie's shoulder.

Hughie shook his head. "You should have left me alone. He deserves to die."

"Aye," said Alex. "But not in front of the law, ken?"

Hughie nodded in reluctant agreement. He clenched and released his jaw as he glared at the wall.

"We dragged him into a close before anyone saw us. We'll finish the job on another day, won't we, Hugh?"

Charlie watched, understanding. With a sudden shift of mood he said brightly, "Hugh, is it?"

"Aye," said Alex. "This lad's too braw a fighter to go by Hughie. He needs a man's name. It's Hugh now," he said proudly.

With a bashful smile, Hugh shook off his lingering anger.

"You should have seen him bouncing that haggis head down four flights of stairs. By the time we reached the street, we had to heave him over Hugh's horse, arse to the wind, so we could give him a proper disposal."

"Which was...?" said Charlie.

Hugh said, "He's having a wee lie down. Across town. In the street."

"Aye," said Alex. "I dinnae suppose he heard that woman calling out "Gardyloo!" Alex shook his head and shrugged.

Hugh stroked his chin thoughtfully. "I thought he looked quite good in brown."

Alex considered for a moment. "*Och*, he was just showing off what he's got for brains."

They all laughed, except Mari.

"He said he'll come back," she said softly.

The room was silent as the men exchanged looks.

"If he dares, he'll be taking a swim in the Nor'loch face down," said Alex, lifting Mari's chin as he searched her eyes. His fierce protectiveness brought Mari solace. "I can promise you that."

Charlie gave Mari's shoulder a comforting squeeze.

Hugh leaned on the wall, his arms folded. A brooding look clouded his usually bright eyes as he studied the street down below.

Chapter 23

First Footing

After cold days of gray skies, a morning came with warming sunshine. Mari leaned out of the window and shook a quilt in the chill morning air. A floor down and a few windows over, another quilt billowed over the sill and the landlady's head soon appeared. Mari leaned down and said, "Happy Hogmanay, Mistress Durie."

"Thank you, Mistress McEwan, and the same to you!"

Mari gathered the quilt back into her arms. "Em, I was wondering, Mistress Durie." She glanced about, not wanting to be overheard. "About the rent... "

"Aye?" Mrs. Durie pulled her own quilt back and held it in her arms as she turned to give Mari her full attention.

Mari said, "I'm fearing I dinnae ken what the arrangement was for the rent. What I mean to say is, do I owe you money?"

"*Och*, no. The gentleman paid it this morning."

Puzzled, Mari tilted her head. "The gentleman?"

"Mr. MacDonell."

Mari's heart caught in her throat for a moment. Her

first thought had been Callum, until she realized that, of course, there were four other Mr. MacDonells. "Which Mr. MacDonell?"

"The one who wears trews. The sailor."

"Duncan?"

"Aye, I believe that's what they call him." Mrs. Durie's face brightened. "Would you please ask him to stop by after midnight?"

"I'm sorry?" Mari could not help revealing her confusion.

Mrs. Durie laughed and said, "For good luck. At first footing." Still seeing Mari's confusion, she said, "If the first person to step foot in your house after midnight is a tall dark stranger, you'll have good luck for the year." She leaned closer. "A man braw as he is ought to be good for two years' good luck, at least!" She winked at Mari.

At last understanding, Mari smiled and said, "I'll tell him."

They waved and closed their windows. As Mari started to spread the quilt over the bed, she thought of the landlady's comment. Braw? Aye, she supposed Duncan was that.

"I'LL BE BACK SOON after dark," Charlie said, as he stood at the threshold looking down the stairway. "Duncan's on his way up, dearie."

"Goodbye, Charlie!" Mari called from the bedroom. She smoothed the quilt over the bed, fluffed the pillows, and then spun back toward the door with a gasp.

"You startled me."

"Charlie told you I was here, did he not?"

She smiled. "Aye, Duncan, he did. I just didnae expect you to be right there. I didnae hear you come in." She put her hands on his arms. "I'm sorry. I'm a wee bit skittish these days. The lads told you?"

"Aye."

She rolled her eyes at the foolishness of her question. "Of course. That's why you're here."

She made some tea and they sat down together.

Duncan set down his tea and leaned back, but he watched her with dark eyes. "How are you, Mari?"

His gaze unsettled her. Why was it only now that she realized how seldom their eyes met? "I stay busy. I get through the days. I'm never alone. The lads do their best to keep me amused. We go for walks. We play cards—"

"Aye." He interrupted her prattle. "But how are you?"

She set down her tea and looked at him candidly. "Are you sure you want truly to ken?"

He looked pointedly at her. "I wouldnae have asked otherwise."

She met his gaze. "I miss him. Each day I busy myself as though that could distract me."

Duncan's eyes softened.

As hard a man as he could be, Mari sometimes caught glimpses of a gentler nature. She said, "It's an ache that that I dinnae want to heal. If it does, I'll have lost him completely."

Duncan barely talked. He did not try to cheer her. He just quietly listened.

Mari curled into her chair and spoke frankly. "And now there's the fear. I awake in the night thinking that Kilgour is there. I ken that you all do your best to protect me, but I feel him out there in the dark, and I ken that he's there in the daylight. I feel wicked for wishing him dead, but I do. It is wrong. But what he did was wrong, and I cannae forgive it." Mari forced a faint smile. "So, you see, I'm becoming quite cold and heartless."

With a soft look and a smile, Duncan said, "You could never be that."

"And the lads try to help. But they want so much to make me happy again that I feel I must try to be so—just to please them. But I'm not. And I'm weary from pretending that I am. At night, I go into my room just to be alone with my moods where the lads willnae worry. And that's how I am. I'm sorry, but you asked, and I warned you."

"I wanted to ken. You dinnae have to pretend with me, Mari."

She saw in his expression that he meant it. And then the tears came.

Duncan quietly sat beside her. "There, now." He reached out and almost smoothed her hair from her brow, but thought better of it. He stood and assumed a bright tone of voice. "It's a bit early, I ken. But I am tall and dark. Now, mind, I'm no stranger, but I'm strange enough to make up for that." He gave her one of his rare grins that spread into his eyes. "And I've brought some whisky. If I promise to step outside long enough to step in for first footing after midnight, will you take a wee dram with me, lassie? For the sake of tradition?"

"I will." Mari smiled for what seemed like the first time in weeks.

"Easy, lass," he cautioned a few minutes later, as she poured a second glass of whisky.

"Why, Duncan, I've seen you pour more than this."

He smiled patiently. "But you are not used to strong drink."

"No, but I think I should like to be. It warms me, and dulls the ache," she said, taking a drink from her glass.

"Aye, it does that," he said as lay his hand on her wrist. "But it comes back to bite you."

Mari slipped her hand free and gave up. As she leaned her head back to rest against the chair, she turned her head to face Duncan. "I just want one night where I dinnae feel sad."

"I ken how you feel, lass. I do."

"No, you cannae ken how it feels to love so much that your love turns to agony."

Her words stopped Duncan short. He let go of the bottle and leaned back in his chair, catching sight through the window of clouds in the moonlight. "Can I not? If you think that I havenae known love, you'd be wrong."

Mari looked at him, stunned.

With a sad smile, Duncan said, "Aye. I loved someone. She betrayed me." He paused as though he might say more, but thought better of it.

"I'm sorry, Duncan. You never mentioned it."

He met her warm gaze for a moment, and with sudden cheer picked up the bottle. "Shall we have another?"

With a guilty grin, Mari said, "Just one before I start cooking supper."

"There's no need to cook. The lads are bringing supper to us," he said.

"Oh, how grand! I'm beginning to like your wild heathen traditions."

"I can see that," he said with a wry look.

ALEX, Charlie, and Hugh arrived with bundles of food and drink. They refused to let Mari help. Instead, they laid out the food and set the table. And when it was ready, they brought Mari to sit as though her chair were a throne from which she could reign over them. In truth, they might have let her.

Some looks were exchanged as they saw Mari's unnatural ebullience. All it took was a defiant glare from Duncan to shut down any discussion.

After supper, out came the fiddle, pipes, and *bodhrán*. Mari shook her head as Charlie tried to coax her away from the wall, but he had a firm grasp of her hand. The whisky had loosened her resolve, so as Alex rolled up the rug, Mari followed Charlie to the center of the room. He taught her a few basic steps and said, "Follow me, lassie!" And they were off. Around the room they whirled. When she stepped on his foot he seemed not to notice. Mari laughed and the music was lively. Alex took a turn, and then Hugh.

Before long, Alex, Charlie, and Hugh stood at the door.

"Come with us, Mari. We'll show you a Hogmanay you will never forget," Alex said, kissing her cheek as he held her hands.

"I can only imagine, which is why I'm not going," she said with a laugh.

"*Och*, Mari, you wound us," said Charlie with a sigh. "Well, as you are the bonniest lass in all of Edinburgh, we shall have to settle for the second, third and fourth bonniest lassies. Well, I myself shall settle for second. These louts may fend for themselves."

Alex laughed as he grabbed Charlie's right arm and twisted it upward behind his back. "'Tis a pity about your arm—not to mention your face," he said, adding a sharp twist at the end.

Hugh chimed in. "The laugh is on you, old men. Have you not noticed the pretty ones like their men unspoilt by wrinkles?"

Alex and Charlie ceased their struggles and gaped at Hugh. A few moments passed as Mari watched, smiling. Alex looked at Charlie. Unspoken words seemed to pass between them. They both turned on Hugh, who took off running down the stairs with the other two close at his heels.

"Goodbye, dearie!" Charlie called out.

"We'll bring breakfast," said Alex.

"It may not get here 'til supper, though," Charlie added.

Shaking her head, Mari closed the door behind them. She turned back toward Duncan. "I'm fearing you drew the short straw."

"Not so," Duncan said, smiling.

Duncan brought the last dish to Mari. The supper dishes were clean, dried and dispensed with. "You ken," Mari said with a twinkle, "this could destroy your reputation."

"For you, Mari McEwan, I would risk that and more." His smile lingered.

"It's your good fortune, then, that I am no risk to you."

A half smile formed as he averted his gaze.

"Shall we go sit by the fire?"

Duncan added a log, and they pulled their chairs closer. "'Tis a cold night."

"Aye," answered Mari. The silence between them grew awkward. "Duncan, what troubles you? You look like you carry a burden."

Duncan looked suddenly at her. "No, it's no burden."

Mari studied him. "Then what is it?"

"We'll not speak of it now."

"But we must. Duncan, I consider you a dear friend. If there is something that stands between us—"

"No, Mari." His voice sounded harsh as he leapt to his feet and walked to the window. More calmly, he said, "You need not worry."

But everything in his stance told her otherwise. "Have I done something, Duncan?" She went to stand by the window beside him. He would not look at her.

One heartbeat later, he bounded out of the door. "Bolt the door, Mari!" Down the stairs he bounded, and across the road to the wynd, where he disappeared into the shadows.

Minutes later there was a knock at the door. "Mari, it's Duncan."

He came in and secured the door lock. "What is it? Duncan, you're scaring me."

"It was nothing."

From the look on his face, Mari knew this was far from the truth.

"I thought I saw something. I was wrong." He turned back and smiled. "Let's warm ourselves by the fire."

There they sat for an hour or so, until the chimes of St. Giles began ringing in the new year. They went to the window and looked down at the street below, full of people. On the twelfth chime, people stopped and embraced.

"There's a good deal of kissing down there," Mari said.

"Another tradition," Duncan said, standing beside her.

"We knew nothing of this growing up," she said as she looked down below with a wistful expression. An unexpected silence filled the air between them.

Mari looked up at Duncan with a faint smile that did little to hide how she missed Callum. Duncan took her face in his hands. With a gentle smile, he bent down and gave her a chaste kiss on the forehead. "Happy Hogmanay."

Mari lifted her eyes. She looked as though she might say something, but all that came out was, "Happy Hogmanay to you, Duncan."

They turned back to the window, and Mari's mood lightened. "Oh—I nearly forgot, Mistress Durie asked if you would stop by her apartment for first footing." A smile lit her eyes. "She thought that since you're so handsome, you might bring an extra measure of luck."

A trace of a grin crept into his expression. "Oh, she did, did she? The poor woman is daft."

"Aye. But not so daft as a man who would pay someone's rent." She leveled a knowing look at him.

"*Och*, that. It was nothing."

"But it was something."

"No, Callum asked us to look after the things he used

to take care of." He looked out the window and studied the crowd down below.

"I thank you, but I cannae let you keep doing things for me."

"Even if I want to?"

"I'm not your responsibility."

"You could be."

Mari flashed a questioning look.

Duncan hastened to add, "If you'd just let me help you. Just for now, until you ken what you want to do."

Mari's eyes drifted away. "I dinnae feel right about it."

"What would Callum have wanted?"

Mari offered no answer, for she knew that Callum would have wanted just this, for her to be cared for.

Duncan said, "He would want things just so, and you ken it."

Mari followed Duncan's gaze to the street as her eyes filled with tears. "I dinnae ken what to say. At some point, I will need to make plans."

"Give it time."

Mari was troubled, but said no more about it.

With a deep breath, Duncan shook off his dark mood. "Come, lass. Shall we go see Mistress Durie?" he said with a reassuring wink.

Mari reluctantly smiled. "Aye."

"Good. Now, we'll need some whisky, of course, and some coal."

Duncan gathered all that they needed to ensure the landlady's good luck. He held the door for Mari, and the two headed on down the stairs to call on Mrs. Durie.

Chapter 24

The Visitor

Duncan lay asleep on the floor outside of Mari's closed bedroom door. The knob twisted and the door to the apartment gently opened. A floorboard gave way with a creak. In an instant, Duncan clamped a tight hold onto an ankle and gave it a yank. A large body fell to the floor with a thud. After a scuffle, Duncan held the intruder pinned down with a dirk poised at his throat.

"Duncan, it's Charlie."

"Dammit, Duncan!" said Alex, as he gripped Duncan's wrist.

"Dammit yourself! You woke me from a sound sleep," Duncan complained as he released Charlie with a shove, and returned his dirk to his belt.

Charlie lifted a brow. "Did I, now? I had plans for my own peaceful slumber just before you threw me to the floor." He sat up holding his shoulder and rotating and extending his arm for dramatic effect.

Making no apologies, Duncan said, "I was protecting the lass."

"And a fine job you're doing," said Alex as he added a log to the fire's burning embers.

Duncan cast an annoyed look toward Alex. "I was not expecting the two of you back until morning."

"Aye," said Charlie. "Well, on rare occasions I let a night pass without bedding a woman."

"No one would have you, eh?" Duncan said, with a glint in his eyes.

"It was my choice," Charlie protested.

"Aye, choice," Alex said with a smirk.

"Well, I do have my standards," said Charlie.

"Aye, standards," said Alex, as he poured whisky into three glasses.

"Where's Hugh?" asked Duncan.

Alex laughed. Charlie scowled. Duncan's face lit up with a rare ear-to-ear grin. "He's with a woman."

"Aye," said Alex, smiling.

"Not just any woman," Duncan said, studying Charlie. "But the one that you wanted," he said with a triumphant smirk.

"Shut your gob, Duncan, or I'll shut it for you," said Charlie, who was in no way amused.

"Will you now?" Duncan smiled and folded his arms, standing ready.

Knowing he was no match for Duncan, Charlie shrugged and grumbled, "At the moment I'd rather drink than fight. But dinnae try my patience."

Duncan merely grinned, having nothing to prove. After Charlie walked away to sit down, Duncan took his drink and went to the window. He leaned his shoulder against the frame and looked into the night.

Alex said, "You should have seen our Hugh tonight.

The lassies all fancied him, and he looked like Charlie used to look back when the girls fancied him." Alex was turning to smirk at Charlie when he heard something from the bedroom. "What was that?"

Duncan was first to reach the bedroom. "Mari?" He rattled the door latch. It was locked. "Mari!" When she failed to answer, he kicked the door in.

Alex stopped at the doorway, with Charlie beside him. Mari stood on the other side of the bed facing them. Her white linen nightgown was crimson with blood. Clenched in her fist was a sgian dubh from which drops of blood fell to Lieutenant Kilgour. He lay struggling to take halting breaths. Duncan shot a look to Alex and Charlie, who moved toward Kilgour, while Duncan rounded the foot of the bed to reach Mari. Kilgour took a few halting gasps and lurched toward her. Alex reached for Kilgour just as Mari lifted her arms and sank the sgian dubh into his chest. She struggled to pull it back out, then she stabbed him again. He fell back, lifeless.

As she pulled the weapon back, Duncan slowly drew closer behind her. "Mari." He spoke in a low, soothing voice. Firmly but gently, he gripped her wrist while he circled her waist with his other arm. "Mari, let it go, darlin'." He spoke quietly in her ear until she let go and it dropped to the bed.

"Mari?"

She did not respond. Duncan coaxed her away from the body and into his arms.

An instant later, something caught Alex's eye at the window. "The son of a bitch used a grappling hook to climb in through the window."

Charlie pulled the bedding over the lifeless body.

Duncan cast a dark look at the others as he circled Mari's waist and led her out of the room, leaving the others behind to clean up.

She began to tremble as Duncan brought her to stand by the warmth of the fire. For a long while she was silent.

"I'm so cold."

Duncan pulled her into his arms and held her, wrapping the end of his plaid about her.

Her teeth chattered. "I woke up and he was in my bed. He came in through the window."

"I know, darlin'."

Duncan held her tighter and cursed himself for not thinking that someone might scale the wall several floors up to the window. The thought of sleeping inside her room had been out of the question for a number of reasons, so he had decided to sleep outside of her door, thinking he'd keep her from danger. He stroked Mari's silken hair and held her head to his chest. "I'm so sorry."

"I've been sleeping with Callum's sgian dubh."

"Aye."

"I had to stop him. I had to stop him. He would have killed me just like he killed Ellen."

"You did what you had to. You're a brave lass."

Duncan heard a scuffling sound and kept his arms about Mari, shielding her from the sight of Alex and Charlie carrying Kilgour away. They had wrapped his plaid about him to cover the blood, and carried him out to the street as though he were a drunken friend who had passed out. From time to time, they passed people, most of them too drunk or tired to notice or care about the three drunks who clung to the shadows. Along the way, they gathered rocks in the folds of Kilgour's plaid, where they tied them. They walked along the Nor'loch until they found a small boat, which they rowed out to the middle. There they rolled Kilgour's weighted body over the edge and watched him sink into the dark water.

With that business done, they returned to the apartment and burned what they could of the bedding. What they could not clean or burn, they took back to the Nor'loch and bundled tightly with rocks, and then dropped it into the middle of the loch. They returned to find Duncan by the fire with Mari asleep in his arms.

By morning the apartment was clean of blood, except that which had dried on Mari's nightgown.

MARI AWOKE with a start and lunged forward. "No!"

"He'll no harm you again." Duncan pulled her back and said softly, "He's gone. It's all over."

"Are you sure?"

"Aye, very sure. The lads took him away."

She looked at Alex and Charlie, their clothes stained with Kilgour's blood.

Alex followed her gaze and looked down at his leine. "Mari, are there any of Callum's leines we could wear? I'd rather we not draw suspicion."

"Aye, there are some in the bedroom." They turned to leave, but Mari hastened to add, "Not the one hanging on the nail. I'll get you some clean ones."

Alex and Charlie changed into clean leines while Mari washed their plaids with a feverish vigor.

Duncan watched her with a troubled expression. "Mari, I'll do this. Go take care of yourself." He took over the washing. His eyes drifted down to the dried blood on her nightgown. "Get cleaned up, lass. We'll want to burn that."

Duncan finished washing the plaids and laid them out by the fire to dry. They were dark enough to mask any blood stains remaining, and as they were dragoons who had fought in recent battles, blood was not an unexpected sight on the men's plaids. Mari bathed and emerged in clean clothes.

Alex and Charlie spoke quietly by the fire, while Duncan went to Mari and said, "How are you, darlin'?"

She shook her head. "I killed a man."

"To defend yourself. You had no choice."

His words did little to ease her troubled soul. There was little talk after that. Duncan took the last seat, next to Mari. He reached over and squeezed her hand for a moment to reassure her. He started to slip his hand from hers, but she held on. There they sat, staring into the flames.

THE FOLLOWING DAY, Mari sat in St. Giles Cathedral and prayed. Duncan sat beside her, concerned. For a long while they sat there, until Duncan leaned over and said gently, "It's time to go."

She looked at him with round shimmering eyes, and she nodded.

As they left, she accepted his offered arm and clung mournfully to him. They stepped into the daylight. The sun brought into relief the uneven stone road and the shadows it left untouched on the stone walls around them. In silence, they walked. When they came to a close, Mari pressed her palm to Duncan's arm, gently urging him to stay while she went into the shadows and wept.

Duncan followed and stood at a distance as long as he could. Then he lay his hand on her shoulder. "*Och*, Mari."

She spun round as he reached his arms out. She flew to his embrace. When she'd cried herself dry of tears, she said, "Duncan, I pray and I pray, but I feel as though God will never forgive me."

With a force that looked almost like anger, Duncan said, "If there is anything to forgive, He has done so already. If that isnae true, may God strike me dead right here on this spot."

Mari gasped. "Duncan, no! You must not speak so!"

"Aye, well I'm still standing here, so you must believe that He forgives you."

"Then perhaps it is I who cannae forgive myself."

"*Och*, well then, to that I'd say that if God forgives you, who are you not to agree?"

"I ken what you say. It makes sense. But my heart aches with the guilt. I have broken a commandment."

Duncan lifted her chin and gave her a dark, piercing look. "Lass, I have killed men in fights and in battles. I dinnae ken how many lives I have taken, but there's one thing I ken. It never is easy, but sometimes it is necessary."

"A few days ago, I would have said that you're wrong. I dinnae ken anymore."

"Well, I do. We both ken what would have happened if you had not fought back."

"Aye. It was all I could think of. I couldnae let him do that to me."

"Then you did what you had to, aye?" Duncan wiped

her eyes dry with his thumbs. Then he brushed strands of hair from her face. His gaze swept over her face and rested on her lips for a moment. "Give it time, lass." He put his hands on her shoulders and held her at a safer distance.

Reassured, Mari nodded.

A pair of men brushed past them on their way through the close. Their admiring eyes settled upon Mari until Duncan pulled her possessively into his arms and glared at the men. When they were well on their way, Duncan said, "In the meanwhile, you are not alone. Nor will you be. I'll be here."

Mari leaned her head on Duncan's chest. Duncan stiffened and said, "So will Alex and Charlie and Hugh. We will help you through this." With a quick kiss on the forehead, he led her back into the sunlight.

Chapter 25

The Truest Heart

In the days that followed, Mari spent more time asleep than awake. One day she awoke at midday. When the shops opened after Hogmanay, the lads had bought a new mattress and bedding for Mari, and leines for themselves.

Everything seemed to return to their former routine. Life looked very much like before, except at night Mari would not sleep alone in her room. Alex, Charlie, and Hugh took turns sleeping on the floor between the window and bed. It was the only way Mari was able to sleep. For a third time, Duncan made an excuse to avoid his turn, and Alex took note. He talked Duncan into going out for a drink. Hugh joined them, leaving Charlie behind with Mari, so she would not be alone. Before long, Hugh was at the bar, his attentions fully engaged by a pretty young barmaid.

Alex and Duncan sat at a small table nearby. With no warning, Alex asked him, "What are you doing?"

"I'm having a dram."

"Do you think me daft? We've known one another since we were bairns."

"Aye," said Duncan. "Long enough to be sure you're a pain in the arse."

Alex leaned back and watched Duncan with narrowing eyes. "I'm not talking about having a dram, and you well know it."

Duncan looked away as if he had not heard.

Alex narrowed his eyes. "I've seen you look at her."

Duncan cast a dark look sideways at Alex. "And I've seen you look at her, too."

"Aye. We all love her a little. But you love her a little too much."

Duncan stared into his drink, his face devoid of emotion. After a long silence, he said, "Did you never wonder why I went to sea?"

"Well, no. I suppose that I thought you liked sailing."

"I hate sailing. It's a wonder I havenae boaked my guts into the North Sea."

"How long has this gone on?"

"Gone on? Nothing's gone on."

"You went to sea to avoid your feelings for Mari."

"I went to sea because I needed the money to send home for the rent."

Alex nodded, unconvinced.

"If left to my father's care, my mother would lose her home, as you well know."

Alex said, "Aye, but that's not all there is to it." His gaze was relentless.

Duncan met his eyes. "No." He stared into his glass. "When I'm away, I think of Jenny."

Alex lifted a brow. "Jenny?"

Duncan nodded.

"The Jenny that Tavish was boasting about? Who promised herself to him the day after you left to come here?"

"I hated her, and then I saw Mari and Callum and I hated Jenny even more. Mari was everything Jenny wasn't —constant and true. She loves Callum. There will be no other for Mari."

"And yet you torment yourself." Alex's look bordered on pity, and Duncan saw this and glared.

"Having never lost love, you couldnae understand."

"Perhaps not. But you seem no better."

With a bitter chuckle, Duncan said, "No, I just know what I want."

"And that's Mari?"

"For awhile I thought it might be." Duncan shook his head slowly.

"Then what is it you want?"

"I want love. I want love like Mari's for Callum. Jenny loved me that way, at least for a time, and I miss it. It left a hollow ache inside me, and I see that in Mari."

Alex's eyes narrowed. "And you think you can fill her hollow ache?"

Duncan met Alex's eyes with a caustic glare. "I willnae dishonor Callum, if that's what you're afraid of. And you denigrate Mari by even suggesting she might. I'll take the insult myself. Once. But I willnae let you shame Mari. She knows nothing of this. Nor will she, because we'll not speak of it again."

Alex was stunned. He had suspected that Duncan might have grown fonder of Mari since Callum's death, but he'd had no idea to what depth. He could have imagined this coming from Charlie, perhaps. Even Hugh. But Duncan? He was always the one with his feelings in check. He did nothing without careful thought.

Duncan finished his drink and got up for another. He brought another for Alex. "I couldnae sleep in her room. I dinnae trust myself with her. I might do something rash."

With a sharp look, Alex leaned forward. "Like what?"

Duncan saw Alex's alarm and hastened to say, "By my sword, I'd not force myself on her! How could you think that?"

Alex had seen Duncan this angry few times, and that was just as well. "Aye, sorry. It's just that—"

"It's Mari," he said, finishing Alex's sentence.

Alex barely hid his relief.

Duncan stared at his drink with sad eyes. "I would never touch Mari without her wanting me to, but she is as lonely as I. Just as I have, she could easily confuse that with other feelings. I'm not sure whether I would be honorable enough to help her to see the difference."

Alex did not disagree.

Duncan leaned back and stared into his drink. "I've kept my distance from her, but it was easier when Callum was here."

"Callum?" Alex was troubled and made no effort to hide it. "You've felt this way since before Callum died?"

"Aye. And each time we're alone, I'm fearing I might tell her. In time, anyone else would have noticed. Not Mari. She sees only the best in people. But Callum would have sorted it out. In that instant, two loves would have been ruined. A love between friends would have been lost to a love that would never have been. I never had Mari, and I couldnae betray Callum and lose my best friend. So I went away. It was better for everyone then."

"And now?" Alex asked him.

"Now? It's worse than before. I've lost Jenny, but Mari is here. It wouldnae be the same sort of love but, knowing that, together we might not be as lonely."

Alex leaned forward. "That, my friend, is a very bad plan."

Duncan nodded, offering no argument. "Can I steal her heart from a ghost? No. Nor will I torment myself by lying an arm's length away in the dark."

Alex eyed Duncan with sympathy. How had he not noticed?

Duncan said, "In the end, we could never be happy. I would never be Callum, and she—as much as I've tried to forget her—would never be Jenny." He looked straight at Alex. "There is no help for me, but I wonder each day about Callum."

Alex's face grew ashen. "Wonder what?"

"Callum was in my hands when the ship went down. Sometimes I wonder if I could have done more to save him."

Alex made no effort to hide he alarm. "Are you saying...?"

"No!" Duncan shut his eyes as though he could shut out the truth. "But I thought of it."

More for himself than for Duncan, Alex said, "But you didnae act on it." Desperate to hear the right answer, Alex said, "Tell me you didnae act on it."

"No! But it haunts me. I had hold of his arms. I looked at him as I gripped his arms, and I held on. The force of our friendship was so powerful that I was certain it would see us through. Live or die, we would do it together. Then the wave hit, and tore us apart. I see his face every morning and night. And I wonder if I did enough."

"What more could you have done?"

"Not want Mari."

Alex looked at Duncan, eyes fixed on the floor, and he wondered how Duncan had managed to hide it this long. But then, Alex knew of no secrets deeper than those of the heart. Nor was there a place further from logic. But logic had to rule now. Mari needed them all. She had left her home for a man who was gone, and she could not go back.

"She depends on you now. But you know that," said Alex.

"Aye. She depends upon me to be a true friend. And I've betrayed her."

"So what will you do?"

Duncan finished his drink. "I'll stay here until she is stronger. After that, she'll have you and Charlie and Hugh. Take her home to the Highlands and see that she's settled. She needs a home, and a family."

"And you?"

"I'll go back out to sea. While we've sat here, my father's probably gambled away the next quarter's rent." Duncan got up and went to the bar for more drinks.

THEY RETURNED HOME to find Mari's brother there, talking with her while Charlie eyed Jamie warily.

Jamie said, "Richard Cameron's going to save Scotland."

"Let him do what he will. We'll not talk of it here," said Mari.

Duncan knew that tone of voice. She did not express anger easily, but it was there, just the same. Duncan took Charlie's arm and pulled him into the other room. "Damn it, what were you thinking, letting him in here?"

"She let him in. He's her brother. What was I to say?"

"No." Duncan leveled a glare that made even Charlie uneasy.

"Duncan, he's the only family she's got."

Duncan growled, "We're the only family she's got. We were the ones here with her when she needed him most. Where was he?"

Charlie met his bitter glare without flinching. Alex said quietly, "Calm yourself, lad."

"He posed no threat to her," Charlie said, as he put a few steps between them.

Duncan barely bit back his rage. "Callum's dead because of what her brother did—or have you forgotten?" He looked away. The damage was done. All he could do was stand by and be there when she needed him. And she would. And each time that she leaned on him, his heart would break just a little bit more.

Tense silence sparked between the three men.

In the other room, Jamie pled, "I cannae work to support myself. Marion, please, I'm doing the Lord's work."

Mari said, "When did killing become the Lord's work?"

"A long time ago." Jamie's jaw tightened.

"And when will it stop?"

"When evil is banished."

"Oh, Jamie. There is no gun with the power to do that."

"I willnae stand idly by while the kirk is attacked. And our people."

"And why not, when your actions solve nothing?"

His jaw clenched. "Mari, don't stand in my way."

"I willnae do that. No one can, for you've always been stubborn. You'll do as you want, but I'll have no part in it."

She stood and started to go to the sitting room, but he grasped her wrist, forcing her to stop. "I need money, Marion."

She looked back. "I'm sorry, but I cannae help you."

"At least give me money for food."

"Take the loaf of bread there on the table, and go."

"Mari—"

"No. I've no money of my own, and I willnae dishonor Callum by giving you his."

"Marion, please!" He gripped her shoulders until Mari winced.

"Let me go, Jamie."

Duncan lunged toward him, but Hugh reached him first, gripping his collar and swinging a punch that knocked Jamie to the floor.

"Hugh, no!"

Hugh turned to her. "Mari, I willnae stand here and allow him to treat you—" He stopped with his mouth open, and looked down. He touched his side and looked at his hand, red with blood.

Charlie pinned Jamie face down to the floor, while Alex forced a knife from his hand.

Hugh looked at Mari as if puzzled, then reached his

bloody hand toward her and fell into her arms. Duncan helped lower Hugh to the floor.

Charlie gripped Jamie's neck. "You damned weasel!"

Alex pulled Charlie off. "Think of Mari."

Mari cradled Hugh in her arms. "Jamie, what have you done?"

Pinned down, Jamie struggled to answer. "I didnae mean to. They attacked me."

"On your feet, you wee bastard!" Duncan joined Charlie in practically lifting Jamie into the air. Duncan jabbed him in the side and swung at his jaw.

Duncan said, "I'll take care of him, Charlie. Go see to your brother."

Mari had already started to tear strips of cloth from her shift and wrap it around Hugh's waist. Alex finished the job while Mari rushed to Duncan. "Stop. You'll kill him."

Duncan did as she asked, but gripped Jamie's shirt and said softly, "If anything happens to Hugh, I will find you and finish this."

Hearing this, Hugh said, "Is it bad as all that?"

Alex dismissed it with a smirk. "No. But if ye dinnae lie back, I can make it so."

Hugh obeyed, having no strength to do otherwise.

Duncan and Charlie hauled Jamie through the door and down onto the street. "If you were not Mari's brother, you'd be dead now, you ken?"

"But if we see you again, best come dressed for your funeral," added Duncan.

Jamie scowled, but ran as soon as Charlie released him.

Charlie went back upstairs and found Hugh cradled

in Mari's arms. Doing his best to hide his concern to see Hugh looking so pale, Charlie said, "Well, look at you. Some lads have all the luck."

Mari tried to smile.

Alex said, "I'll need to have a look before I stitch him up, hen. Would you fetch me a needle and thread, and then heat up some water?"

Mari brought a pillow and gently slid it beneath Hugh's head, and then saw to the rest.

She had just put the kettle over the fire when Hugh said, "Callum? Does this mean I'm dead?"

Chapter 26

The Long Journey

"No, you're not dead, and neither am I," Callum said, as he stood in the doorway and forced an encouraging grin. Then a movement caught his eye.

Mari had been stirring the coals, but the sound of that voice made her halt.

Callum now had a beard and strange clothes, and he wondered if she would even know him. Each weary step of his journey back to her had been driven by longing for this moment.

Mari turned slowly, reluctant to find out that she was mistaken. "Callum?"

He held out his arms. She flew to him and buried her face in his chest and sank into the feel of his body against hers. Her lips grazed his neck as Callum held her face and kissed her.

With eyes fixed on the reunion, Alex held a flask out in Duncan's direction. With a quick glance, he said quietly, "You'll be wanting this."

Charlie overheard and said with a smirk, "Why?

Hugh's the one being stitched up." He looked at Callum. "By hell, where have you been?"

"Not far from it, as it turns out."

Duncan drank and offered the flask back to Alex, who took one look at Duncan and pushed the flask back.

Mari led Callum to a chair, while Alex began stitching up Hugh's wound. Mari brought Callum a dram and then sat on the floor beside him. She rested her head on his knee, but looked up often to convince herself it was real.

He told of his journey, and when he had finished, Mari said, "No more talk. I'm taking you to bed."

Charlie lifted an eyebrow.

"He needs sleep. He's exhausted," Mari said, as color flushed her cheeks.

"Ignore these unmannerly rogues," Callum said, as he rose to his feet with no small effort. "I'll deal with them later. I can see nothing's changed," he said over his shoulder with a smile. But despite his good spirits, he was weary and weak. He put his arm over Mari's shoulder, and leaned on her as she held him by the waist and led him to the bedroom.

After closing the door, Callum lay on the bed, clothes and all, and reached out for her. "Come here beside me." She pulled a quilt over Callum and slipped into bed, fitting her body against his. He drew her close and held her in the sturdy arms for which she had yearned so many nights. "*Och*, my Mari, I missed you." His worn body dragged him into a deep sleep. Mari lay on her side and did not tire of watching him until she drifted into her own sleep.

"MARI." Callum slid his hand under her neck and cupped her head in his palm. She slept. Brushing his lips to her ear, he spoke in a deep, quiet whisper. "So many times just the thought of you kept me alive. Mari, love, I want you so." He pressed his lips to her neck and trailed kisses back to her ear as he whispered, "Wake up, lass." He rolled onto her gently and slid his hand to her breast.

Mari's scream cut through the air. Duncan burst through the door. "Mari!"

He found Mari trembling in Callum's arms.

Callum held her shoulders and searched her face. "What is it, love?"

"I thought it was—" She stopped as her eyes drifted to Duncan. Feeling Callum's eyes on her, her eyes darted back to him. "It was a bad dream."

Duncan opened his mouth to speak, but thought better of it as Callum enfolded Mari into his arms. It was not his place to comfort her now. He went to the window and checked to make sure no one was outside. Then he left, closing the door gently behind him.

As he watched the door close, Callum said, "'Twas more than a dream."

Mari pushed her hair back from her face with fingers that trembled. "I woke up and you were on top of me. I didnae know it was you."

Callum's eyes darkened. "And who would it be?"

Mari stared at the window in silence. When Callum inhaled to speak, she said, "Kilgour."

"Who in hell is this Kilgour that you'd think of him

before your own husband?" Anger quickly overtook his concern.

"Kilgour was the highland dragoon who shot Jamie. He raped and killed Ellen, and he tried to do likewise with me."

Callum's anger turned to concern. "Lass, do you still dream of that after so many months?"

"No. It was not that I dreamt of it. He was here."

Callum gripped her shoulders. "By my sword, I will kill him."

"He's already dead." She told Callum the story of how he'd climbed in through the window. How before he could rape her, she'd stabbed him with Callum's sgian dubh. Callum listened. He was quiet, but his jaw clenched. When she was finished, he sat on the edge of the bed.

She put a gentle hand on his shoulder. "Please dinnae turn from me."

Painful silence hung in the air as Callum tamped down the rage and the guilt that kept him from being able to think or speak. "I wasnae here to protect you."

"I protected myself."

"That's not what I wanted for you."

"No. But you're all that I've wanted, and you're home. So come back to bed and show me what you want for me now." She put her arms about his neck, and he spun about to hold her and lower her onto the bed.

Duncan sat by the fire in the sitting room while the steady creak of the bed in the next room punctuated the gentle rain outside. He finished his drink and went out to the dark rain-soaked street.

The next morning he was on a ship bound for Barbados.

"HERE'S SOME BROTH, lad. Try and take some." Hugh looked at Mari, then closed his eyes. As the hours went on his face drained of color. Helplessly, they all watched over him.

Charlie brought in a doctor.

"It's a hell of a time for Duncan to go sailing," said Charlie.

Alex was quick to defend him. "How was he to know Hugh would take a turn for the worse? He'd already signed on."

"And why is that?" asked Charlie.

"Charlie," cautioned Callum, "it's not Alex's fault."

Alex glared at Charlie. "I'm sorry. In spite of your high estimation of me, I cannae walk on water; nor can I guide Duncan's decisions quite yet. He did what he felt was best. That's all I need to know, and it is enough."

The doctor came out of the bedroom looking somber.

"How is he?" asked Mari, rushing to him.

"He's weak. The stab wound went deep. I've re-bandaged the wound. He needs rest. Keep him comfortable."

"But he'll get better," said Mari, looking for confirmation.

Alex eyed the doctor, but asked nothing. He had seen too many men after battle, as had the others.

Callum walked him to the door. Before leaving, the

doctor turned back and spoke softly. "You're Highlanders, aye?"

Callum nodded.

"Catholic?"

Callum nodded, this time more slowly.

The doctor looked at Callum and said with alarming frankness, "You'd best send for a priest."

Callum's brow furrowed as he nodded. He closed the door and stood facing it, trying to regain control of the rising emotion and the deepening grief. He knew Mari's touch on his arm, and he turned around, a false smile on his lips.

"What did he say?" she asked, worried.

"He'll be back tomorrow to check on him."

Mari nodded, but caught a glimpse of the truth in Callum's eyes. "Will he?"

"Aye." He put his arm about her and drew her back toward the others.

In the morning, Hugh opened his eyes and looked up at the sun shining in through the window. He lifted his head, as though he might sit up, but gave up the effort. Mari sat beside him and reached around from behind to prop him up against her.

"I'm cold, Mari."

As she wrapped her arms around him, he asked for Charlie.

Charlie gripped his hand. "I'm here, Hugh," he said as he clenched his jaw and fought back tears that shone in his eyes.

"Will you stay with me today?" Hugh asked him.

Alex looked on with a clenched jaw and stoic expression.

Charlie forced an engaging smile. "Aye, of course I will, Hugh." He sat on the edge of the bed and took hold of his hand.

A faint smile formed, but faded as he gasped for air and stopped breathing.

Mari froze.

He gasped again, and once more. After that, he was silent.

"Hughie, no," moaned Mari.

Charlie pulled his brother's limp body into his arms and held him. A mournful sound came from deep in his chest as he gently rocked the limp body.

Chapter 27

The Drovers' Road

The men sat in the sitting room while Mari made tea in the kitchen.

Callum said, "Someone's got to tell Nellie. I'll not have her find out from a letter."

Charlie was so lost in grief that he seemed not to have heard, but he looked up at Callum. "I cannae face her until I've made his murderer pay."

Alex signaled for Charlie to lower his voice so Mari would not overhear him.

"I will go," said Callum. "It makes sense for me to go. I'm a wanted man, so I cannae go to the funeral, and I cannae stay here for very long. And unless I leave Mari behind—which I willnae do—I cannae go off to avenge Hughie's murder. So it only makes sense that I go."

"Aye," said Charlie, as the others gave a nod.

"I'll tell Nellie, and I'll take the lass home. Mari's been through enough."

Hearing her name, Mari paused outside of the doorway to hear what plans they were making for her.

Alex said, "Charlie and I can take care of things here. We will find that wee son of a bitch, and we'll give him a taste of Highland justice."

Charlie added, "And if he survives that, we'll let the authorities put his head on a pike."

Charlie looked up too late. Mari stood in the doorway. She had heard, and the damage was done. He met her hurt gaze with bitterness. "Hugh was my brother."

"And Jamie is mine."

Charlie held his tongue and looked down, not from regret for his words but out of respect for her. Hugh had done nothing to deserve the fate Jamie forced on him. But Jamie had earned every bit of what Charlie had planned for him.

Callum excused himself and caught up with Mari, who had quietly escaped to the bedroom. He drew close as she stood at the window, her gaze fixed outside. The percussive rain pelted the glass pane and darkened the sandstone walls of the buildings.

Mari said, "Will it ever stop raining? I'm so tired of rain."

Callum circled his arms about her waist. She leaned back against his chest, and they watched rain drip down the windowpane. There was no further talk of her brother. What more could they say that would not tear them apart?

AND SO IT was decided that Callum would take Mari home to the Highlands. Mari did not protest. She had known too much sadness here. As much as she had loved

Hugh, her presence would not be needed. Only men were permitted to attend funeral services, and afterward she would not be a comfort. For Callum's sake, they would treat her with respect, but every time they looked at her they would be reminded of her brother and what he had done. It was better to keep to herself until they could see her and not think of Hugh's murder. As for Mari, as much as she understood how they must feel, her husband included, Jamie was her brother. And with that came her own feelings, which she could not express to them. Her pain might not be as bitter as theirs, but she too had loved Hugh. Although Jamie had broken her heart, she still loved him. The MacDonells knew that their every bitter word pained her. Her absence would allow them to express their grief freely without having to worry about her feelings.

For Callum, home would be a longed-for relief. She was glad for him, but it meant more change for her. She had lived her whole life on a farm. Life had moved in predictable cycles along with the seasons. But now life was beyond her control. It was changing too fast.

The one constant was rain. It had rained through the day, and was raining after dark when they left.

Alex gripped Callum's hand. "I'm sorry you have to leave like a thief in the night, but it's safer this way."

"Aye," replied Callum, not even trying to hide his grim mood.

Alex's eyes settled on Mari. "Come here, hen," he said with a grin as he held out his arms.

With moist eyes, she hugged him, and then stepped back and rested her hands on his shoulders. "Look after Charlie."

"I will." He looked into her eyes and, as was his gift, filled her with confidence in him.

They left unspoken the truth about how things had changed between them. Alex was able to see past the rift now between them, but Charlie could not. But the same thing that tied families together had somehow been forged between them over these months. Something in Alex's smile and warm touch gave her hope that they might all find their way back together.

Charlie joined them and first said his goodbyes to Callum. He now stood before Mari with a remote look that masked his deep sorrow. "Mari."

She missed the carefree grin he'd always had when he'd call her "dearie". She wondered she'd lost that forever.

"Dear Charlie." She looked into his eyes, but they were distant.

She reached out and put a gentle hand on his shoulder. "I'm so sorry," she said, looking at him through her tears.

Charlie turned his head slightly, hiding moist eyes. "*Whisht*, dearie. Just gie us a hug."

And she gave him just that, along with some tears on his shoulder.

Callum helped Mari onto the horse he had bought her, and then he mounted Storm. Through the dark rain they rode, under the looming shadow of Edinburgh Castle.

Late in the night they took shelter in a shed. They made love in the hay with the passion of two grieving souls who have come close to death, and now cling to life and each other. Afterward, their bodies entwined, they talked softly of where they had been and the people they'd left for a while, and the one they had just lost forever.

"If you hadnae found me that day, so much would be different."

"I cannae think of my life without you," he said, just before he kissed her.

Mari rested her head on his shoulder. "Hugh would be alive."

With a sudden fierceness, Callum sat up and pulled her up by the shoulders. "I forbid you to talk—or even think that again. Do you ken?"

"Aye," she said in a whisper. She had never seen him like this.

"You are not to blame. I forbid you to take on that burden." His stern gaze burned into her.

"But I miss him so," she said, as tears spilled from her sorrowful eyes.

"*Och*, I miss him too." He gently pulled her to his chest and rested his palm on the back of her head. "I've kent Hughie since he was a bairn and I was a wee lad. His great strengths were his flaws. He was trusting and kind."

"And too good to deserve such a young death."

"Aye, but you cannae live your life looking back. How could you have known it would happen? We could think all the day long how he might have been spared, but at days' end, he cannae come back to us. To wonder otherwise is a cruel game that no one can win."

Mari looked into eyes that bore such a somber expression. "How did you become so wise?"

"I learned in one quick lesson." Deep pain haunted his expression.

Mari listened.

"My brother died." He glanced at her, and then looked off toward distant memories. "Losing Hugh brings my brother to mind, I suppose. Robbie was different. He thought and felt deeply. My brother and I were born on the wrong side of the blanket. If anyone tried to remind me, I made them regret it. But Robbie was different. When lads said things, it hurt, but he wouldnae fight back. I dinnae ken why, but the others wouldnae leave him alone."

"Even Duncan? And Charlie and Alex?"

"Nae, but they didnae stop anyone, either." Callum swallowed. "Nor did I.

"I just told him to fight them. He was younger. I should have protected him. But he was bigger and stronger than any of them, so I thought it would toughen him up. But he didnae fight back.

"One day, he flew out of the byre on his horse. I jumped out of the way, and I cursed him."

Callum did not speak for a while. His jaw clenched. Mari put her hand on his shoulder.

He glanced at her and went on. "He didnae come home. We found him the next day hanging from a tree."

Mari choked tears back.

Callum said, "For years I would ask myself, what if I'd stopped them, or said something to Robbie? Why did I not go after him? The last thing he heard anyone say was my cursing. And no matter what I might have done, Robbie was dead. I couldnae bring him back."

"So when you saw me that day at the cliff, you saved me."

His dark gaze met hers. "Aye, I found you in time."

"And you made my life better than it could have been."

"I wasnae looking for a wife at the time," he said, with an unexpected grin which soon faded. "But I saw you at the edge of that cliff, and I was determined to stop you. That's all I wanted. Until I spoke with you."

"I dinnae recall saying anything special."

"No. I suppose I was won over by your kicking and clawing." Callum grinned.

With a self-conscious smile, Mari said, "Aye. How could you not have been charmed?"

With a glint in his eye, he said, "Well, I saw enough emotion in the first two minutes I'd kent you to make me wonder what ten minutes more might bring."

"Oh that's what you thought, did you?"

"It's more what I felt. For by then, I was in love."

Mari put her arms about his neck and pressed her body to his. She whispered her love in his ear, and he took her mouth in a devouring kiss. So much had been lost to them both, but they'd found one another, and they would not let go.

CALLUM WOKE Mari with a light kiss before dawn. "Lass," he whispered into her ear. She stirred a bit, but drifted back to sleep. He moved to her mouth, kissing and whispering, "Mari, my love."

Mari smiled and kissed him. "Not yet," she said, pulling him toward her.

He grinned, tempted, yet knowing that farmers rose

early. But when Mari swung her leg over and climbed atop him, he chose not to deny her. When, some minutes later, they both were blissfully awake, they both heard footsteps outside.

With a curse, Callum said, "Time to go, lass!" They scrambled to saddle and mount their horses. As the byre door opened, the farmer jumped aside as two riders on horseback galloped out of the byre toward the hills beyond.

When they were far enough from the farm to be safe, Mari surprised Callum by racing past him with a joyous laugh. He caught up and rode beside her across an open stretch, until he had to spoil her fun by leading her back onto their route.

"We'll follow the drovers' roads into the highlands. There's a more direct military road, but we dinnae want to risk a chance meeting with the king's men."

So they veered away from the path they were on and crossed over the gentle slopes of fields. Mari shocked Callum by jumping a hedgerow.

He raced to catch up. "God's teeth, lass! I didnae know you could ride like that."

"And how would you?" she said with a bright smile. "But I can!" She urged her horse to go faster as she laughed over her shoulder.

When they slowed down at last, Callum took the lead, and they soon found themselves on a drovers' road.

As the sun rose well into the sky, Mari said, "*Och!* Callum! Are you not hungry?"

"Aye. It's a shame we've so little to eat."

"What? Did we not bring food with us? I thought I saw—"

"Eggs?" Callum pulled a fresh egg from his pocket.

"Where did you get that? Well, I ken where. But when?"

"I went for a walk in the morning and found them."

"Found them?"

"Aye. Under a hen."

"You're a terrible, thieving man, Callum MacDonell."

"Aye. So I dinnae suppose you would stoop to eat one of these. What a shame, for I have six."

"Six eggs!"

Aye," he said, feigning remorse with a frown.

"Your penance is to cook them," she said, leaving the path and heading toward the sound of a burn.

Sometime after they had cooked and eaten the eggs, they were packed up and ready to go when Callum grabbed Mari's wrist and yanked her close beside him, with his finger to his lips. They stood still and waited as the rattling sound of a wagon approached, and then passed them and rode down the road.

Through some overgrown brambles, Mari caught a glimpse of grain sacks on the back of a wagon.

Callum whispered, "It's only a peddler, but we dinnae want to be seen. Mind, I'm still an escaped prisoner, so we wouldnae want him to tell the wrong folk that he's seen us."

They walked parallel to the road for a mile or so to be sure they would not be seen over the hedge wall that lined this stretch of the road. Then they mounted their horses and rode on.

The sun burned high in the sky when he asked, "Are you hungry, lass?" His broad smile proved he knew the answer.

Her answering look left no doubt.

"When we get to Crieff, there's a drover's inn there. We can give the horses a rest while we have a hot meal. If you like, we could sleep there."

"If I like?" Mari rubbed her back and shifted her weight in the saddle. "I've never ridden so much. I may not be able to walk if ever we do stop."

"Dinnae worry, Mistress MacDonell. I can carry you up to our bed."

She flashed a wide-eyed look just in time to see him wink and smile. Her admonishing look soon spread into a smile as she warmed under his gaze. She found herself suddenly keen to reach Crieff.

A MIST ROLLED in and rain soon fell in sheets as they rode into Crieff. The drover's inn was a stone building darkened outside by the rain and made darker inside by the soot-stained oak ceiling. The low rumble of talk came to a halt as they walked in and looked for a table. Callum held Mari's hand with a sure grip and walked to the bar, where he got two tankards of ale. He then led the way to a table not far from the fire, where they warmed away the chill of the rain. A grand fire crackled inside the stone fireplace that ran the length of the wall, floor to ceiling. Mari took off the drenched plaid wrapped about her shoulders and dress, and draped it over her chair. In her weary state, the flames soon held her rapt in their flickering warmth.

Callum studied Mari, with her weary expression, and lay his hand on hers for a moment before he got up and

went to the barkeep to ask for a room. As a shadow overtook her, she smiled and looked up. But it was not Callum
who stood beside her. Instead, there stood a hulking man
who appraised her and smiled and then stood by the fire
with his hands outstretched toward the warmth.

Callum eyed the man as he returned and sat down.
"Wife." Mari looked up quizzically at Callum. He had
never called her wife as though it were her name. He
leaned closer and added in quieter tones, "We've a room."
Callum warmed Mari's chilled hands in his and leaned
closer. "Drink up, love," he said. "It's overly crowded in
here. We'll sup quickly and then away to our room when
it's ready."

A barmaid brought two bowls of beef pottage and
bread with fresh butter. She smiled warmly at Callum as
she set down Mari's bowl. She proceeded to arrange every
item on the table, taking care to lean down to afford
Callum full view of the plump bosom that swelled from
her bodice. As she stood, she faced Callum, with her
shoulder to Mari. With a light touch to her bodice as
though smoothing it down, she looked into his eyes and
said softly, "If there's anything else I can do for you, you
need only ask. I work very late."

"Thank you," he said, promptly turning to Mari and
smiling. The girl lingered for a moment of wistful longing, and then walked away.

Mari was too tired to be even the least bit amused. But
thoughts of the barmaid soon faded as she savored the hot
food. Callum ate, but kept stock of the room, every
window and door, and each person between. It was not a
large inn, and had quickly filled up as travelers sought

shelter from the driving rain outside. The man by the fire returned to the bar and remained there. Mari's eyes drifted closed.

"Mari, love."

She awoke with a start. Her startled look charmed Callum. He could not help but grin. He stood and offered his hand. Mari took it and followed.

Their room was a small one, with mattresses stuffed with hay. While Callum bolted the door, Mari pulled back the quilt and was about to climb in when Callum crept up behind her and said, "It wouldnae be healthy to sleep in damp clothing. Here, love, let me help you." He proceeded to remove each item of clothing with caresses and kisses, but she barely responded. With a hopeless grin, he picked up the pace and had her in bed moments later. Callum unbelted his plaid and climbed into bed beside her. Mari nestled against him and, exhausted, fell soundly asleep.

CALLUM WOKE and found Mari awake. He watched her as the rain drizzled outside. "Come, love. Let me ease those dark thoughts of yours." He nuzzled into the crook of her neck and brushed soft lips along her collarbone as he slid his hand to the hem of her shift and gathered the fabric in folds. "*Och*, lass. I cannae touch you enough." As his touch quickened her breathing, he rolled onto her. They panted and breathed out deep sighs full of all they had kept safe in their hearts during the long, lonely months they had loved alone and apart. Long after, they held on, entwined and complete. Callum watched a tear trail down Mari's temple and brushed it aside.

"'Twas a long time alone," Callum said in a low throaty whisper.

"Aye, love." She turned and rested her head on his shoulder.

Chapter 28

The Blackhouse by the Sea

The drovers' roads avoided the towns, which suited Callum's plans for travel. At this time of the year, they would meet with no drovers and few travelers, all the while staying clear of gathering places where they might draw undue notice. From time to time they would veer off of the road to avoid other travelers. When encounters could not be avoided, they simply rode past and did nothing to draw undue notice.

After eight days of hard travel, they followed a path through the trees that lined the shores of Loch Oich. They were looking into the hills for the castle when Callum held out his hand to signal Mari to stop.

"Ho, there, strangers!" From the dark shelter of trees rode three well-armed men.

The one in the lead said, "For a man with the face of a six-month-old old tattie, 'tis a gey bonnie lassie he travels with."

The others offered grunts of approval until they were interrupted.

"Aye, my wife is gey bonnie, and my fist is gey strong, so we'll not be discussing it further," Callum said with a stern look, but a glint in his eye. The three men laughed as they sheathed their swords and came closer.

"We were fishing, but this is a far finer catch than we'd hoped for."

Callum smiled and introduced Mari to Ranald, and then to his companions, Ivar and Sandy. Although the men focused their attention at Callum, they were keenly aware of the woman with him, and made no secret of staring with admiration when conversation allowed. If their attention before had been unsettling, Mari found their current scrutiny almost unbearable.

"Go to, lads. Cease with your stares at my wife, and let us be on our way. We're in need of a meal and some rest."

With final admiring glances at Mari, the men turned and led the way to Invergarry Castle.

As they caught first sight of the castle, Mari looked at Callum, amazed. "This is your home?"

"I grew up here, but it isnae my home anymore."

"You will always be welcome here," Ranald said, with a direct look at Callum.

Callum smiled in return, but Mari saw it was forced. He leaned toward her and explained, "Someday these lands will be Ranald's. He's the Glengarry's cousin and heir."

"Aye." Ranald nodded toward Mari with a roguish smile that made her mistrust him. "But you'll not be far away, will you, Callum?"

Callum smiled almost sincerely as Ranald rode on to catch up with his men.

Callum turned to Mari and said, "The chief granted me land on Loch Garry. I'd begun building a home before we left for the lowlands."

"He granted you lands?"

"Aye. I am his son."

"You are? But if you are his son..."

"Aye, well, I am not his heir." He watched her, patiently waiting for her to catch hold of his meaning. "My mother was not his wife."

She raised her brows and said, "Oh."

"Does it bother you, Mari—that you've married a bastard?"

She looked at him frankly. "Do you not recall how you met me? Have I reason to judge?"

He half-smiled, but remained serious. "He acknowledges me as his son. Even if he did not, everyone knows it. But I willnae inherit. I've little to offer to you except what he has given to me." He studied her, giving her time to absorb it. "I'm sorry, Mari."

Mari glanced over to him as he rode alongside her. "You're sorry? You rescued me from a shame of my own doing. You gave me love, a home, and a family, and you're sorry?" She smiled warmly. "I am not."

Callum drew close beside her and gave her hand a squeeze, and then they rode on to the castle.

No one arrived by surprise at Invergarry Castle. Scouts had seen them approaching for miles. Callum had expected an escort to greet them. What he had not expected was for it to be led by the chief, whom most called Glengarry.

"Lord MacDonell and Aros," said Callum.

"Callum, lad," said the chief, with a warm smile. Callum was his only son, a son whom he seemed more than willing to treat as his own. Mari saw deep warmth in his eyes as he greeted Callum. Lady MacDonell soon joined her husband with welcoming words, but hers were decidedly cool.

The chief said, "Come, lad, dismount. Let us talk."

With a nod, Callum dismounted. The chief turned to assist his lady wife down from her horse with care. As she set her feet on the ground, Mari saw what the folds of fabric had until now concealed. She was with child, a fact which, she saw with a glance, had not escaped Callum's notice.

Callum took a step toward the woods, but stopped as Glengarry took both of Mari's hands in his and smiled at her warmly. "Welcome to Glengarry." He turned to Callum. "She's a beauty, lad."

"Aye," Callum said, pausing and turning to Mari with glowing regard.

But Mari could not help but wonder what sort of welcome this was, on the road leading up to the castle. The chief had to understand they were weary from riding, and would be in need of rest and refreshment, and yet none were offered.

While Glengarry exchanged conversation with Callum, Ranald and his men lingered within sight, but just out of earshot. Lady MacDonell watched her husband with his son. Mari could not help but wonder at how she viewed Callum. A woman in Lady MacDonell's position was expected to provide her Lord and husband with a son and heir, but she had not. Callum must be, for her, a reminder of this personal failing, not to mention her husband's infidelity. The weight of this seemed to have taken its toll on her countenance over the years. Although clearly a beauty at one time, her eyes held little light and her lips were drawn slightly down at the corners, all of which left her looking quite grim. Mari wondered how much of the decision not to name Callum as heir was the result of Lady MacDonell's influence. A man's guilt could be a powerful lever when artfully manipulated. In this case it would be at Callum's expense.

As it was bound to, given the circumstances of their unusual meeting outside of the castle, the conversation faded. Awkward silence stretched out until, at last, the chief pointedly said, "You're a wanted man, Callum."

Callum's eyes widened, but he otherwise hid his surprise. "Aye, I am."

With a wry smile, Glengarry said, "There's little that doesnae reach me sooner or later."

"Aye, that doesnae surprise me."

"But I dinnae ken your side of it, lad."

Callum told him the full story of how he had taken the place of an escaped prisoner, leaving out the fact that it was Mari's brother. Glengarry showed little reaction, for most of the story had been reported to him. When Callum was finished, Glengarry said, "What you did was a noble thing, taking the place of young Hugh. I admire you for it. But still, in the eyes of the King, you're an escaped prisoner."

Callum nodded. "A fugitive. Aye, I am that."

The chief looked him in the eye. He was well-practiced at concealing emotion, so his warm look spoke more than his words. "And I cannae harbor a known fugitive in my home."

Callum nodded.

Although others would miss it from this far, Mari saw a change in Callum's demeanor.

With a firm hand on Callum's shoulder, the chief led him away from the others, while Mari lingered behind with Lady MacDonell. They spoke of the beauty of the area, the loch in particular, anything but what was foremost in their minds. Mari imagined herself in Lady MacDonell's position, and decided that she was more gracious than Mari might have been. She found herself warming to Lady MacDonell, if only out of compassion.

"Lad, if I welcome you home I defy the King, and that is something I cannae do."

Callum nodded. As much as he might understand, it hurt to know he was no longer welcome at home.

The chief went on, "If questioned by the crown, I'll deny having seen you. And I'll deny giving you leave to remain on my land, ken?"

Callum nodded. "I've been on my own for a long time." He looked away, lest his face accuse even more than his words.

This was not lost on the chief, but he ignored it. "If you keep going west, there's a croft by the sea where you can bide." Anyone looking on would have seen Glengarry reach out and grasp Callum's hand. They would not have seen the pouch of coins that he pressed into Callum's hand.

"No, my Lord. I cannae take that."

"You can and you will. You fought hard for the clan, and we owe you your due. It's your pay. Take it, lad."

Callum did, with his thanks. But the mention of fighting was only a painful reminder that he would no longer fight for his clan. Fighting was the one thing he had done well. It had brought honor to him and the memory of his mother, as well as the clan. Now he was wanted by the very men who had fought by his side. He had come down in the world, and brought Mari down with him.

Callum returned to Mari's side and said farewell to the Lady MacDonell, and once more thanked Glengarry.

As they rode away, Mari said, "I suppose he was as kind as one could expect, given the circumstances."

"Aye," Callum answered, but his brooding silence said otherwise.

"And the Lady MacDonell?"

"What of her?"

"Was it not kind of her to come with him to greet us?"

"Kind? I think not."

"Oh?"

"She tolerates my existence, but only because she has little choice. No, she was here to make sure that I saw she was pregnant."

Before Mari could say more, Callum said, "That's Nellie's cottage there."

The chief gave them leave to linger long enough to tell Nellie the sad news of Hugh's death, and then they were forced to move on, leaving her to her grief and the comfort of friends. She was not alone, but it saddened them to leave her, broken and weeping, behind them.

THEY RODE CAREFULLY over hills and rugged terrain. Callum's only words were warnings about difficult spots here and there. Mari followed and tried not to think of what troubled her most. The day before had brought unexpected revelations about Callum's background, made worse by the reception they had received at the castle. The fact that he was illegitimate concerned her least of all. That he had withheld this troubled her more. She had always been honest with him, and expected the same in return. And yet, had she borne a child, what would her own child have endured? And how would it have shaped him? She could not judge Callum too harshly for hiding what had been the source of childhood heartache, for it was that very childhood burden that had led him to not judge her pregnancy harshly.

Unused to long journeys on horseback, Mari's patience wore thin. By the time the ground leveled out, deep fatigue had set in. Hours of rough riding and troubling thoughts had taken their toll. Mari swatted a bothersome tree branch away and cried out in frustration, "Might I ever ken where we are going? Or at least might we ride on a path, for a change?" All that she had held back rushed out with a harshness she had not intended. When Callum turned to answer, she saw how weary and preoccupied he was. She now regretted her tone.

"Aye. We're to go to a croft by the sea. It's far enough that no one will find us without someone coming ahead to warn us to move on."

Callum said little else, but dark thoughts shaded his

expression. The sun sank to the horizon, and the horses needed rest. They stopped to make camp for the night.

Callum sat alone on a fallen tree trunk by a burn. The water rushed along, finding its way over the small rocks and around the large boulders.

Mari left him alone for as long as she could. Unable to bear it any longer, she sat down beside him.

The words choked in his throat. "I'm sorry, lass." He would not turn to face her.

"And why are you sorry?"

"I've let you down."

Mari took his face in her hands and forced him to look in her eyes. "Callum MacDonell, you willnae talk so. What you did for Hugh was the right thing. And let us not forget that it was my brother whose actions forced you to it. You promised to take care of Hugh, and you did."

Callum turned with a guttural scoff. "A fine job I did of that."

Mari recalled Nellie's cry upon hearing of Hughie's death, and the pain in Callum's eyes at having brought such news to her. "But Callum, what could you have done? You are but one man."

Callum stared at the water that rushed over the rocks of the burn.

Mari took his hand in both of hers. "Callum, my love, everything that you've done since I've known you has been the right thing." When he did not reply, she said, "You married me." Tears pooled in her eyes. "And I married you, everything that you are, because you are part of my soul. So I'll hear no more talk of your letting me down."

He did not move, except to tighten his hand about hers.

Mari said sternly, "You'd best kiss me now, or I will make you sorry."

With that, Callum smiled and swept Mari into his arms.

THE NEXT DAY they rode through long stretches of quiet. Mari watched Callum. Although he thought he concealed it, his disposition had improved little from the day before.

Mari's thoughts went to the source. "The chief seemed to think highly of you."

Callum merely offered a brief sideways glance.

Mari went on. "But Lady MacDonell is rather aloof, is she not?"

"She is that," he said, seeming annoyed, though whether with Mari or the mere thought of Lady MacDonell, Mari could not quite determine. One thing she was sure of was that Callum was in a dark mood, one that he was not eager to share with her.

"We'll stop over there by the water," he said, changing the subject.

With that, the discussion abruptly ended. Mari set her mind on preparing food. The horses drank from the cool water of the burn and then grazed while Mari and Callum shared some bannocks and ale that the chief had sent with them. Callum withdrew further. When she could take no more, Mari got up to go walking alone. Callum clasped hold of her hand. "Wait. I'll come with you."

Without a glance, Mari nodded. She would not stop him, but she found his heavy mood hard to bear and wished to be free of it. They walked for a bit, until Callum paused by a thick oak and pulled Mari beside him to lean against it. He stared at the sky, which showed hints of gray through the clouds.

"I'd intended to tell you as we approached the castle, but the chief met us before I had the chance." He shook his head. "I should have told you long before that."

Mari studied his face as he struggled to tell her what burdened him so. He looked so remote as to be out of reach. The next moment, he looked at her and softened to melancholy that made her heart ache.

Callum said, "My mother and father were childhood playmates. They grew up together. My mother once told me she did not recall falling in love because it always was there. When they grew old enough, they were lovers."

Mari had not realized how heavy Callum's burden felt on her shoulders until now. She was relieved just to lean back and listen.

"Life in the Highlands is different. Peace is fragile. Our life depends upon the strength of the clan and our loyalty to it. I know that, for you, we must seem very coarse. But what you dinnae see is the cord that ties all of us to one another. We live and die for each other. It is in our blood. A man's honor means everything here, and my father understood his. He had a duty to his people from which he couldnae—he wouldnae—shrink."

Mari knew Callum. As much as he might have believed what he said, she saw how doubt gnawed within him, never healing. Had it truly been duty that drove his father's decision, or had he chosen the life he preferred?

"My mother was pregnant with me when he told her of his upcoming marriage."

Mari thought back upon her first meeting with Callum. Most men would have viewed her with disdain for her pregnant condition, but he never had. He had never questioned her worth, or even her virtue, for having been with another man first. Now she understood better the ease with which he was able to love her with no regard to her past.

Callum went on. "His marriage was arranged. There was no turning back. At least, that's how he saw it. My mother defended his choice to the end. But the truth was, she was lonely.

"He didnae lie to her—or to his wife. Lady MacDonell always knew about my mother. On their wedding night, he warned her not to love him. But she did. And she hated my mother."

"It must have been hard for her."

He cast a sharp look that softened at once. "Aye, and for us. Not long after his wife lost her first child, my brother was born. He was healthy. My mother was happy. And Lady MacDonell was not. She lost another child, and then another. And then the pregnancies stopped. And all along there we were, my brother and I, to remind her of how she had failed to produce an heir for my father. The chief was good to his wife, but he never stopped loving my mother."

"And you?"

Callum smiled with a haunting pain in his eyes. "*Och*, I suppose that he loved me too, in his way. But Lady MacDonell played on his guilt, so he never dared show it. She made sure that everyone knew that my brother and I were bastards. And they didnae forget—nor did the lads we would play with and train with. We grew up with the taunting, and I learned to fight. But my brother had a gentler soul. And in time it killed him. After he took his own life, my mother was never quite the same. She lived on for a few years more, but it had broken her spirit."

Mari touched his hand and he closed it around hers.

"She deserved more. And yet, as she lay dying, she said she had loved and been loved, and had borne two fine sons. Her life and her heart had been full." A bitter look clouded his face. "But my father was not there even then. She died alone."

"Callum," Mari said, wanting to tell him how sorry she was, and to promise that he would not be alone. She would love him forever. But he held her and kissed her before she could say it, and somehow the words were no longer needed.

Callum took Mari's hand and led the way back to camp. "So you see, Lady MacDonell would not have missed the chance to ride out to greet us. Not only was she able to show me that she was pregnant, she was able to watch the chief send me away. After long years of waiting, she finally saw me get put in my place."

"Callum," Mari started to disagree, but looking back, she could not.

His voice had a hard edge as he said, "She need not have bothered. I've been reminded of it every day of my life. I will never forget what I am."

THEY ARRIVED at the blackhouse by the sea. There they found peace, warming themselves and each other beside the peat fire in the center of the room. They lived off the oats and smoked beef that the chief had sent with them. After a month, he sent a cow and more food to last them until spring came and they could gather their own. Sporadic days of sun grew more frequent until the spring came. They walked the heath, gathering wild sorrel and nettles, and fishing for salmon and trout in the river. Callum dug peat, and Mari helped bring it back to the house, where they stacked it for fires and to fill in the gaps in the rock walls. She made butter and cheese while Callum hung fish from the roof to smoke over the fire. Summer came and brought long days of sea breezes and sun, and cool mists when it rained. Life was simple and full.

They had been through a long stretch of rain when one morning the sun shone through a thick mist. Mari finished feeding the cow, and they went for a walk to decide if the weather might be sunny enough to make hay.

"No, it's too wet. I'll go fishing instead," Callum said with a look toward the sea.

"The raspberries are ripe. Would you fancy a raspberry cranachan when you come back from your fishing?"

Callum scooped his arm about Mari's waist. "That's not all that I'd fancy," he said as he pulled her against him and kissed her. And there, in the field, he unfastened her bodice and growled into her ear, "Mari, love. It's a shame that the ground is so wet, or I'd take you right here. But that tree over there looks inviting." With a wicked grin, he scooped her into his arms and carried her over to the tree, where he set her down gently, leaning her back to the tree.

"And what about your fishing?" she whispered, as he stroked her earlobe with his tongue. A light gasp slipped out. "And the berries?" It came out as a weak sigh at best.

"Stop talking," he whispered into her neck as he worked his way down the newly parted bodice to the edge of her corset.

She smoothed her hands up his thighs until he groaned and buried his face in her breasts.

As he hoisted her up with her legs wrapped around him, she gave in to the pulse of his body against hers. How she had missed the fit of their flesh together, and his unabashed fervor.

As she caught her breath, he tenderly set her down. "You've made me weak in the knees," she said with a laugh as she tightened her grip on his shoulder.

He smiled. "I'll not let you fall. If I did, I might not get that raspberry cranachan you've promised."

"Oh, I see! So you're just after my cooking?"

He could not help grinning. "Something akin to that. Although you are a fair bonnie lassie. Come gie us another kiss."

"If you were not so handsome, I'd never put up with you!"

"Aye, but I am, no?" He grinned.

"Aye, and modest!" With a light laugh, she picked up her basket and shooed him away. "Go catch us some supper while I pick some fine berries."

"*Och*, lass. Would you send me away?"

"Aye, I would," she said as she set out. With a sudden stop, she said quietly, "Callum."

He went to her side.

"Do you see something there? In the mist?" she asked.

In an instant, Callum pulled Mari behind him and pulled out his dirk. "Hie you inside, Mari."

"Not without you!"

"Mind me, lass. Climb the ladder up into the rafters and hide yourself there until I come for you."

His stern tone and strong arm sent her back to the cottage as two horsemen thundered out of the mist and headed straight for Callum.

Chapter 29

The Legacy

Callum steeled himself, gripping his dirk. Defensive moves raced through his mind. He had to keep himself between the horsemen and Mari. He could use his agility to his advantage, but against two horsemen, that would only get him so far. He could shift direction to dodge their blows, at least for a while, but he was in the more vulnerable position. He knew it well, as would they. His mind raced.

"You'll be wanting this," Mari said, as she put his basket hilt sword in his hands.

"You're a brave one, Mari MacDonell." With a proud look, he said, "Now get back inside."

"I've a dirk, and I'll use it before I go back inside." As she spoke, her eyes remained set on the horsemen's approach. "Callum? Are those—"

"Aye." He started to laugh. "MacDonell plaids. Aye, that they are."

Mari ran up to greet them as Alex and Charlie dismounted. Alex first caught Mari in an embrace, and then released her to Charlie. She hesitated, unsure of how he would receive her after the way they had parted. Her doubts vanished as he offered a warm smile and open arms.

"Come here, dearie."

After a hug that put tensions behind them, she said, "*Och*, look at the two of you. Come in and rest, and I'll get you some ale. Are you hungry? Of course you are." She arranged herself between the two men and hooked her arms through theirs as she led them inside. "I'm so happy to see you!"

"Mari," said Charlie, as she sat him down at the table.

Mari was too excited to hear the serious tone in his voice. "Did you go by the castle? Of course you did. How is Nellie?"

"Mari," Charlie repeated, a bit louder.

She looked at him with surprise, but his look told her that something was not right. Her eyes flashed to Alex, who was silently watching her, with a somber look that alarmed her.

Callum watched and drew close beside Mari.

Alex met Mari's gaze with a directness that made her shudder. "Your brother's dead, Mari."

She did not move, nor did anyone else. Having seen death and brought news of it before, they knew better than to speak yet. Mari seemed not to have heard him.

Callum took hold of her arm. "Come, lass. Let's sit down."

Mari looked at Alex, and then Charlie. "Did you kill him?"

Charlie met her eyes squarely. "I tried to."

Mari started to nod slowly.

"Alex stopped me," said Charlie.

Her eyes darted to Alex, who looked downward.

Charlie's words caught in his throat. "Jamie was there at Airds Moss. He had joined up with Cameron. They were praying." Charlie shook his head, not believing.

Alex said, "Our orders were to surround them. Barely a man escaped."

Mari said, "And how did he die?" She looked plainly from one to the other. "Just tell me."

Charlie said, "I dinnae do it, if that's what you're thinking. I would have, but Alex stopped me. I'm sorry, Mari, but he killed my brother. I had my dirk at his throat, but Alex reminded me that we had to take him back to Edinburgh. We needed to return him so Jamie could take his rightful place in prison. Then Callum would be free."

"And we did that," said Alex. "We took him back, and secured your freedom, Callum."

Callum gave a slight nod to Alex, but said nothing out of deference to Mari. Regardless of what Jamie had done, he was Mari's brother, for whom she was grieving. He would not express his own joy at her brother's expense, but he let Alex know with a look that he was deeply grateful.

Alex went on. "We were sure he would get transportation, his original sentence."

"But he didnae," said Mari softly.

Alex shook his head grimly.

Charlie said, "Airds Moss was a bloody business. They cut off Cameron's head, and—"

"We dinnae need all the details," said Callum, his eyes darting toward Mari.

"When we got back to Edinburgh, Jamie was put on

trial." Alex lifted sympathetic eyes to Mari's. "He was sentenced to death."

"Oh, Jamie." Callum guided Mari to a chair. "All alone."

Charlie said, "It all happened so fast. We couldnae get here to tell you and bring you to him. But your parents were there."

Startled, Mari looked up. "Were they?"

Alex said, "Aye. He didnae die alone."

"Good," Mari said, but an odd look came over her. Callum took hold of her shoulders. "Mari, lass?"

"For all that he's done, with all the men he has killed, they went to him." She tried to fathom it. "With Jamie, no sin was too great for their forgiveness." Her lips spread, almost smiling. "But for falling in love, I am dead to the people I love. At least Jamie died with their love. They left me with no family."

Callum said quietly, "Except us."

IN AN EFFORT TO get her mind off her grief, Mari spent the afternoon staying busy. She went out to get berries and came back to cook. The men went fishing for supper and returned ready for the mugs of ale Callum kept filled. When the eating was done, the talk turned to the future. In the fire's warm glow, Mari set her mind toward happier matters. It was good to see Alex and Charlie. Although it hurt to think of Charlie with a knife at Jamie's throat, she knew he had fresh in his mind the vision of Hugh's death by her brother's hand. As much as Jamie's death grieved her, Hughie's grieved her as well. She could not fault Charlie for harboring bitter feelings. They had done the right thing in bringing Jamie to justice to restore Callum's freedom. Mari could not blame them for a result no one would have expected. Perhaps Callum was right. They were family, and family forgave if they were to stay together. She needed to feel there was family about her. She glanced around the table at the men as they laughed over something she'd missed. The three men looked so happy. She would always miss Jamie and her parents, but this was her family now.

The men spoke of more cheerful matters. "It was Glengarry who did it," said Alex.

Callum lifted his chin and stared, unbelieving.

"Aye, when he learned of Jamie's capture, he dispatched a letter to each man on the Edinburgh Privy Council. The man isnae without influence. Your pardon was signed and then we were charged with delivering it back to Invergarry."

Callum leaned back. "Glengarry did that for me?"

Alex nodded, content to see how much the news must mean to Callum.

Callum reached over and grasped Mari's hand. "No more hiding, my love. We can go wherever we want."

She looked at him, and shared not only relief, but new hope for the future. Their lives could move forward.

Callum said, "Where shall we go, lassie?"

"Invergarry," said Charlie.

"I was not asking you," Callum said with an arch look. "Unless you answer to 'lassie' now."

Alex leaned back and laughed. "What a bonnie lassie he'd make."

"Aye, far more bonnie than any lass who would have you," Charlie said, with a sideways glance.

Alex grinned, and turned to Callum. "I hadnae meant discuss it this evening, but the subject seems to have come up." He rolled his eyes in Charlie's direction. "I ken that you've had enough news for one night." Alex paused.

"May as well tell me now," said Callum.

Mari slipped her hand into the crook of Callum's arm, where it leaned on the table.

"Lady MacDonell died a sennight ago," said Charlie.

"I'm so sorry to hear it." Mari slipped her arm into Callum's, whose somber expression conveyed his conflicting emotions. Both he and his mother had suffered at the bidding of Lady MacDonell.

Mari asked, "What of the bairn?"

Alex said, "The wee thing was stillborn, and his mother was gone the next day."

"A son? She once told me, when she thought I was too young to remember, that one day she would have a son. And when she did, the chief would forget all about me."

Unable to hide her dismay, Mari looked to the others, excepting the same. But she saw from their faces that this was not news. "She must have been so unhappy to say such a thing."

"Aye, but she had no cause to make a child suffer for it. And suffer I did." Callum showed little emotion, but it was there underneath.

Mari stroked Callum's arm, wanting to soothe him, but he covered her hand with his.

"And how fares Glengarry?" said Callum.

"He's not been himself," Alex said.

Mari nodded. "Understandably."

"Aye, true enough." Alex studied his interlaced hands for a moment, and then looked up at Callum. "We're to bring you back with us."

WHEN THEY ARRIVED AT GLENGARRY, the chief greeted them, shared a meal, and retired to his rooms. Callum did his best to conceal his surprise when he and Mari were given a room in the castle. While Lady MacDonell was alive, he had never been invited to stay in the castle. He had never dared hope for this sudden inclusion in castle life. Even so, the chief spoke little to them, and never of why they were here or how long they would remain.

In the days that followed, The Glengarry was scarce, grieving alone and not leaving his rooms except to oversee the most pressing matters. But the days passed, and he emerged from his grief and began to spend time with the people around him. On one such evening, he invited Mari and Callum to the solar. The late summer night had grown cool. They had gathered about a large fire. A glowing log sparked and crackled.

Glengarry said simply, "I'd like you to stay."

Callum lifted his eyes toward his father's. His throat thickened with emotion. How many times over the years had he wished for these words?

"As my son," he added, meeting his eyes squarely.

"Aye?" Callum answered. He was too stunned to say more. He had spent his life as an outsider, a bastard. It had shaped who he was as a man. He had turned years of emptiness and sometimes ridicule into strength of heart, mind and body. And now, when he had finally resolved who he was as a man, he was given the chance to be something he had not dreamed of since childhood: Glengarry's son.

"Think on it," said his father.

Callum nodded. He could not shake the feeling that there was something more. It was in Glengarry's manner, something to which Callum had become attuned over the years. He chastised himself for being so reluctant to trust. After all, it was a simple offer. And why would Glengarry not long to have family about him?

"You honor me, sir."

LATER, a fire warmed the night air as the men sat about it outside on a bright moonlit night. Mari had gone to sleep, but Callum was restless. He came to join them with a sudden longing for their simple life as dragoons, when few problems loomed from one day to the next. He told them of his father's offer. They were not surprised.

Charlie said, "When we were sent to bring you back, we expected it. After all, he's lost his only heir."

"Only legitimate heir," Alex corrected. "There are rumblings in the clan. The chief knows this and wants to secure the clan's peace and stability after he's gone."

"Is he ill?" Callum asked.

"No, but the death of a loved one reminds us of our own mortality, and I think he is weary. He wants someone to keep the clan together in peace."

"Ranald could do it," said Callum.

"Aye. So could you."

Callum met Alex's eyes, but could not share his confidence.

Charlie said, "There is talk that Clan MacKenzie would attack, given the chance."

Callum said, "*Och*, that talk has gone on for the last hundred years."

Alex raised an eyebrow. "Aye, well, when you trap a congregation in their kirk and send your piper marching about it merrily playing a tune while it burns to the ground, people tend to hold a wee grudge."

They all stared into the fire in silence. It had not been their clan's finest hour.

Callum said, "Leaders do terrible things."

"And sometimes they do great things," said Alex. "That choice would be yours." He looked at Callum with confidence.

GRAY and misty days followed in which Callum spent hours with the chief learning about the workings of the castle and clan. Mari thought she should be learning as well about running a household, but whenever she broached the subject the chief put her off, so Mari felt idle and restless. When the sun at last rose, Callum took her out riding. It was a crisp autumn day, and the hills were brilliant with color. At a sunny clearing beside the loch, they stopped and spread out a spare plaid that Callum had brought. Mari leaned back into Callum's cradling arms and they stared at the loch and the hills, and they talked. Despite how busy Glengarry had kept Callum, Mari was happy to see him forming a bond with his father and finding his place in the world.

"And what of you, love? How is your life here?"

She rested her head on his chest. "It is quiet and good to watch you. You are where you belong."

He smiled gently. "Am I?"

"Aye."

"I belong beside you, as well, and I've missed you, my Mari." He leaned down and breathed in the scent of her hair. Gently, he removed the combs that held it in place, until it cascaded in thick lengths that spilled over her shoulders. He combed his thick fingers through her hair and lifted enough to expose her bare neck. There he pressed soft lips upon it until Mari shivered.

"Are you cold?" He pulled the plaid over her shoulders.

With a warm look, Mari said, "No, not as long as you keep your arms about me just so." She nestled into his arms as she pivoted around and thoroughly kissed him. Her breath brushed his neck as she whispered, "I have missed you." She reached down and pulled his plaid up the length of his thighs. "And I've longed for you." She turned and straddled him. With a throaty growl, he gripped her hips as she guided him into her. His hands slid up to her breasts, and he fumbled to unfasten her bodice. With a curse, he curled his fingers over the edge of the fabric as Mari laughed lightly. She unfastened her clothing and bared herself to him. With a deep sigh, he brushed his hands over her satin skin, and then lifted her off him and lowered her onto her back. He touched her and watched her face flush with the bliss he brought her.

When Callum collapsed beside her, he lay his head on her shoulder and stretched his arm over her.

Late in the afternoon, Mari opened her eyes to see clouds rolling in over the sun. She stirred, and Callum awoke. "Now I'm cold," she said, pulling her clothing about her. She looked down and smiled wistfully at him as he watched her. "It's late."

"Aye." He sat up with a regretful sigh.

They shared a last lingering look, and then Callum patted her hand and they got up to leave. As Mari shook the plaid and began to fold it, he circled her waist and pulled her against him. "I love you," he whispered into her ear.

She returned his embrace. "I know. But you should continue to tell me—in case I forget."

"I'd rather show you."

Mari lifted her eyes and grinned. "You could do both."

And he did.

IN NO HURRY, they returned to the castle. But as they entered the bailey, there was a flurry of activity and new horses being led to the stable.

"Lad," called Callum to a young stable boy.

"Sir?" said the lad as he led two of the horses.

"What is all this?"

"Visitors." He lowered his voice and leaned closer. "MacKenzies."

Callum nodded and sent the boy on his way. He said to Mari, "MacKenzies dinnae just happen by to visit

MacDonells. This cannae be good." But as he looked about, everything looked as it should. There were no signs of alarm, or of guards preparing for battle.

As they were about to enter the great hall, one of Glengarry's men approached Callum. "Glengarry wishes to see the lass."

With a sharp look, Callum snapped, "The 'lass' is my wife. And you may call her Mistress MacDonell."

The man looked down. "Aye, sir. It was only what he said, so I—"

"So you now know better than to address her so."

"Aye, sorry, sir."

"Glengarry will see her inside, if you'll just let us pass," Callum said, losing his patience.

"He told me to bring her to the solar without you."

Callum took Mari's hand firmly in his. "Did he, now?"

"Aye, sir."

Charlie joined them and said quietly, "I heard him say it. I will go with her, if you like."

"Aye." Callum frowned.

Mari said, "Callum, I'm sure it is nothing. I've been asking when I would learn of my duties here. I am sure it is that, nothing more."

Callum considered for a moment, and then lifted her hand to his lips and released her into Charlie's care, but not without a look of caution to Charlie. After watching her walk down the hall on Charlie's arm, Callum turned and went into the great hall.

Chapter 30

The Arrangement

Glengarry spied Callum as soon as he entered and called him over to the fire. There, Callum was introduced to Lord Kenneth Mackenzie, 4th Earl of Seaforth and his sister, Lady Aemilia. Upon hearing her name, Aemilia turned from the fire to face him. She was a beauty, a very young one, with fair hair swept back from her face to reveal limpid eyes. Callum thought he saw something quite sad there, despite her cordial smile. As he went through the motions of greeting them and sitting together by the fire, Callum's mind was with Mari. She was by now in the solar, waiting to meet with Glengarry. Why had the chief sent her there, knowing that he would be here, along with Callum? But there was no time to guess at Glengarry's reasons, nor could they discuss them right now. In the best times, relations with MacKenzies were strained. If they were to form some sort of peaceful alliance, as appeared possible now, all parties would need to speak and act with great care.

Cousin Ranald stood guard at the door. He had made

himself scarce since Callum moved into the castle. Callum understood why, and was watchful of him. Callum had, after all, usurped Ranald as the heir apparent of Glengarry's power and fortune. Now that Callum was in line as the next clan chief, Ranald had to feel displaced at best, and resentful and bitter at worst. Now being relegated to guard duty must have been a harsh blow to receive, unless Ranald had volunteered for it. But the choice was a sound one on Glengarry's part. Ranald was Glengarry's finest warrior. Who better to have close when meeting with the enemy?

They had been sitting and talking of small matters. Their trip had been uneventful, which was always a good thing. They had talked of the weather. At last Glengarry turned to Callum. "Why dinnae you take Lady Aemilia outside for some air?"

Callum fought back the pained look that had instantly formed on his face. She had been riding most of a day from Castle Chanonry of Ross. If anything, the poor girl would be weary of fresh air, and in need of some rest. But Glengarry returned a strong look that cautioned him not to argue. So he offered his arm and led Lady Aemilia outdoors for a walk. Ranald followed closely behind. Whether to protect or to chaperone, Callum was uncertain. He was sure that it was not needed. They were within the well-guarded walls of the castle, made more so by additional men posted while the MacKenzies were here. A person could not go anywhere without being seen by at least one guard. If Ranald thought he was protecting the Lady Aemilia from Callum, then it was an insult. She was lovely, but so was his Mari, with whom he was deeply in love—Mari, his wife, who was trapped in the chief's solar on what seemed like a fool's errand. At least Charlie was with her and would entertain and look after her while she waited for Glengarry. However, if she was not downstairs by the time they returned from this walk, he would go to retrieve her.

Driven, no doubt, by Callum's silence, Lady Aemilia and Ranald had become engaged in some sort of idle conversation about the plants and the weather, or some such dull nonsense. Out of politeness, Callum made an effort to pay attention. Ranald surprised him with considerable knowledge of gardens and flowering herbs. He would not have expected it. She seemed quite entertained, a fact which also surprised him as he suppressed yet another yawn. As he watched Lady Aemilia's red curls bob as she spoke, his mind wandered to why she was there. MacKenzies did not simply visit MacDonells for the pleasure of their company. There was too much bad blood going back for generations. So what was the reason?

"Do you not agree, Sir Callum?"

Torn away from his thoughts, Callum looked at her, feeling at a loss. All he had heard was, "Sir Callum."

"I am not 'Sir' anything, Lady Aemilia."

She smiled sweetly and said, "Master MacDonell, then."

Just as Callum was thinking there was no end to her poise, she stifled a yawn.

"I'm so sorry!" She appeared truly shocked.

With a warm smile, he said, "My Lady, you have had a long trip, and a very long day. Shall we go inside and find someone to show you to your room? You will no doubt wish to rest before supper."

A broad and genuine smile bloomed. "Aye, I would. Thank you."

Callum felt Ranald's scrutiny and glanced toward him. Callum caught a dark look before Ranald's eyes darted away. Lady Aemilia followed the exchange and studied Ranald for a moment, and then took the arm Callum offered.

After Ranald headed off toward the stables, Callum found a housemaid to show Lady Aemilia to her room. Then he went up the back stairs to find Mari. He swung open the door and found Glengarry seated and watching her as she stood at the window. She smoothed her hands over her face and then turned to face him as he entered the room. He could read little in her expression, but her cheeks were moist with fresh tears. Callum rushed to her side. "What is it?"

With a light shake of her head, she looked at Glengarry, who appeared deeply concerned. He looked down, and then lifted his eyes to meet Callum's. "We've a chance to end the feud with the MacKenzies."

It should have been good news. Callum glanced at Mari, and then asked his father, "At what cost?"

Ignoring the question, Glengarry went on. "Ranald went to see Seaforth some time ago, and it looked like we might find common ground. But after Bothwell Brigg, MacKenzies sided with the Covenanters, and I'd let go of hope. But it seems, now that the fighting is over, he is willing to talk once more."

Callum said, "Aye, well that's good, is it not?" But he knew there was more. He was troubled, even more so when he took Mari's hand. She was trembling.

"Yes," Glengarry continued, "it's a good thing. But

alliances are never strong without blood—of one kind or the other. If we dinnae wish to spill blood, we must join the two bloodlines." He stopped and looked frankly at Callum.

Callum followed the inference and shook his head. "I dinnae ken what sort of scheme you've concocted, but it cannae involve me."

Glengarry leaned forward. "Listen, son."

"Oh, 'son' is it now?"

"Yes. You are my son, and you've got to accept what goes along with that."

Callum glared at his father.

"Callum." Mari put her hand on his arm.

He looked at her with an angry and desperate look. Dragging her by the hand, he led her to the window. In quiet words that stuck in his throat, he said, "Mari, what has he told you?"

She looked at him with as brave a look as she could muster and said, "We're not married."

"*Och!* I have pledged my life to you, woman."

"But not before a priest, or clergy of any kind. No matter how much we want it to be, in the eyes of the law—"

His voice rang out. "Law be damned—and you, too, if you truly believe that!" He gripped her shoulders as tears trailed down her cheeks.

"Callum!" His father barked it out as an order, with a harshness Callum had rarely heard.

Callum let go at once and looked down at Mari. He stepped back, shaking his head. He was too shocked to voice words for a moment. "Mari?" He stumbled against a chair and sank down, burying his face in his hands. When he lifted his head, his face was void of emotion. "I went through hell for you, Mari. I took the place of your brother in prison. I walked back from that hell of a shipwreck. I lived to see you, because you are my life and my heart bides with you."

"Callum, please." A tear fell from her cheek.

He gripped her shoulders. "You are my wife. And you now take those words that we pledged and you say they're not real?"

Her only answer was a helpless look from tearful eyes.

Callum's eyes burned into Mari's. When she could no longer bear it, she cast her eyes downward.

He glared, his wrath mounting. "So if we are not married, then what does that make you? My whore?" He abruptly arose, knocking over the chair, and stormed out of the room.

HOURS LATER, Callum appeared at Nellie's cottage. He knocked at the door and it opened. Charlie stepped outside and closed the door gently behind him, then swung back around and punched Callum in the chin. Callum took it without fighting back.

Charlie said, "How could you say that to her, you bloody maggot?"

Callum quietly asked, "Is she here?"

"If she is, you'll not see her. Even if she would see you, I would not let her. Now go to! Back to your ivory tower, you bleedin' fool!"

Callum gritted his teeth and glanced at the door. He could fight his way through Charlie and storm through the door, but it would only upset Mari and make matters worse. Callum turned and walked away.

LATE INTO THE NIGHT, Alex found Callum on a spot overlooking the loch where they used to go as children to play, and then later as young men after they had gotten into mischief and needed to hide out for a while.

Callum glanced up and then back at the loch, which was lit by the nearly full moon. "Did you come to take a swing at me too?"

Alex gave a half smile. "I think Charlie did a fine enough job of it. Whatever he left undone, I've no doubt that you've finished." He paused and looked at the path of the moon's reflection over the loch.

"How is she?" asked Callum.

"Her heart's broken."

Callum looked up, visibly pained at the thought. "Charlie's right. I am a bloody fool. She said only what Glengarry had convinced her to say. She did nothing to deserve what I said, and I dinnae deserve her." Callum stared over the loch to the hills.

Alex sat down beside him.

Callum rubbed his face wearily and let out a deep sigh. "My father wants me to marry Aemilia."

Alex had pieced together much of what had happened, but he had not heard Callum's side.

Callum said, "We're all tired. We fought for the crown, and we'd all do it again, but everyone's weary of fighting. MacKenzies fought against us on the Covenanters' side, and they're tired, too. People were killed on both

sides. And now there's more tension than ever between
the two clans. If we go on fighting, more lives will be lost.
A marriage would bring the two clans together, and
everyone would live happily ever after. It's quite simple,
really."

"Except that you're already married."

With a wry sideways look, Callum said, "Well, I'd
thought as much, aye."

"And Mari? What does she think?"

Callum's eyes shut for a moment. When he opened
them, he was clenching his jaw. "I didnae give her much
chance to tell me." His anger faded to sorrow. "And now
I've broken her heart."

"You've hurt her. But it's Glengarry who's broken her
heart."

"And mine with it." With a false smile, Callum said, "I
thought he'd accepted me as his son." He took a moment
to regain control of his emotions. When he could speak
with even tones, he said, "He just needed me for a
purpose."

Alex said in a low voice, "As purposes go, it's a noble
one."

"Peace? Aye, it is. Even if he must destroy lives to
achieve it."

"But your lives are not lost."

Callum's anger rose back to the surface. "Are you
agreeing with him?"

Alex measured his words. "No. And yet, I cannae
entirely disagree. Nor can you."

Bitterness flashed in Callum's eyes, but he reluctantly
nodded. "Peace between the clans. For that, I would fight

any battle and give up my life. But how can I give up Mari?"

"I dinnae ken."

Callum said, barely able to speak, "Nor do I. I love her. How could I hurt her like that?" Frustrated, he combed his fingers through his hair as he thought of his last words to Mari. "I called her a whore."

Alex said, "Mari told me, you bastard."

It was a raw nerve, and Alex knew it. Callum overcame his initial reaction and said, "I deserved that."

"You did. But, knowing Mari, she has already forgiven you."

"She would. And that makes me feel worse."

"As it should. But from what I heard from Nellie, what wounded her most was the thought that she'd lost you."

"She will never lose me. I willnae let her go."

Alex stared at the pre-dawn shadows the leaves cast about them. "But the question is, how will you keep her?"

"I'll not keep her like my mother was kept, if that's what you mean. No, I am not going to marry the Lady Aemilia."

"But how can you not?"

"Simple. As soon as Mari will see me again, I will take her away. I will marry her again and again, in every town from here to London, until everyone knows that we're married, if that's what it takes."

"Unfortunately, it isnae quite so simple."

Callum shook his head, but Alex continued. "Glengarry and Seaforth have agreed. Plans have been made."

"Aye, and he expects me to live as he did, with Mari as my mistress."

They sat in silence for a long while before Callum spoke. "I always believed my mother's version of how things were. But now I know that he did not love her in the same way she loved him. He cared. But it was not like the love I have for Mari."

Alex quietly said, "You cannae know what goes on in a man's mind and heart."

"And what if I cannae? What matters is what a man does." Callum looked at Alex. "I must see her."

IN THE MIDMORNING, before seeing Mari, Callum talked with his father alone.

"I cannae marry her. I belong to Mari now."

"You've a duty to your clan."

"And to my wife."

"Unless you can produce proof of the marriage, she isnae your wife."

"She is by my word, and I willnae let her go."

"There's no need. You just have to marry Aemilia, and after the wedding you can set Mari up in a little cottage and see her whenever you want."

"I willnae live like that."

"It's done all the time, and you ken it."

"Aye, it is, but not by me."

"You have no choice."

Callum narrowed his eyes and looked straight at the chief. "There is always a choice. You just made the wrong one."

The chief was furious. "Have you forgotten all I have done for you, unappreciative bastard?"

"Bastard, yes. But unappreciative? No. I have not forgotten one thing you have done over the years. I have never forgotten how you broke my mother's heart. She loved you, but you used her for your convenience. You made her your whore. And you raised me as little more than a stable boy. I was ridiculed and attacked by every child in the clan until I fought them off one by one. Only after I'd fought every warrior here did you elevate me— and then only to serve your purpose. I fought to protect you, but I did it for her—for my mother. But she's gone now, and I owe you nothing."

"You little whelp. I gave you land."

"But no name. And the land you took back."

"Out of loyalty to the crown."

"And what of loyalty to the woman who loved you, and to your son?"

The chief glared at Callum and said, "If this is how you repay me, then I have no son."

"Aye? Well I never had a father, so it's all the same to me!" Callum turned his back and stormed out, slamming the large oak door behind him.

With a face red with rage, Glengarry watched Callum leave.

Chapter 31

For Duty

Callum did not wait for Alex to arrange a meeting with Mari. Instead, he strode out of the castle and went straight to Nellie's.

She met him with scolding. "You deserve what you get, Callum MacDonell. Mari isnae one of your soldiers. You cannae talk like that to her."

"I know. I was wrong, and I'm sorry. But if you willnae tell me where she is, how can I tell her so?"

Nellie gave him an admonishing look, and then nodded her head toward the meadow. "She saw you coming and went for a walk. She doesnae want to see you."

Callum took hold of Nellie's shoulders and planted a kiss on her cheek. She tried to look stern, but it melted to worry as he turned and started to run.

Mari was picking wildflowers when she saw Callum coming. Gripping the flowers like a closely held shield, she watched him approach.

Callum slowed down to a walk, afraid she might run if he approached her too quickly.

"I was a brute and a damned fool to speak to you so."

"Aye, you were," Mari said softly. She lifted her eyes to meet his. "I've never known you to be either."

"Lass." He reached for her hand, but she moved it only slightly from him, but enough to cause him to drop his hand to his side. Her withdrawal wounded him deeply. He looked at her with the eyes of a broken man and spoke in a low voice. "It was the thought of losing you. I could not—I cannae bear it." He swallowed and looked off to the distance, unable to speak. When emotion overcame him, he looked away to hide it from her. When he was able to speak, he said, "Have I lost you already?"

The light touch of her hand on his shoulder was all he needed to spin around and sweep her into a strong embrace. They clung to each other. Mari sobbed herself to exhaustion.

"I cannae bear to lose you," he said as he clutched her against him.

"I dinnae ken how to leave you," she whispered. "But if we do not part, there will be a clan war."

A moan escaped from his throat as he leaned down to kiss her. "You are my wife."

They sat, half concealed by tall grasses, beside one another. Callum circled his arm about Mari's shoulder as she rested against his broad chest. Mari spoke first. "You have a duty."

"My first duty is to you."

"And how happy could I be if by putting me first, a clan war broke out? Lives would be lost. They are your friends and your loved ones. Your duty is to them as well."

"I willnae let you go."

"Callum, I will never leave you. I vowed it once before, and I meant it." She looked plainly at him.

He met her gaze, and knew what she was thinking. "No."

"Callum, listen. Let me bide here. I dinnae care about anything but to be with you."

"No, Mari. I willnae have you live like my mother. I saw what it did to her."

"It's the only way."

"No."

Resigned to her fate, she stopped arguing with him. One look and she knew that he saw she was right.

"No, Mari," he said, but his words were futile. He held her in his arms as all around them the grasses yielded to the cool evening breezes.

DUNCAN CAME HOME from the sea. His parents lived in a small cottage near Nellie's. They told him all the news of the castle.

"And Jenny?"

His mother's kind eyes were almost too much to bear. "She's away to Inverness with her mother to shop—"

"For the wedding." Duncan finished the sentence.

"Aye." She reached for him, but Duncan waved her off and changed the subject. "What of Callum and Mari?"

By the time they were finished, he'd learned that Callum was to be married. As for Mari, no one seemed to know what would become of her. All they knew was that she was staying at Nellie's.

After he'd finished the midday meal his mother had prepared, Duncan went for a walk straight to Nellie's. Mari was bringing in a pail of milk when she saw him. Setting it down, she ran to him and threw her arms about him. He could not help but return the embrace.

"Nellie's having a wee lie down. She tires easily lately. I worry about her," said Mari. She picked up the milk pail, but Duncan took it from her and carried it into the cottage. As he set it down, Nellie sharply inhaled and then settled to sleep. Mari grasped Duncan's hand and led him outside. "Let's go for a walk. I want to hear everything that has happened to you."

They walked holding hands through the grass and along a path into the trees. Mari laughed at something he said and her hand slipped away as she brushed hair away from her face. Duncan forced a smile, feeling its loss. When they came to a fallen log, they sat down. It was easy to talk, but he had no desire to entertain her with stories of the sea and port cities.

"What has happened?" he asked, suddenly serious.

Mari's expression dissolved and her eyes filled with tears. "So you've heard?"

"Not from you."

"Aye, well, there isnae much to tell, is there?" Mari glanced at him and then looked away, into the shadows of trees.

Duncan waited, content to be with her.

Mari said, "Callum's father has claimed him as his own and taken him in. He never spoke of it much, but he longed for it deeply. Now he has a home, and a place he belongs."

"And you by his side?"

Sad eye settled on his. "Not beside him, but not far away." She could not hold his gaze. As she cast her eyes down, a tear dropped to her chest and soaked into the cloth.

Without thinking, he reached for the same strand of hair that the breezes kept blowing onto her face, and he brushed it back over her ear. He lifted his hand, nearly stroking her hair, but pulled back. Instead, he leaned his elbows on his thighs and clasped his hands while he stared at the ground.

Mari said, "He must marry a MacKenzie to bring peace to our clans. There is no proof of our marriage, so if no one disputes it, it doesnae exist."

"But you exist. How can he do this to you?"

With limpid eyes, Mari met Duncan's gaze. "Because I told him to."

Duncan could not speak without telling her what he really thought, so he said nothing.

Mari looked straight ahead and spoke as though she were convincing herself more than Duncan. "It's the right thing to do. All the fighting must stop, and this will end it."

Duncan started to speak, but Mari went on. "If he stayed with me, there would only be more fighting and more people killed—perhaps Callum—or you."

She turned to face him, and her sadness disarmed him. He disagreed, but he would not argue. To do so would change nothing. But he could not help but wonder how she would manage it. How could she watch Callum marry another, and live as another woman's husband? How would she endure it? As strong as she was, such a burden could crush any spirit. She could not be alone, and she would not. This was something Duncan could do for her. He could be there for her to lean on, if she would have him. But now was not the time to talk of such things.

They emerged from the woods, and Duncan was suddenly self-conscious. He and Jenny had walked through these same woods as young lovers stealing away together. "I had not thought how it might look for us walking alone. Some will say 'tis not seemly."

"Let them think what they will," Mari said, having resigned herself to her fate. "Before all this is over, they'll think worse of me, of that I am certain."

There was little late afternoon light left when they arrived back at the cottage. Nellie was awake and beginning to prepare supper. Mari insisted on taking over so Nellie could rest.

"Duncan, you'll stay?"

"If I know my mother, she's preparing a feast for me. I could not disappoint her."

Mari smiled. "Aye, well come back later, if you like."

He gave a halfhearted smile.

"Please? It would be almost like our evenings in Edinburgh. Have you seen Charlie and Alex?"

"Not yet."

"Well, perhaps I could send one of the boys to the castle to fetch them."

When he hesitated, Mari said, "Good. Then I'll see you after supper. Please?" She looked almost her old self as she gave him a pleading, and most charming, look.

"For you, darlin'." He grinned, and they felt once more easy together.

A rap at the door broke their lingering gaze.

Mari opened the door to find a young lad. "This is for you, Mistress," he said, holding out a small bundle.

"Why thank you. Who sent you with this?"

"Mr. MacDonell."

"Callum?" she said, more to herself than to the boy.

"Aye, Mr. Callum MacDonell."

Mari gave him some shortbread she'd made that morning. After he'd thanked her, he went running away.

Duncan watched the lad with a smile, recalling his own youth. When he looked back at Mari, the bundle was opened and Mari was still. Duncan closed the door. "Mari, what is it?"

She set down a small pouch full of coins. With false cheer, she said, "Well, I'd best get to supper."

Duncan and Nellie exchanged looks while Mari pretended that nothing was wrong. He went over to her and gave her shoulders a squeeze. "I'll be back later."

AFTER STOPPING at home to tell his mother he would be late for supper, Duncan strode up to the castle. Before he reached Callum, Alex and Charlie stopped him. They exchanged greetings, which Duncan cut short. Given the time he had been gone, it seemed odd.

When Charlie became distracted by a maid on an errand form the kitchen, Alex pulled Duncan aside. "What is it? You've a look in your eyes I've only seen before battle."

"Aye, well, I've been to see Mari."

Alex nodded, now understanding.

"Callum just had a boy deliver a purse full of coins to

Mari, as though she were—as if it were her wages." He stopped and swallowed.

"Now, Duncan—"

"He's broken her heart."

"From what I understand, she broke his." Alex gripped Duncan's shoulder. "I've been here. It's not nearly as simple as you seem to believe."

"I'll hear that from Callum." He pushed past Alex, but Alex grabbed hold of his arms. "He's about to sit down to supper."

"With Seaforth and that woman?"

"Lady Aemilia," Alex said with a nod. "Let's talk after supper. After that, in the morning, you can talk to Callum."

Duncan gritted his teeth and reluctantly nodded. "*Och*, I forgot. Mari asked me to invite you and Charlie to visit this evening."

"Good. We can talk then."

Duncan gave barely a nod before turning to leave. Alex gave Charlie a light slap on the head to draw his attention from the pretty young maid he was charming. Alex kept walking without looking back, while Charlie gave her his most charming grin and bounded off to catch up with Alex.

CALLUM TOOK his place beside Aemilia for supper. The past few days had left her looking weary. Framed by flaming curls, her wan face appeared almost ghostly.

"Lady Aemilia, has the weather been to your liking?" asked Callum.

Her eyes darted back toward him with a startled expression. "I'm sorry?"

"Do you not think the weather has been sunny and fine?"

Lady Aemilia forced a weak smile. "Oh. Yes, I suppose it has." Her eyes met his, and then flitted downward to her food, which she stared at, making no effort to eat.

Callum looked out at the great hall from his seat at the dais. Everyone looked in good spirits. He glanced over at Glengarry and Seaforth. Even they looked close to tolerating one another's company. This wedding would make friends from foes. More importantly, it would save lives. And although it would cost him his own, or the life he had wanted, it would serve a greater good. He reminded himself of this often, otherwise he could not go forward with this. This was his duty, to his clan and its people.

And right now that duty would be served by making conversation with his betrothed. After all, this was no more her fault than his. "Have you been outside for a walk or a ride?"

Lady Aemilia glanced toward him, barely meeting his eyes. "Aye."

"And how did you find it?"

"Woods, a loch, and steep hills. I have seen these before." While she did not speak with impatience, her gentle tone did not hide her disinterest.

Callum arched an eyebrow. "I see." He looked away to hide the smirk he could barely control.

She turned her head to face him directly for the first time this evening. Callum was once more struck by her fragile beauty, more vivid perhaps because this was the first time she had looked into his eyes. She was lovely, to be sure. But in this moment she gave him an unshielded view of her sadness in all of its depth. Her voice was quiet and smooth. "I have ridden through woods and trod down the rough path to the water. My toes have been wetted. I have sat in the solar and pulled needles through cloth, a task I confess I do loathe. And I have discussed every possible aspect of the weather, from sunrise to sunset, since I have been here. I feel that I now have a full measure of life here. While I cannae fully express how I feel about it, I feel certain you can imagine, for you feel no more affection for me than I do for you."

This was more than she had spoken to him since they had met. He was not quite prepared to respond.

"Lady Aemilia—"

"Please, sir. It would be better if we didnae pretend."

He could not quite decide between offense, annoyance, or sympathy. "I have offered no pretense. I, too, agree it is good to be honest. Although supper may not be the best place or time, while we are in full view of our clansmen." He took in the glances and whispers that spread down the tables below.

She said, "I am sorry. From what I can tell, you are a kind man. But I cannae live day after day lying to one another. Our marriage will be lie enough."

Callum leaned back and studied her, and she knew it.

She would not meet his eyes. "I ken that I've been blunt."

Callum smiled wryly. "Well, if we're to be honest, you have."

She peered into his eyes. "You seem like a good man, but I shall never love you."

Callum stared blankly at her. "I shall keep that in mind."

"Sir, I am feeling unwell. Please excuse me."

She rose and left, stopping long enough to make her apologies to her host, and then to her brother.

As she walked away, Callum almost wanted to smile. In some ways, he could not blame her. She knew her mind and her heart, and was honest with a startling frankness. However, she ignored what was best for her people. She was selfish. He could not admire that.

DUNCAN, Alex, and Charlie sat around Nellie's fireplace with Mari. Having arrived after supper, they had talked through the evening. Nellie nodded off in her chair while soft voices peppered the silence that settles at the end of an evening. The fire drew Mari to stare and remember. The happy memories had become sad reminders of what she would lose after Callum was married. In passing, Duncan's hand settled on Mari's shoulder for a moment, and then he sat down. Mari barely lifted her chin to acknowledge him there.

Charlie was the first to stand and bid Mari goodnight, and the others soon followed. But before they could say their goodbyes, a knock sounded.

"Mari."

She straightened the instant she heard Callum's voice.

Alex first looked to Mari for her permission. As he opened the door, Duncan moved over to stand beside Mari. If this was meant to provide any sense of support, Mari failed to notice. Her attention was on the opening door, and the man in the doorway. In the silence, unvoiced thoughts charged the air. Callum took a step toward her while the other men instinctively stiffened their posture, as though Callum posed some sort of threat. This did not escape Callum's notice as he glanced at Alex and Charlie. And then his eyes met Duncan's unwavering look. Callum's mouth quirked in wry amusement that went instantly somber. He looked down for a moment, and then lifted troubled eyes to Mari and let his gaze settle there, soft and heavy.

A light metallic clinking sounded as Mari lifted her hand. In it she clutched the coin purse that the boy had delivered to her. "You sent a boy to deliver this?" She stepped toward him, extending her hand, and impulsively threw it at him. This caught Callum off guard. Only reflex allowed him to catch it as several coins fell onto the floor.

Confused, Callum opened his mouth, but Mari went on. "Have I become an errand you are too busy to attend to yourself?"

Callum's eyes burned with anger. "I will answer your questions alone." He directed a pointed glare to Alex, who looked first at Mari for her consent, and then wordlessly left, followed by Charlie. When Duncan hesitated, Callum gripped his arm and looked pointedly at him. "You need not worry. I can take care of my wife."

Duncan's eyes flashed. "Aye, I have seen how you take care of your wife."

Callum took a step closer, but stopped as Mari called out. "Callum, if you have something to say to me, say it now."

The two men exchanged a look. Alex called Duncan's name in a quiet, firm voice. Duncan glanced sharply at

Alex but hesitated before turning from Callum, closing the cottage door firmly behind him.

Callum held out the pouch in his hands. "I didnae send this."

Mari looked away as her indignant face melted to despair.

Misreading this as disbelief, Callum took a step toward her. "I didnae send it. Believe me or not, it is true. I have never lied to you. How can you think that I would begin now?" He braced himself for more doubt. Instead Mari turned back to face him. He wanted to sweep her into his arms, but resisted. "My father must have sent it. I dinnae think he meant any harm by it."

"No, I am sure he was merely falling into old habits."

Although she had spoken them softly, her words made him ache with the memories of such purses. He had brought some himself to his mother. How must she have felt to receive them from him?

Callum stepped closer. She stiffened, but he would not relent. He took both her hands in his and lifted them to his lips. Glancing up, he caught sight of a tear as it slid down her cheek. With tender hands, he brushed her tears away and kissed her cheek. With that, Mari gave in to his enclosing arms.

He said, "You'll recall, this was your idea."

She nodded, but would not lift her eyes to meet his.

"And a bloody awful one it was," Callum added.

"Aye, but it's the only way I can have at least part of you."

"No, lass. We could pack up and say our goodbyes and leave it all behind us. I could go tell my father to call off the wedding and leave him to sort it all out."

She shook her head in disbelief. "He would disinherit you."

"Aye," he said plainly.

"You'd lose everything."

"If I stay, I lose you. And you are the one thing I cannae live without."

Mari sighed with relief, but felt guilty for it. "Do you think it is wise?"

"No. It isnae wise at all, but it is the only choice I can live with." Callum stroked her hair and pressed his lips to her forehead.

"I'm afraid," she whispered.

Callum smiled his most reassuring smile. "I will keep you safe."

"I dinnae doubt it. But if we were to do such a thing, how would you feel months from now? You'd have lost everything you'd ever wanted, and I'd be the cause."

He took her face in his hands and smiled at her. "My love, when I was a boy, I wanted many things, but now that I am a man, all I want is you."

Mari could not argue against her heart, when all it wanted was Callum.

Callum kissed her and said, "Seaforth willnae take it well. Of that, you can be certain."

"He could lock you in the dungeon."

"Aye. I have thought of that, too. But I'd still have to tell him in person."

Mari gripped Callum's leine. "You're no good to me in a dungeon. Please, love, dinnae do that to me."

Callum considered her words. "I dinnae like sneaking away like a coward."

"Then send him a message, if you must. But I willnae let you risk telling him in person."

Callum looked with surprise, and a hint of a grin. "You willnae let me?"

She looked at him with stern resolve. "No."

Suddenly serious, his eyes softened. "Very well then, my love. As you wish."

Mari rewarded Callum with a long and heartfelt kiss.

When at last she released him, he said, "He'll send men after us. We'd have to make haste."

"Alone? Just the two of us?"

"Aye. It is better that way. We risk both our lives. There's no need to risk more."

"But the lads would want to come with us."

"Which is why we willnae tell them."

This troubled Mari, but she knew he was right. If they told Callum's friends, they would insist upon coming along. And their lives would be ruined. They would lose their homes, their families and their clan.

Callum said, "It is too much to ask of them."

Mari nodded, agreeing.

He put his hands on her shoulders. "And I cannae help but wonder. Is it too much to ask of you?" His dark eyes searched hers.

"Whether you ask or not, it will be the same. I must be with you, and I believe that you feel the same."

He pulled her to his chest and kissed her forehead. "You need never doubt that."

Mari's hopeful tone weakened. "But what of the clan? What would become of them if we did this?"

Callum's gaze darkened, but he said nothing.

Mari said, "Our happiness would come at a price.

Others would pay in sorrow or with their lives." She slowly shook her head.

She was right, but Callum did not yet have the heart to say it aloud. Taking her face in his hands, he put his mouth on hers in a soul-quenching kiss.

Nellie stirred in her chair as she slept. Neither moved until they were sure she had settled back to sleep. Then Callum grasped Mari's hand and led her outside. They went around to the back of the cottage and sought out a shadow beneath the full moon.

"Callum." The sound caught in her throat.

"*Och*, lass. How I've missed you." Guiding her until her back was against the wall, he leaned the full length of his body against hers and kissed her until her body swayed against his.

"Mari, you are all that I want." He devoured her mouth with his kiss, and opened his palms over her shoulders and slid them slowly down to find their way to each curve they had missed. Mari clutched the folds of his plaid in her fist as she pulled him against her. He groaned and leaned into her, touching her until her breaths grew uneven. As she gripped his shoulders, he lifted her so her legs wrapped around him. He took her, heart pounding, against the side of the cottage as she clung to him, arms circled about his neck, breathing the scent she had longed for and feared she had lost.

When their desire was spent, Callum set her on her feet and held her close. Despair cloaked them. With his forehead against hers, he said, "We cannae leave, can we?"

"No, my love," she whispered.

"Callum!" Duncan's voice sounded from around the corner.

Callum whispered, "Dinnae lose heart." He called back to Duncan, "Aye!"

She kissed Callum, not knowing when she might have the chance again.

"Mari, how can I ask this of you?"

She said sadly, "We ask it of each other, because we have no choice."

When Duncan called out again, Callum hooked his arm about Mari's waist and kept her close. Hair and clothing disheveled, they rounded the corner to the front of the cottage.

Duncan took in the sight of the couple. Lit by the full moon, there was little doubt as to what they'd been doing. He averted his eyes for a moment to recoup his composure. "Callum, you're wanted at the castle. Lady Aemilia is missing."

Duncan stood awkwardly by while Callum gave Mari a hug and planted a kiss on her forehead. He combed his fingers into her hair and cradled her head in his hand as he whispered into her ear. Leaving her standing by the cottage door, Callum gripped Duncan's shoulder and set out with the others for the castle.

Chapter 32

For Love

On the way to the castle, Duncan said, "Her maid went to her room to attend to her after she left supper."

Callum recalled the moment well.

Duncan continued. "She told her maid she was going to sleep and didnae wish to be disturbed. When her maid went to check on her later, Lady Aemilia was gone."

"Perhaps she's gone somewhere to be alone." As he said it, Callum knew how unlikely it was.

Duncan shook his head. "They have combed the castle. She isnae there. Of that they are certain."

Callum said, "She didnae want this wedding."

With a frown, Alex said, "And what makes you think that?"

"I have talked to the lass. She made no secret of how she feels."

"So you think she might have run away to escape you?" asked Charlie.

With a wry look, Callum said, "To escape being married."

"'Twas a foolhardy thing for a woman to flee all alone," Duncan said.

"What makes you think she's alone?" asked Charlie.

Callum flashed a surprised look.

Alex said, "What?"

"She's a bonnie lass," said Charlie. "Or had you not noticed? I've no doubt she'd be able to find some willing escort."

"One willing to turn from his clan?" Alex asked.

Charlie shrugged. "She's very bonnie. For some, it would take little more."

"For you, perhaps," Alex said, smirking at Charlie.

Charlie chuckled. "Aye, well, I wouldnae run off with her, but if the lass lost her way and wound up in my bed I'd not send her away."

Alex said, "I cannae say I recall your sending anyone away—or anything, for that matter."

Without even a glance, Charlie backhanded Alex in the gut as he finished the sentence.

THEY ARRIVED at the castle to find the bailey in a flurry of stable boys and horses being readied to ride. Glengarry spied Callum and pulled him aside. "Find her, Callum. If anything happens to her, all hell will break loose."

Callum nodded. They both knew this could cause a new clan war. Peace depended upon his finding her safe and returning her. And when that happened, new cause for clan war would erupt if he told Glengarry and Seaforth of his wishes to honor his heart and stay married to Mari. But that matter would wait. Lady Aemilia was off wandering in the woods. There was no telling what danger she was in.

Callum and Alex took the lead, followed by Charlie and Duncan. Alex was the best tracker among them. No one doubted that they would find her; the only question was whether she would be alive.

Darkness fell and the trail became harder to follow, so the men stopped and made camp.

Before dawn, they were riding again. She seemed to be heading south. "You were right, Charlie," said Alex. "She isnae alone." He dismounted and studied the tracks. "There are two horses."

The men rode through the day. In the evening it began to rain lightly, which made the trail easy to follow at first. But soon the rain fell in sheets that washed away the tracks.

"We may as well stop and make camp," Alex told them.

"What if she's lying somewhere hurt, and needs help?" Charlie asked.

"All the more reason to wait until morning, when we can find her trail. We could spend the night heading in any number of directions, and all of them wrong."

Duncan said, "And remember, she isnae alone. In the darkness, they have the advantage. They can lie still and listen for us to approach."

CALLUM SAID, "Alex is right. We'll rest here and be back on her trail in the morning."

The rain had stopped overnight, leaving a mist rising

up through the trees that grew light with the first hints of dawn. The rain had washed away hoofprints, so they continued south on foot, leading their horses and hoping to pick up the trail again. Alex's efforts were rewarded when a broken twig and an indented leaf on the ground set him back on the trail.

Callum muttered, "If she's been kidnapped—"

Charlie said, "She'll bring a fine ransom."

"No she'll not, because we'll find them first," Alex said.

Soon they came to a glen. The sun shone through the mist to a cottage below, from which smoke curled out of the chimney. Beside it was a byre. They dismounted and walked their horses in near silence to the byre. Slowly, they opened the door just enough to creep in. Inside, two Highland stallions were tied to a post. Alex looked at Callum and shifted his eyes toward the hayloft. Bits of hay floated down as the rafters creaked in muted cadence. Soft womanly moans and a masculine groan proved false any kidnapping theory. Charlie made a point to share a smug look, for this was as he had expected. She found some willing lad to whisk her away. Callum was first to climb up the ladder. Sword drawn and dirk at the ready, he positioned himself to his best fighting advantage and then cleared his throat. The man reached out to the side for his sword, but before he could grasp it, Callum pressed his sword point onto the man's back. The man withdrew his hand.

"Slowly," barked Callum. "Turn around." The man rolled off of Aemilia and turned to face Callum.

"Ranald?"

Ranald spied his dirk nearby and started to reach for it, but found Callum's sword poised point first on his chest.

Ranald said, "Kill me then, but dinnae harm the Lady Aemilia. I forced myself on her."

"No, it's a lie! Dinnae blame him! 'Tis all my fault!" cried Aemilia.

"Aemi, you dinnae ken what you're saying." Ranald gave her a look that was meant to be stern, but only softened upon gazing at her.

"Good God. They're in love?" Charlie said from below.

"So it would appear," Callum said, as he studied Ranald.

Ranald glanced about and assessed his situation. Callum watched him, confident he had little chance of escape. If he got past Callum, there were three others below, which he might brave alone, but with Aemilia here he would not risk it.

Callum said, "There's no use, and you know it. Climb down. I'll throw your clothes down to you." He did not trust Ranald to gather his clothes without bringing a sgian dubh as well. "Go on." Callum prodded Ranald with the tip of his sword. "I'll see to Lady Aemilia."

With a bold look, Ranald said, "You'll not touch her." It was a command, and it might have been more had Ranald not known Callum since childhood and trusted his honor.

"You have my word."

Ranald met Callum's steady gaze with his own piercing look, and then barely nodded.

While Ranald climbed down the ladder from the hayloft, Aemilia started to whimper.

"*Och!*" Callum was losing his patience. "You need not worry, lass. I'll not touch you."

"What will happen to Ranald?"

"Given the fact that he's bedded my betrothed, you can be certain he'll get far less than he deserves."

"And how do I know that?" Aemilia clutched her gown to her chest and looked up at Callum with eyes burning with both anger and fear.

"If I were going to slay him in a jealous rage, I'd have done it already." With a dismissive wave of his sword, he said, "Now get dressed. We've a long ride ahead."

"I cannae get dressed with you looking at me!"

"Well, I'll not turn my back on you, lassie, if that's what you're hoping."

When Callum did not move, she covered herself with her skirt, and then slipped her shift over her head, taking care to stay as covered as possible, then stepped into her underskirt and pulled it up to her waist. Callum rolled his eyes as she went through the elaborate process of maintaining her modesty, which under the circumstances seemed a wee bit absurd. By the time she'd pulled up her stockings, he was simply amused. This was short-lived, for as she slipped on her shoes, Aemilia started to sniffle.

"And what is it now?" Callum said, biting back his annoyance.

"My ribbon's come untied," she said, pointing to the lacing at her shoulder.

"God's teeth, woman! Let me see." With a sigh of disgust, Callum sheathed his sword and tied her sleeve to her shoulder.

Aemilia looked up to thank him with a demure smile, and then poked a sgian dubh against Callum's ribs.

Callum looked down at the blade, and then back up at her. He tried not to grin at the brave look she had so unconvincingly assumed. In an instant, he had her spun about, her arm and wrist twisted behind her until the knife dropped to the floor. While he gripped her two wrists in his hand, he yanked out the ribbon he'd tied on her sleeve and used it to tie her wrists behind her. "Climb down, milady."

"But I cannae—not with my hands tied. I will fall."

"Charlie, should my ladylove lose her footing and fall, will you catch her?"

Charlie grinned. "It would be my pleasure."

Ranald stirred, but by now had his hands tied and was held in Duncan's firm grip.

Charlie climbed up the ladder and step-by-step helped a flustered Aemilia descend to the ground.

THEY RETURNED to the castle under cover of darkness. They had split into two separate parties, with Callum, Duncan, and Ranald in one, and Alex, Charlie, and Aemilia in the other. While they could not hope to avoid being seen, they at least hoped to conceal the connection between the two lovers. Should they not cooperate, each was threatened with the other's exposure and punishment, the threat of which secured an uneventful trip home. Callum sent one of his men inside to make sure Seaforth had retired, and then the lovers were separately brought to the solar.

When Glengarry came into the room, he stopped short. "Ranald?"

Ranald met the harsh look with the noble grace of a man being watched by the woman he loves.

Callum drew Glengarry aside. "Before you speak, hear me out."

Speaking as though they were not in the same room within earshot, Glengarry said, "They've made a mockery of me, and of you for that matter."

"Not yet. No harm has been done."

"From the looks of the lass, I'd say you were wrong."

"Oh, that. Aye, we found them in a hayloft. But no one knows of it yet, save you and my men."

"One of our men has defiled Seaforth's sister while they were guests under our roof. There is harm enough there."

"We could let it be known that we found her alone. She went out for a ride and lost her way. Ranald was elsewhere, and returned separately with Duncan and Alex."

"Elsewhere? Where exactly is that? And how was it that he happened to encounter Duncan and Alex? Do you really think no one will wonder why those two left with you, but were inexplicably separated? And then, as luck would have it, just happened upon Ranald and returned the same evening as you? I'll wager by tomorrow the truth will have been pieced together."

Callum thought for a moment, cursing himself for having made such a poor argument. He said quietly, "Aye, but what if we convinced Seaforth that Ranald is the better choice? News of that would so outweigh talk of our wee hunting party that no one will bother to wonder about it."

A dark, thoughtful look came over Glengarry. He softened his tone. "We agreed that his sister would marry my heir."

Callum drew Glengarry further away from the lovers and spoke softly. "But what if Ranald is your heir?"

Glengarry looked genuinely wounded. "I've made you my heir."

In this moment, Callum felt closer to his father than he had ever been. He could not fully mask his sadness. "But you've taken my wife from me."

Glengarry said, "I ken that I've given you every right to doubt my motives, but I always wanted for you to be part of my family." His eyes moistened as he swallowed. He did not go on.

"My Lord, I thank you. It was always my wish, as you must have known. But I have new wishes now. My heart is with Mari."

"You would turn all of this over to Ranald for her?"

"Aye, I would." The words came out with such ease. Callum had wondered, when the moment came, how it would feel to give everything up. Would he really be able to give up a lifelong dream out of love for one woman? But that woman was Mari.

Glengarry looked out through the window overlooking the loch. For a long while, he was silent. "I once came very close to doing what you have just done. But I could not let it go. There were times—many times—over the years when I sorely regretted it." He looked Callum straight in the eye. "I did love her, you know."

Callum swallowed back emotion. "I wanted to think so, but I never was sure."

Glengarry's eyes darkened. "That was a cost that you

both had to bear, and I'm sorry for that." He gripped Callum's shoulder.

They turned to take in the view through the window, sharing the peace of the still night.

Stirring from across the room drew Glengarry's attention back to practical matters. "So what am I to do with those two?"

"They're in love," said Callum.

"So I gathered," Glengarry said with a wry glance in their direction.

"And what of Seaforth? He'll take offense at your spurning his sister."

"It was she who did the spurning. She ran off with Ranald."

"It was she who ran off," Glengarry corrected. "And she did it alone. Seaforth cannae learn of Ranald's involvement."

Glengarry thought for a moment. "She ran away and left you, wounding your pride if not your heart."

"And I was wounded enough that I had to leave the scene of my disgrace."

Glengarry studied Callum with a sad resignation. "After that, I had no choice but to make Ranald future chief and heir to half of my estate."

Callum met his eyes with an unanswered question. *Only half?*

Glengarry answered with a faint smile, which soon faded. "The other half of my estate may not be enough to make up for the past, but it can shape your future."

Callum looked at Glengarry and saw a father's love. It so moved him that he had to look down. He took a breath and contained his emotions. "Do you think Seaforth would agree to the change?"

"Aye, he'll accept our proposal if it means we'll keep quiet about his sister's behavior. When I'm through, he'll feel lucky we'll have her at all, after what she has done."

Callum said, "She followed her heart. It's not so bad as all that."

"Perhaps not, but we willnae share that opinion with Seaforth." Glengarry lifted a brow.

"In the end, he will have what he wants. His sister will marry the heir to the chiefdom, and there will be peace between our two clans."

Glengarry looked over at the two nervous lovers and spoke loudly. "Ranald, what in God's name were you thinking?"

He looked plainly at Glengarry and said, "I love her."

"My Lord, please dinnae blame him. I begged him to take me away." Aemilia glanced nervously toward Callum. "I'm sorry, but I could never love anyone but Ranald. I could not face a life without him."

Callum folded his arms and looked at Glengarry.

Ranald said, "Forgive me, but the lady said she would leave with or without me to escape the wedding. I felt I had no choice but to keep her safe."

With a jaundiced look, Glengarry said, "Aye, from what I understand, you were keeping her quite safe in your arms when they found you."

Ranald clenched his jaw and bit back his reply.

Aemilia looked from Callum to Glengarry. "Have you never been in love?"

Glengarry seemed to ignore her question. Instead he

turned to Ranald. "It appears that Callum doesnae want the chiefdom."

Ranald looked sharply at Callum. Callum shrugged in reply.

Glengarry said, "Until now, I have always known you to be a man of honor. This was entirely out of character for you. It is the only lapse I will ever allow without grave consequences. Do you understand?"

"I do, my Lord."

"It will take some convincing to get Seaforth to agree to his sister marrying a different heir."

Aemilia's eyes filled with tears. Ranald could only manage a muted, "Thank you, my Lord."

Glengarry turned to Callum. "You must leave now. Seaforth cannae see you. You will need to stay away for a year, perhaps two." He gazed at his son for a moment, and then gripped his shoulder. "Goodbye, lad."

Callum looked into eyes that shone with the love he had longed for since childhood. He managed a fond goodbye and left while he still could control his emotions.

Glengarry watched him leave, and then told a guard to go and wake Seaforth from his slumber.

SEAFORTH STORMED IN. "WHERE IS SHE?"

"She's in here. Tread lightly. She's had a long and trying day."

"So I hear," Seaforth said, fuming. He caught sight of her and shot her a fiery look. "Foolish girl."

Glengarry said, "I'm afraid she wounded Callum irreparably."

Seaforth could not hide his alarm as he looked at Glengarry and waited for what might come next.

Glengarry proceeded with care, taking note of Seaforth's every reaction. "I could not stop him. He's gone."

The news drew a grim look to Glengarry, and a more piercing look to Aemilia.

Glengarry said, "He has relinquished the chiefdom."

Seaforth's face reddened as he shot a scathing look at Aemilia.

She looked back at him boldly. "It could not be helped."

He walked over to face her. "Could it not?" Then he slapped her with the back of his hand.

Ranald leapt at him and landed a blow that threw Seaforth off balance and sent him to an awkward sprawl on the floor.

Ranald pulled Aemilia into his arms as he smoothed her hair back and peered at the red handprint on her face. As Seaforth stirred to rise up, Ranald pulled Aemilia behind him.

"Ranald, please," she whispered, urging caution.

Ranald bit back the words that he wanted to say, and instead said, "I will marry Lady Aemilia."

Seaforth was on his feet now, blotting the blood from his lip with a handkerchief. His eyes swept over Ranald from head to toe. "You'll do no such thing." He leveled a sharp look at Glengarry. "Our deal was for her to marry the heir to the chiefdom."

"Aye," said Glengarry nonchalantly. "With Callum gone, I'm of a mind to change my heir to Ranald."

Seaforth looked as though he might spit, but he held himself back, with a long glare at Ranald.

Ranald glowered back, unrelenting.

For a long while, no one spoke. With one last swipe of the handkerchief, Seaforth looked at Glengarry and casually said, "Very well. I will need it in writing that he is to be chief. I'll not wait for the banns. Pay the priest off. I want them married this Sunday."

"Agreed," said Glengarry.

"Good." Seaforth looked at Aemilia, who clung to Ranald's arm. Ranald made no effort at pretense as he slipped his arm about Aemilia's waist and protectively held her.

This prompted an unexpected laugh from Seaforth. "I would say you could have her, but it appears that you already have." With a cruel laugh, he bade Glengarry goodnight and walked out of the room.

FOUR HORSEMEN RODE down from the castle with a spare horse in tow. Mari heard their approach and flung open the cottage door.

"It's all over." Callum dismounted and opened his arms. Mari flew to him.

Charlie grinned. "So you'd throw yourself away on this sorry lout?"

Mari smiled broadly as she turned to Callum and brushed a stray lock of hair from his brow. "Yes, I would. I would have him forever."

"And you will." Callum consumed her with a kiss that drew out until Alex cleared his throat.

"Em, Callum, you ken we're still here?"

Callum glanced over his shoulder. "Aye, but I dinnae care." And he kissed her again.

Alex clapped his hand on Callum's shoulder and led the way inside to bid Nellie goodbye. She tried to be brave through her tears, but the leaving was hard. It was hard for them all. But they had to be gone before morning, so they were on their way, with a nearly full moon lighting their way.

Chapter 33

Forever

One Week Later

Callum turned Mari about in his arms so they both faced the window looking out over the Edinburgh street where Alex, Charlie and Duncan strode toward the nearest pub. Mari leaned back against Callum's sturdy chest and sighed with contentment.

He rested his cheek on her head. "Out there is our life, Mari. We'll not waste time looking behind us anymore."

She turned her head back toward him. "But I quite like the view behind me at the moment," she said with a mischievous grin.

"Aye, do you now? Well, there's no accounting for taste. But I willnae complain as long as I've got you to look at."

"Just look?" She glanced up and gave a wistful nod. "Hm."

"Aye." Callum pretended to ignore her demure hint. "And to hold—except when I let you go to the market."

She cast a narrow-eyed look over her shoulder.

He made no effort to hide a mischievous grin. "And to cook me grand meals."

"*Och*, of course. Those grand plates of neeps and tatties."

"And the sweeping and washing."

She pivoted around and looked up through her lashes. "Aye."

With a mischievous spark in his eye, he said, "And the children. I was thinking at least nine or ten."

She nodded, now smiling herself. "I see." Mari placed her fists on her hips. "That's a grand picture you paint of our life."

With a teasing grin, he said, "It is grand, is it not?"

She nodded, suppressing a smile. "Aye. I'd best be about it." She took a few steps away, and then turned back as if a thought had just occurred to her. "Of course, with all the cooking—"

"Of grand meals," he added, sauntering toward her.

"Aye, the grand meals, and the sweeping and washing..." Mari sighed.

"Aye, lass?" He looked deeply interested as he inched closer.

"I was just wondering." She peered into his eyes.

"Well, it's good that you're thinking. Keeps the mind active, no?" He seemed barely to listen as he pulled her to him and nuzzled close to breathe in the scent of her hair.

Mari looked at him sweetly. "Aye, but with all of those grand meals and all, I'm fearing I'll be very tired." She paused to heave a huge sigh and to wipe her brow with the back of her hand. Callum buried his face in her neck and trailed kisses along it as Mari continued with a frown, as though deep in thought. "Aye, I'm quite certain I'll be far too tired to make all those bairns you've got planned."

He lifted his head to take in her broad smile. "Now, Mari, there are some things a body is never too tired for."

"Really? I cannae imagine to what you're referring." She turned to look toward the kitchen, but looked back at Callum. "Well, I'd best get to work on that grand meal I've got planned for this evening."

"Now, lass, not so hasty. Let me show you to what I'm referring. I'm referring to this." He kissed the base of her neck as his hands slid from her shoulders. He slipped his fingertips along the inside of her neckline. "And this." He untied the ribbon holding her hair and combed his fingers into the strands, and then he leaned down to give her a slow, head-spinning kiss. He kissed her until her arms went limp and rested gently about his neck. He whispered into her ear, "Damn the cooking and washing. Let's just make bairns." He proceeded to busy his hands.

Mari smiled. "We've got one on the way. It's a wee bit soon to be making the next one."

Callum pulled back and held her by the shoulders as he searched her eyes. "A bairn?"

With a light laugh, she said, "Aye." But as quickly as the laugh came, it went as her eyes shone with tears.

"*Och*, Mari." His eyes looked a bit moist as he smiled and then kissed her. He circled his arms about her waist and held her close. His full lips brushed her ear as he said, "'Tis a good life we'll have."

"Aye, I ken it." She looked up at him while he smoothed back her hair.

His hands slid to her shoulders as his fingers resumed

their exploration of the edge of her neckline. "You've been on your feet too long today."

She looked at him as though he were daft. "I'm just fine."

"No, my love, you must rest—for the sake of the bairn."

"Must I?" She frowned, sure now that he was daft.

"*Och*, aye, you must." In one sudden move, he had her up in his arms, and he carried her off to the bedroom. When she tried to protest, he kissed her—deep kisses that made her forget to resist. Gently, he set her down on the bed. "Have I mentioned that I love you?" he asked as he lowered himself onto her.

"Once or twice," she said, as she helped pull his leine over his head.

"That's not nearly enough. Let me show you."

And he did.

Author's Note

Highland Soldiers is a work of fiction; however, much of the background is rooted in history. Following are some of the customs and events I researched while writing this series:

The Stool of Repentance was a very real part of the 17th Century Scotland church. People were known to commit suicide rather than face the ordeal.

In 1670 King Charles II declared it illegal to worship in any church other than the Church of Scotland. Those caught doing so could be summarily executed on the spot. To enforce this decree, as many as 8,000 Highland soldiers were brought down to the lowlands. So began the period in Scottish history known as The Killing Times. For a moving account if these times, I recommend *Scottish Covenanter Stories: Tales from the Killing Times*, by Dane Love.

The song lyrics in Chapter 6 are from Child Ballad 110, Collected by Percy Grainger from the singing of Mr William Roberts at Burringham-on-Trent, Lincolnshire,

July 1906. Printed in the *Folk Song Journal* No. 12, vol. III, p.222, and reprinted in Bronson's *The Traditional Tunes of the Child Ballads*, vol. II, p. 540.

On May 3, 1679, Archbishop Sharp was murdered by a band of Covenanters, which included some lairds, a weaver, and a handful of tenant farmers.

On June 22, 1679, the Battle of Bothwell Brigg was fought. Following the battle, prisoners were marched to Edinburgh's Covenanter's Prison in Greyfriar's Kirkyard. They were kept there for four months, where, according to the Scottish Covenanter Memorial inscription:

> *Some of the prisoners died here, some were tried and executed for treason, some escaped, and some were freed after signing a bond of loyalty to the Crown...In November 1679 the remaining 257 men, who had been sentenced to transportation overseas, were taken to Leith and placed on board a ship bound for the American colonies; nearly all were drowned when this ship was wrecked in the Orkney islands (where there is a monument in their memory), but 48 of the prisoners survived.*

On June 24, 1679, the Privy Council issued orders that, among other things, directed:

> *If any of the prisoners escape, the sentries may assure themselves to cast the dice, and answer body for body for the fugitives, without any exception; and the officers are to answer for the sentries, and the town of Edinburgh for the officers. And if any of the prisoners escape, the Council will require a particular account, and make them answerable for them.*

The next day, the Privy Council directed that no one was to go near the prison gates, except to bring charitable donations of food, which would be distributed equally among the prisoners.

On December 10, 1679, The *Crown* was wrecked off the coast of Orkney. The captain and crew made no effort to rescue the prisoners locked below deck, presumably because his insurance would cover prisoners who died, but he would receive nothing for escaped prisoners. One crewmember took an axe to the hatch, which allowed fifty prisoners to escape. While most were recaptured and later sent to Jamaican plantations to work, some did escape and make their way home to mainland Scotland.

On December 25, 1679, five Covenanters who had refused to divulge information about the murder of Archbishop Sharp were hanged, despite not having been directly involved with the murder.

The Highland Soldiers Series

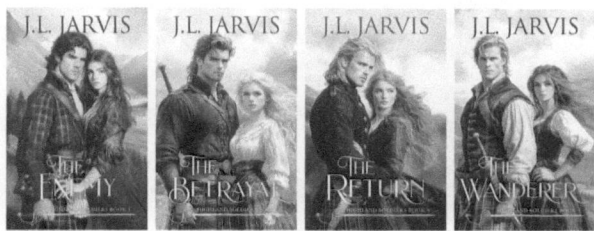

Highland Soldiers: Scottish historical romances set during turbulence seventeenth-century Scotland

Thank You!

Thank you for reading! If you enjoyed this book, please consider leaving a review or a rating. Your feedback on bookstore, Goodreads, and Bookbub websites helps other readers discover books they'll enjoy.

instagram.com/jljarvis.writer
facebook.com/jljarvis1writer
x.com/JLJarvis_writer
youtube.com/@jljarvis-author
goodreads.com/jljarvis
bookbub.com/authors/j-l-jarvis

Also by J.L. Jarvis

Waterfront Summers

(Can be read in any order)

The Cottage at Peregrine Cove

The House on Serenity Lake

Moonlight on Mariner's Bluff

Drake & Wilde Mysteries

(Reading Order)

Love in the Time of Pumpkins

Secrets in the Hollow

Shadow of the Horseman

Standalones

(Can be read in any order)

A Cowboy Kind of Love

A Christmas Eve Stop

Christmas by Lamplight

A Kiss in the Rain

App-ily Ever After

Once Upon a Winter

The Red Rose

Highland Vow

Short Stories

The Holiday Hideaway

Highland Passage

(Can be read in any order)

Highland Passage

Knight Errant

Lost Bride

Highland Soldiers

(Reading Order)

The Enemy

The Betrayal

The Return

The Wanderer

American Hearts

(Can be read in any order)

Secret Hearts

Forbidden Hearts

Runaway Hearts

For more information, visit jljarvis.com.

Get monthly book news at news.jljarvis.com.

About the Author

J.L. Jarvis is a left-handed former opera singer/teacher/lawyer who writes books. She now lives and writes on a mountaintop in upstate New York.

jljarvis.com